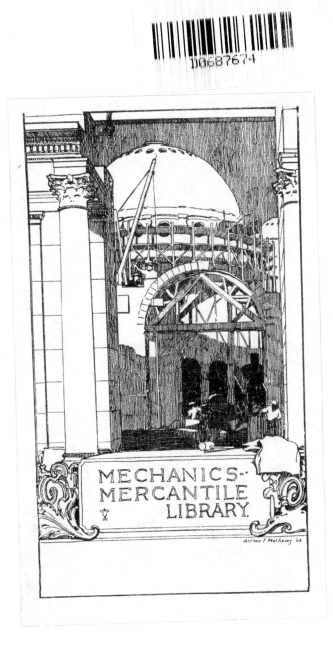

MECHANICS-
MERCANTILE
LIBRARY.

Arthur F. Mathews '06

FAITH
WITHOUT
DOUBT

Also by Anna Blundy

Every Time We Say Goodbye
Only My Dreams
The Bad News Bible

ANNA BLUNDY

FAITH WITHOUT DOUBT

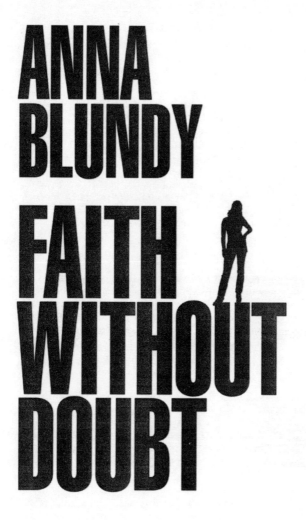

review

First published in 2005
by HEADLINE BOOK PUBLISHING

A REVIEW hardback

10 9 8 7 6 5 4 3 2 1

British Library Cataloguing in Publication Data is available from the British Library

ISBN 0 7553 02974 (hardback)
ISBN 0 7553 22266 (trade paperback)

Printed and bound in Great Britain by Clays Ltd, St Ives plc

Papers and cover board used by Headline are natural, recyclable products made from
wood grown in sustainable forests. The manufacturing processes conform to the
environmental regulations of the country of origin.

HEADLINE BOOK PUBLISHING
A division of Hodder Headline
338 Euston Road
London NWI 3BH

www.reviewbooks.co.uk
www.hodderheadline.com

'For Joshua F. Klein and Eden Jones. If you only existed.'

ACKNOWLEDGEMENTS

With thanks to Rosie de Courcy, Deborah Rogers, John Lee Anderson (whose brilliant pieces from Baghdad were an inspiration) and the people of Brandeglio (especially Carolina), San Cassiano (especially Ornella) and Bagni di Lucca (especially Ilario).

CHAPTER ONE

Three-quarters of an hour ago I sat down on a high chrome stool and drank a couple of shots of vodka. A man called Graham told me to 'enjoy'. I doubt that many people doing neat vodka shots in a DC bar at eleven o'clock in the morning are enjoying.

I thought it might pull me together. But I think it pulled me further apart. I came to see someone important. I went and stood outside his building and I felt my face get wet. It took me a second to work out what was happening. I actually looked up at the sky. I haven't cried since I can't remember when.

I fished around in the pockets of my jeans but I'd run out of quarters for the phone boxes. 'You have reached the phone of Joshua Klein. Please leave a message.' Yes, well, I'd already left two hundred messages. What did I want him to do? Hit me over the head?

I don't know now what I was doing there. It already feels like years

1

ago. I suppose I was thinking about another life. A life in which I was in there too, wearing one of his shirts, drinking coffee, reading bits out of the paper and laughing. And I wondered to myself, is he at home? Doing up a silk tie? Polishing a Savile Row shoe? I needed to find out but I never meant this to happen.

I must have been crouched here on the fire escape for a long time. Twenty minutes? Half an hour? I'm shivering but I know it's hot because I can see all the steam from the air conditioners billowing out the back. These buildings, so grand and brown with their boxes of red geraniums on the street side, are dark and grimy behind. There is a deep well of a courtyard reeking of rotten cabbage and cats.

I'm frightened to put the gun down and I'm frightened to keep holding it. There is congealed blood all over my hand and I'm afraid to peel my fingers away from the metal, to hear the wetness and to breathe in the smell. And I'm afraid, irrationally I suppose, that if I do put it down, here on the ridged black iron of the fire escape, that it might go off again, that a deafening crack might split my eardrum in two.

My shoulder is still searing with pain from the kickback. I thought my arm might break. Even in the horror of the moment I registered how odd it was that it should surprise me. I've seen people fire their weapons a million times, but that the force of one bullet from a . . . some kind of handgun. Police-issue thing, I suppose. I can't look now. Not now.

I can't stop shivering either, I think there is blood in my hair. I feel I should do something but I don't know what. I hope he is dead. I hope there wasn't too much pain. Is that a ridiculous thing to think? His eyes seemed to roll back in his head with the impact. Green eyes with flecks of gold in them. A spray of his blood spattered the curtains and he looked as though he was turning to see. He wore only a shirt and tie, boxer shorts and socks. One cufflink. He must have been getting dressed. He was listening to *La Traviata*. Playing our song. I wonder if it's still playing, Maria Callas screaming into the room. I wonder if he can hear it.

He looked his age suddenly, lying there, soaking the carpet with his blood. An old man dying, pink foam spewing from his mouth as his punctured lungs filled with fluid.

And I remembered, standing over him holding the gun, I remembered the first time I asked him about the age gap between us. 'Doesn't it bother you?' I said.

'No. Why? It happens,' he said. Sometimes he speaks so quickly you could miss it, and he changed the subject. His final comment on the matter.

I feel as though I stood there for hours, my dirty boots on the carpet. But I didn't. I wanted to lie down next to him and die too. I wanted to kiss his eyelids and tell him all the things I'd ever wanted to say. But I ran, like they all do. And here I am waiting to be found. Is that what I'm doing? I just looked down at my free hand, covered in drying blood, and I threw up over the edge, on to the clanging ladder, on to my boots. I can smell bile and vodka and blood and sweat. I can hear a siren and I'm glad.

CHAPTER TWO

If only I had known that first day in Baghdad I would have shaken his hand and walked away. But the fact is, I did know. It only takes a second. Hey, a million songs will tell you that much.

This war had been brewing for ages. Since the first Gulf War, I suppose. Or, more accurately, since George Bush won the election because of a couple of confused old ladies in Florida and some inscrutably bumpy ballot papers. I stayed up all night in a hotel, I forget where, watching the count, hiding under my duvet and popping out again when it looked like Gore might have taken it. Anyway, I suppose Dubya just wanted to finish off what his dad started and get it right this time. None of us could have imagined then the Abu Ghraib prison horrors or those pictures of Saddam Hussein having his teeth examined like a horse, bearded and defeated, mad and old. But people get old suddenly, not slowly as we all like to think, but overnight in a hole, like a facelift that drops one day.

5

A veneer slips and all of a sudden the raw flesh of the truth is exposed.

I'd been naffing about in London for ages waiting for something big. When I got back from Jerusalem they didn't seem to know what to do with me. I think I'm a bit of an embarrassment in the office now that newspapers have gone all corporate and slick, no smoking and a bottle of sparkling mineral water with lunch. Weird. That happened suddenly too, though I suppose it has to have been Murdoch. One morning you're a huge profit-making or -losing business and every glass of claret on expenses is checked and signed. No more glasses of claret. Most people these days seem to actually go to the gym. No, honestly.

I rapped my fingers on the foreign editor's desk and muttered 'Iraq' in her ear as often as was seemly. You'd have to have been blind not to see it coming.

Everyone knew the Americans were about to start bombing. I've got a friend in shipping who called me months earlier to tell me America was moving tons of military supplies to Kuwait and that it must mean war. This was before anyone had even started discussing it, let alone saying 'not in my name' and lying down on Whitehall and what have you. Not in my name. I ask you. As if Colin Powell cares what your name is.

I know it might seem odd for someone in my line of business (actually, it's not), but I find political discussions tedious. Basically because they are always negative and whining. You don't get a tableful of people sitting around and saying, 'Gosh, isn't Blair doing an excellent job!' 'Don't you just love President Bush?' It's always a self-righteous 'I could have done it better/could have told you/should have voted for the other bloke/shouldn't have voted at all'. I think once you stand between two sides who are trying to kill each other, you realise that it is all endlessly complicated. Everybody is wrong and right. Having a strong political viewpoint seems to mean being angry, self-important and judgemental.

Me and McCaughrean got in a couple of nights before things really got going, blood pumping with the prospect of war, not that we admitted it.

Don (never any of the above things) was on great form on the plane. He was very, very pissed before we even checked in and by the time we left the ground he was stroking his camera bag and saying he was going to change his name by deed poll to 'War On Terror' in the hope that the US government would accidentally pay some huge amount of money into his account at Barclays, High Street Kensington.

'Hey, Eff Zed,' he slobbered into my ear when he felt my attention waning. 'You want to keep alert. There's a war on, you know.' Well, not quite, there wasn't, but the boys were on their way from Alabama and Alsager and the British tabloids were already running pieces about what they'd be having to eat and what sort of desert training they had (or, more importantly, hadn't) had.

'Thanks, Don.' I nodded twisting my peanut packet into a cigarette shape and putting it into my mouth. How is it possible that you are not allowed to smoke on these things? The radiation is more likely to give you cancer than a couple of wafts of cigarette smoke, for God's sake.

Let's face it, something's going to get you one day. It might be that you've been on too many planes or smoked too many cigarettes or you might just get engulfed by a landslide on your idyllic mountainside where you spent your whole life drinking spring water and eating mushrooms. When you've got to go, you've got to go.

'Still, I shouldn't trouble yourself too much, Faithy,' he went on. 'After all, what do you fucking foreign fucking correspondents do anyway, eh?'

I didn't feel this question needed dignifying with an answer. I nodded at the stewardess who was offering me another vodka.

'I'll have a couple of those, thank you, darling,' McCaughrean bellowed at her.

'Of course, sir,' she muttered, screwing up her face in revulsion.

'Fucking dogs these days, aren't they?' Don said, while she was still very much in earshot.

It's funny that there are still people who expect stewardesses to be pretty. Such an old-fashioned thing somehow. A bit like calling women popsies and seeing nothing wrong in slapping a juicy-looking bottom when you see one. Come to think of it, Russia is still a bit like that. I once did a piece about a lawyer who was trying to get some sexual harassment cases to court in Moscow. The whole thing was absurd. The idea that a male boss didn't have the right to insist his secretary wear a see-through blouse and fuck him on a regular basis if she wanted to keep her job never occurred to anybody. People were at a loss to understand what exactly the complaint was.

I hoped Don might have forgotten his train of thought. No such luck.

'I mean, what? What do you really do?' he asked again, trying to shift about in his seat. The American airlines are apparently widening their seats because everyone over there is so fat. Perhaps Don should consider moving to the States, because he was definitely spilling over the sides of this one. And we were in Club.

Not too shabby for Faith Zanetti.

The paper was feeling generous towards us because we might die. Biiiiiiiiig upheavals since Martin Glover got killed in Jerusalem. OK, let's face it, he paid someone to kill him because I found out he was a murdering paedophile, but I didn't let that become entirely public knowledge. Why torture his family when he's already gone? I think there were people at work who worked it out, though. He was supposed to have died a hero but nobody ever, ever mentions his name. Normally if you die on the job you become a bit of a legend for six months or so. My dad's name was still knocking around nearly a decade after he died.

Nowadays they've started actually checking the facts on people's CVs and running the data past the police so you only get the perkiest, jolliest, sanest and most education-saturated types. There used to be some kind of meritocracy on the go, but now we're basically talking Oxbridge. I like Tamsin though. She's a good editor. Not that she is any more inclined to put actual news into the paper than anyone else, but she doesn't try to pretend either. She is very straightforward about ideas not being sexy enough and tells you to sensationalise the intro without making out it's to make things clearer. And she let me come to Baghdad.

It's weird, the beginning of a war. We know for sure that some of us probably will die. A few journalists usually do. Will it be me? I've been shot before, that time in El Salvador when I won the award, and my own father was killed in Ireland when I was little, but even then it's hard to swallow as a real possibility. But it *could* be me and on a rational level we know that, and that's why we are thundering with adrenalin and high-spirited mania. This is the game.

'Personally, Don, I write articles,' I said, without much enthusiasm or engagement. I know where he's going with this rant. Not, to put it mildly, the first time I have heard him expound on this theme.

'Yeah. Yeah. What? Five, six hundred words? A bit of Reuters wire and a quote from your driver? That's not work, Zanetti. I risk my fucking life on a daily fucking basis to get those images back. Those images that change public fucking opinion.'

He was having trouble with his headset. I think it was difficulty focusing rather than anything more mechanical.

'Yes, you do, Don,' I said and patted him on the arm.

Someone behind us was listening in. It was Grant Bradford, his orange hair gleaming in the gloom. He works for a tabloid. Not known for news coverage, but they do like a war. Especially a rabble-rousing one like this with a proper scary villain, a whole people wronged and our brave boys going in to face the music. Actually, I don't know why I'm being self-righteous about it since *The Chronicle* is no different. We just use longer words and excuse our lurid front page with a pompous leader or two way inside. Only the left-wing press felt they were on a mission. A mission to prove that military action is wrong. Well, it's not hard. A couple of pictures of dead babies and the readers are up in arms (so to speak) if they weren't already. Making war look bad is not difficult. It's justifying it that's the tricky area, though in this case made a lot easier by the leeringly Satanic baddy and his diabolical sons.

'Hey, lard arse. I have made a good, honest, twenty-year career out of a bit of Reuters and a quote from my driver and I won't hear a word said against it,' Grant said, leaning in between the seats to make his point. 'If anybody has any better suggestions as to how to put a piece together then I'd like to hear 'em.'

'Tosser,' McCaughrean muttered.

The plane was almost completely empty apart from journalists. Not many people flying into Baghdad at the minute. It's one of those destinations where you get disinfected on the way back. They tell you to put your hands over your face and then a steward walks up and down spraying everyone and everything with some sort of insecticide or something. Really weird.

I noticed that woman, whose name I can never remember, who had half her face blown off in Bosnia was sitting at the back drinking Drambuie. It looks like a mask (her face, not the Drambuie). Half beautiful and serene, half hideous and deformed, all twisted and stretched like bubblegum. Janet Fischer, the CNN war woman, had a thing with her. I think she works for a wire service.

'Welcome to Saddam International Airport.' Oh, please. McCaughrean rolled along behind me wheezing and gasping, and a mustachioed psychopath dressed like one of the Village People spent forty-five minutes trying to find discrepancies between the information on my visa and the information in my passport. He can't have thought my passport photo wasn't me. My frizz of curly blonde hair always looks pretty distinctive in photos. And the general scruffiness and tan. Presumably his fingernails would be pulled out with pliers if he let me in without the right documentation.

Amazing they'd given us all visas, really, but the myth was that they were going to win and we should all come and watch the glorious Iraqi victory.

10

Nasty regimes have a lot in common. Mainly that everybody is frightened. I remember when I married my Russian husband (a way of getting away from England) and I had to stand at customs for two hours. I was eighteen and the Cold War was still on. A boy in a hat looked down at me from his box and although there must have been a thousand people in the dark airport, it was almost completely silent. You felt that the KGB were poised behind the nearest door, just waiting to take you off to a gulag until the end of time. A woman spoke to ask me to heave her case off the carousel for her and she leaned in so close I thought she really was passing on some political secret. So the quiet and the gloom in Baghdad were familiar.

There were huge pastelly portraits of Saddam Hussein everywhere, hazy in the cigarette smoke and the fluorescent lights of an airport that would very likely be rubble by this time next week. Or didn't they know that? The man himself had apparently disappeared, though he was rumoured to be touring his capital in a taxi and hopping out to hug children whenever the opportunity arose. On the other hand it could have been one of his doubles. We didn't know it at the time but I guess he was probably already at that farmhouse with his stash of cash and his Mars Bars, leaping into his hole whenever a plane went overhead.

Is it obligatory for mad dictators to be such tasteless bastards? I mean, why would you want paintings of yourself all over the place that look like something off the side of a whirling waltzer or an advert for an obscure Egyptian film? Why does he smile like that? These things are terrible and the statues are worse. Lenin and Stalin were just the same, although at least the Soviets seemed to have slightly better artists at their disposal. Or maybe they didn't. I must say the early posters of Gorbachev with no birthmark were ridiculous. They were like something you get done of yourself outside Notre Dame for fifteen quid. A choice between that and a caricature, the result of either somewhere between the two.

Our taxi driver had done an engineering degree in Birmingham. 'I love

Birmingham,' he said, the warm air whooshing in from the city with smells of burning garbage and desert dust. We drove past a eucalyptus copse and they really do smell a bit like Vicks inhalers. 'It is the most charming place in the whole world. One day I will take my family back there to live happy forever.' I thought Don might actually choke to death laughing.

We drove along the bank of the Tigris, normal evening traffic gliding past the biblical palms. A lot of honking, a lot of swirling neon signs, a lot of crap electricity pylons with tangled wires draped low between them. Concrete. Baghdad is big on concrete. And roundabouts that stretch out to the horizon. No reason why it should, but it somehow doesn't look like the place where everything began. You know – Ur, the world's first city, Tower of Babel, hanging gardens of Babylon, the place where writing was invented and all that. More like somewhere you might get your hands cut off. Saw that monstrous sculpture that's supposed to be Saddam Hussein's enormous hands holding defiant swords. Defiance is always the stance of a loser, I thought. Of the person who doesn't have the power. You get defiant children and defiant pupils, defiant little republics and defiant tinpot dictators. If you've got to be defiant you might as well just surrender immediately.

'Oral Roberts,' I said to myself, looking at those hands.

'You what?' McCaughrean asked, scratching some eczema on his wrist.

'It reminds me of the Oral Roberts university in the American south,' I told him. He's a TV evangelist whose prayer tower got struck by lightning. No, really. It was this space pod on a stick in the university campus and God just struck it down. Quite rightly, of course.

When we pulled up at the Corona Hotel I gave the driver a packet of cigarettes as well as the fare. 'I prefer Benson and Hedges,' he said, and drove away, the radio wailing Om Khalsoum and her plaintive love songs into the night.

CHAPTER THREE

Check-in at the Corona is one of those procedures that involves confis-
cation of your passport and a brief interrogation. The whole world's press
was checking in. Japanese television crews, former Soviet hacks from
the ends of the earth, Belgian, Norwegian, Mexican reporters all excited
and chattering. One of the South Americans slapped me on the arse. I
kicked him. Don and I smoked impatiently and I clomped the heels of
my cowboy boots up and down on the marble floor, rapped my fingers
on the counter and pulled at coils of my hair. We were dying to dump
our bags and start drinking. There is something about walking into the
bar on the first night (in this case Carly Posner's room – prohibition in
Baghdad and all that. 'Return to Faith' they call it. Ha!) – like the first
day back at school. I slapped hands with Eden Jones – we were going
through a pretending to be matey phase. This is the man who would
probably be my husband if I were a normal person. And if he were.

13

'Hey, Zanetti. Thought you were embedded,' he said, grinning. He is always tanned and looks as though he's been sleeping in his clothes for a week, but the smile lines in his face and the shambling hunch of his shoulders are home. We are liable to fall into bed with each other when things get really bad – there was an incident in Jerusalem last year – but on the whole we spend most of our time trying to forget that we tried to be a couple once. The idea of either of us forming half of a couple is laughable. Let alone both of us. Absurd.

Lots of people were embedded, in fact. They place you with the army and you have to hand them their ammunition and stuff and write about how great our boys are. You don't get killed though, which is the advantage.

'Yeah. I didn't want to wear the uniform so they ditched me.' I winked and sat down to talk to Carly who I haven't seen since Bosnia when we spent the day on the beach in Split. I first met her in Moscow in 1993 when the White House was burning. She was a camerawoman in those days, crouched on the twenty-ninth floor of the Ukraine Hotel, poking her lens out of the window. Her sound man was killed, just standing there in a hotel room across the river from the action and at least fifty metres above it. He was drinking a Styrofoam cup of coffee. She is thin and wiry, more masculine than feminine, though she wears red lipstick that she reapplies every ten minutes in a compact mirror she keeps in her back pocket. It is a nervous tic, not vanity. She never washes her hair and it is dark and lank. She would say she doesn't care but I think she is just afraid that if she made the effort she might fail.

She always has these disastrous relationships with men she picks up in war zones, suffering from post-traumatic stress and wanting to be saved. When my friend Shiv was still alive she used to take the piss out of Carly. 'They are for having sex with, you know,' she would point out. Most of Carly's were barely capable, what with the horror and all that. Her most recent boyfriend shot himself last year so she told me about that and how she's had to adopt his teenage son. Fat lot of good she'd be as a mother, I pointed out. Quite, she agreed. We talked until we saw the dawn start to come up over the river, smudgy against the presidential palaces in the distance. Someone said they could hear a B-52 and we all perked up a bit but it was McCaughrean snoring. Al-Shabab TV, on silently in the corner, was showing a long documentary about some mosques. Gripping stuff.

I went to my room, had a burning hot shower and stood on the freaky Star Trek-design balcony in the requisite robe (these can be purchased from reception for $250 US) to watch the day begin. Middle Eastern cities seem to shimmer at dawn. Perhaps it's the dust or the pollution or both. A few boats were bobbing on the river and cars had started honking along the banks. I could squint and see what must be the Al Rashid Hotel where they have the disco with the naked singer and pink lighting, and Saddam's crappy half-built mosques, the spindly telecommunications tower with the giant saucer on top and the pyramid-shaped mansion that belonged to Saddam's late brother-in-law Adnan. Did he have him killed? I think so. There was the military marching field with giant sabres looming over it. And the oil fires that had already been started on the outskirts. I crouched down and leant against the sliding doors to smoke in the orange mist. I had managed to lull myself into a kind of stupor when suddenly a building exploded in front of me. I hadn't even seen a plane. Briefly, I considered the possibility that I had imagined it.

I stood up and flicked my cigarette off the side of the balcony, leaning over for a better view. The bombardments had begun. Suddenly the whole city was wailing with air raid sirens and I could see and hear the crackle of anti-aircraft fire. People must be running downstairs with their bottles of water and torches. Babies crying.

I wish I could say I was unimpressed or, more politically correct, appalled. But it was sort of cool to see gleaming American F-14s swooping out of the sky and deafening the city with these earth-shaking explosions that left a cloud of smoke and dust in the place of what might have been the Ministry of Defence. Your first thought, my first thought, isn't the casualties, though God knows there will be time enough to think about, to see, to grieve for them. My first thought was, fuck me, they're good. Here they are, these Americans, ruling the world. For better or for worse. The come-and-get-me glint of those planes in the smoking sky made me glad not to be Saddam Hussein. It never took a genius to see that the Iraqis didn't stand a chance.

Eden's batty theory is that Saddam, realising he was toast in terms of military hardware, was going to capitulate, end the whole thing in a few days and then start country-wide anti-American insurrections, making the whole place ungovernable. Welcome back, Saddam. All a bit conspiracy theory for my liking. But cute.

Pip Deakin, Mr BBC Serious, was out on his balcony too, shouting and swearing at his producer and getting ready to do a live piece to his videophone in pyjamas and flak jacket. His camera crew were showing him how to use the phone, their own equipment idle at their feet. He could have done a proper piece with lights that the viewers in England would actually be able to see. He preferred, however, the grainy out-of-synch intrepidness of the videophone. Thought it made him look braver. He wiped some grease into his hair and smoothed his eyebrows down. More like a soap star than someone standing in the middle of a doomed city. He muttered to himself, practising.

'From where I stand here in central Baghdad,' he began (yeah, not actually that central – they put us in this hotel because it's not too central and therefore NICE AND SAFE). 'I can see F-14 and F-18 jets pounding Republican Guard strongholds with cruise missiles. These planes are coming from the USS *Theodore Roosevelt* in the Eastern Mediterranean . . .'

'Looking foxy, Deakin,' I shouted over to him as another explosion seemed to rock the city. 'Don't duck.'

'I'll take that blow job whenever you're ready, Zanetti,' he yelled back, adjusting his pyjama lapel. Idiot.

I pulled myself together (that is, put my jeans on) and went down into the lobby, hauling my flak jacket and helmet with me. My helmet had 'Press' written on the front of it. Mmm. That should do it. They'd given us goggles too, for some reason. It's a war, not a chemistry experiment. I hope. (Weapons of mass destruction or no weapons of mass destruction, that is the question. Or rather, will they be used on me?) It didn't seem a great time for my lunch date, but I'd set it up from London and I was planning to keep it. My dad had this Iraqi girlfriend, Nur, before he met Evie. She'd been to England and I remembered her and liked her. On the phone she had sounded a bit distant – I could hear her smoking in a languorous way – but she said she'd come and get me from the hotel.

Pandemonium in the lobby. The press rushing about tugging wires and shouting in a clipped, organised way. Then from outside the sound of real panic (more 'my house is on fire' than 'got a deadline to meet'), cars honking and tyres squealing on asphalt. The Middle East is very heavy on asphalt, mainly, I think, because it makes your driving sound more macho, screeching under rubber.

I saw Eden walking through the revolving doors to the street. He had a notebook in his hand and was writing in it, fag clenched between his lips. He spat it out and trod on it. One of the hotel staff was watering spiky plants with a green hose. He had his trousers rolled up and his feet were getting wet.

'Look at that.' I nudged Eden, but he was looking at the sky.

'Hey, Faithy,' Eden said as though I hadn't spoken, excited, agitated. 'Look how fucking low they're coming in. They really don't give a shit.'

He took my packet of cigarettes out of the back pocket of my jeans and put one in his mouth. Then he put the packet in his shirt pocket, along with his red Bic lighter.

17

'Hey, arsehole, they're mine,' I said, snatching them back. He hadn't even noticed where they had come from.

'Oh, sorry.' He flinched, and stared up at the smoking skies. ''Chup to?' he asked me, not caring.

'Lunch with an ex of Dad's,' I told him.

'What? Now?' He squinted. I'd got his attention. Maybe he was jealous that I was being more war blasé than he was. Pathetic? Yes. But a lot of that kind of competitiveness goes on out here.

I nodded. 'This instant.'

'Fuck me, Zanetti. If you're going to go round the world trying to eat lunch with every single ex of your dad's, you're not going to get a lot of work done.'

'Good point,' I said. Never mind me, how the hell Dad ever found time to file his pieces or take his shirts to the laundry I can't imagine. A black limo pulled up in front of us.

I remembered Nur young and studenty, phenomenally beautiful, rather zealous. Lots of ideas about Iraq and her people. None of them, obviously, involving Saddam Hussein. In fact I think she had a brother she was rather hoping might seize power one day, waiting in the wings printing illegal pamphlets. All very Lenin. So I'm not sure what I expected but the sight of her now was hilarious – big hair and perfectly matching lipstick, bag and dainty shoes, just as if no bombs were pounding down at all. She grinned all over her face, laughing at my clothes and hair.

'Habibi,' she said, kissing me three times. 'God, you look just like him.' At Dad's funeral the church was packed full of wailing women who had flown in from around the world. It sounds like an exaggeration but it's not. Last time I spent more than a month in London I thought I'd try and do something about my flat and went to Homebase. An American woman I recognised from my childhood was loading up her car in the miserable November rain.

18

'Sandy?' I said.

Sandy stood up, looked at me and burst into tears.

'It seems like yesterday when you first came to New York. You were such a tiny little girl,' she said. 'I still miss him, you know. He was the only man who could be a friend, a colleague, a lover . . .'

Hey. I had never known he was sleeping with Sandy too. I mean, we went to her wedding, for Christ's sake.

Nur's driver, sitting behind the dark glass of a huge black beetle of a Mercedes, honked his horn. Not, apparently, as blasé as his mistress. Hotel security were staring at the car and twitching towards their guns. A man in dirty white robes walked along the street by the hotel. He had a big old radio pressed to his ear. He was listening to tinny pop music.

'All this fuss,' Nur scoffed, at her driver, at the media-related chaos. 'If we can survive decades of Saddam bloody Hussein, we can survive this, don't you think, darling?'

She was almost better looking now than when Dad had first turned up in London with her, a student, shy and pretty and completely in awe of this journalist she had been translating for. Translating, my arse. That's the kind of language everybody understands. Now Nur, like poor widowed Evie, Dad's wife, is coiffed and manicured, with glossy tights and a shiny handbag, beige clothes and a smell of money. To be fair on Dad, he had apparently offered to marry her but she hadn't wanted to leave Iraq. And Iraq had clearly been good to her.

'See you later, Jones.' I waved to Eden, scrambling into the back of the car. Leather seats, air conditioning, maybe even a mini bar, though I didn't look. Nur offered me a little tiny cigarette from a silver cigarette case and put one in her own mouth.

'Darling, how are you?' she smiled as we purred away – into the city. The currently being bombarded city. Well, if she didn't seem to care, why should I?

'Good. Good. Same as ever. How's Rashid?' She married a very, very

19

old oil man of some kind. Sent me the tackiest wedding photo postcard I've ever seen. Nur sequinned from head to toe and glowing with soft-focus pink-tinted naffness, standing next to a mustachioed corpse in a tux.

We skidded hard round a corner, nearly killing a donkey, and I held on to the completely useless hanging strap. Nur had somehow managed to just sway with the car.

'Sweety, didn't I tell you? He's dead. I'm sure I must have written.' She flicked her ash into the appropriate compartment and smiled with big chocolate eyes.

'Oh. Sorry,' I said. Had she written? Probably. I can't be expected to keep up with the life details of every last girlfriend of my father world-wide, now can I?

'I'm remarried. You must remember Hugo!' she said, some vast electric gates, perhaps inspired by a trip to Graceland, opening in front of us, a man in a sentry box nodding deferentially to Nur. She had lawns. No, not only did she have lawns (an amazing feat in the Middle East) but the lawns were being sprinkled. Right now. Now. Today. Explosions rock Baghdad and Nur is turning on the sprinklers. Brilliant. Admittedly, it was that grass they have in hot places, very dark green and very thick blades, but it was grass.

'Hugo Greene? You're joking?' I laughed, getting out of the car into some red dust, large potted palms flanking a white colonnaded entrance. God, it was hot. I have seen a lot of houses like this before. A few of them in Beirut but most of them on Bishops Avenue, London's tackiest residential street with unbelievably big houses on it, all Roman columns and statues and security. One of them is called 'Top Rack Mansion' and that pretty much sums it up taste-wise. Porn barons and Russians. Here, though, in suburban Baghdad, it means class, education (probably abroad) and culture.

Someone had heard us drive up. He opened the door – a boozy-looking white bloke in blue linen trousers and a white shirt, sweat-stained despite the expensive chill from within. It was Hugo Greene.

'Faith Zanetti. Good to see you. Fucking hell. Look at you. How old does that make me?' He slapped me on the back and spilt a bit of his whisky on ice. 'Want one?' he asked, glancing up a bit blearily.

'Vodka, please. Thanks.'

Hugo bloody Greene. I think he was on *The Chronicle* with my dad in the seventies. Or no. It must have been a different paper because they were both in New York together. Studio 54, Elaine's and all that, doing stories about crime and race. Nothing's changed. So he'd got dad back at last, marrying Nur. The famous story about Hugo Greene and my dad is that Dad went to visit him in some real shithole posting like Brussels or Helsinki or somewhere and Hugo had left Dad at the bar with his girlfriend, Ruslanka, for an hour or so while he filed his story. Big mistake. Dad and Ruslanka were together for about two years. They had a horrible flat in Hackney and a hamster. I used to have to go and stay the night but I was always sick. The smoke. The fear. Maybe the hamster.

I hadn't noticed the route we'd taken but we must have been miles away from the centre because I couldn't hear a thing. Just Nur's heels on the black and white marble floor. There was a romantic painting of Nur in white underwear hanging on the left of the gilt staircase, catching some of the light from a Hampstead garden suburb chandelier. Hardly Hugo's scene I wouldn't have thought, but maybe, like the rest of us, he never really had a scene. We all spend so much time looking at every-body else's that we forget to rustle one up for ourselves. Maybe this suited him as well as anything.

'Come in here,' he said, and I clomped into a kind of dining room with big French doors on to the garden where the sprinkler was whirring. It depressed me to see Dad's friends. Hard to believe he'd have been this old if he'd survived the shooting in Belfast. He would have hated it.

21

'Your old dad would have fucking hated being old, Faithy,' Hugo said, sloshing some vodka into a crystal glass. I assumed this was Rashid's house. 'Look at me. Eyesight's going, organs are failing.'

'Leave it out, Greene. You're not that old.' I laughed, but not with much enthusiasm. He looked dreadful. But that was more the brain-boiling sun and the booze, wasn't it? He couldn't have been much over sixty, if that.

'Older than I once was, younger than I'll be,' he sang. Simon and Garfunkel, I think.

'How do you know Nur?' I wondered, standing in front of the drinks cabinet, listening to Nur issuing orders to someone who would be bringing food to the meticulously laid table.

'Nur? Fuck. I can't even remember. Known her all my life. She introduced me to Iraq. Came here to see her in nineteen eighty-one and never left. Best country in the world,' he smiled, showing teeth that looked as if they wished they'd been to America for some work.

Funny types these. You get them everywhere. Journalists who don't quite manage to leave. It means they lose their jobs with the big papers, of course, and end up stringing for whoever will have them. And then they go totally mad, lose all sense of perspective and start writing ranting humourless columns about the infidel west and Israel, and eventually become the subjects of documentaries. They pretend to themselves, as Hugo was probably doing, that they have fallen in love with a local and can't leave. But in fact they usually go out with a string of locals in that rather imperialist way westerners have and end up pissed and alone in the seediest bars talking to anyone white they can find about their once glorious careers. Hey, it's a type, though they're dying out fast.

A girl in a headscarf and Nike trainers brought some trays of food in and we sat down to eat, away from the blistering heat outside and ignoring the war which was beginning not many miles away.

22

'Maybe we should have gone up to the fountains for a picnic,' Nur smiled, perhaps as an indication that we would be deleting the fighting from our consciousness for the duration of lunch. I pushed some meatballs around my plate and sipped my vodka. One of the nice things about the Middle East is that you can smoke throughout a meal without anyone thinking you are lower than slime.

'Tell me,' Nur said, exhaling her smoke and smiling warmly. 'Have you married an English Lothario without letting Auntie Nur know?'

Auntie Nur, eh? OK.

I laughed. 'Hardly,' I said. 'Not the marrying kind.'

Hugo and Nur scoffed together at this.

'Darling,' Nur told me. 'Everyone is the marrying kind. It's finding the right fellow that might be difficult for someone as . . . as lively as you are.'

'Well, if that's true then I'm still having difficulty. And, frankly, most married people don't seem to have found the right fellow either,' I said, a bit too cross. I hate this tyranny. I would loathe to have someone's relentless presence in my life, someone who feels he has a right to shout at me when I piss him off. 'Evie's got it about right,' I said, picking up a glass of water. 'Hardly ever sees the man.'

Nur took her knife and fork in her hands as though she wasn't quite sure what they were for. 'Ah yes,' she said. 'I had forgotten that she remarried.' Evie could be described as being my stepmother. Not by me though.

There was a long pause during which nobody mentioned that Nur had been in love with my dad and that he had dumped her for Evie. I coughed.

'Are you managing to work at all?' I wondered. Well, I didn't actually but I had to say something.

'Well, everything has come to a bit of a standstill now, but Hugo and I are active politically. My brother . . .' Nur began, but either she thought better of it or Hugo kicked her. This was the brother who was eyeing the presidency. Fat chance. 'There's a friend of ours here you must meet,' she said, changing the subject and looking at my face as though it slightly gave her the creeps. They all do this. I look like my dad. 'Joshua Klein.'

Hugo glanced up expectantly but I didn't know him. Yet.

'Bit of an arsehole but he might be useful,' he told me. 'Might get you both round to the flat.' As well as this place they apparently had a flat in the centre, the old bit where all the writers used to live before Saddam.

'I'd love to meet him,' I said.

'Knew your old man, I think,' Hugo added. 'Yes, I'm sure he did.'

That's the moment I'd like to get back to. Right then. The first mention of his name. I could have said, 'Ooooh, no thanks, too busy. Sorry.' But of course I'd have met him anyway. That day, though, the first day of the bombardments, out at Nur and Hugo's, that's when the poison set in.

I made my excuses as soon as I could. I always look forward to seeing people who knew Dad and it always depresses me. Somehow, the present gets obliterated at these meetings and I start feeling mired in an unhappy past, as though this death, this enormous bereavement is the only thing that ever happened to me. And there is always an empty seat at the table.

I kissed Nur and Hugo sadly, as though I would never see them again, or as though we were parting after a funeral or something. Ugh. I was pleased to be swooshed back to the hotel, flak jacket at my feet. The driver was nervous about being home with his family before dark and who could blame him? He took all the corners in that mad religious way – if God wants to save me, He will. In my view, He often needs a bit of assistance. I couldn't shake off the gloom of Nur and Hugo somehow. He got so pissed he could hardly speak by the time the pista-chio cakes and coffee came out and I noticed that Nur winced whenever she had to get up or sit down. Her ease and sophistication all a kind of desperate act. In fact she was probably morphined up to the eyeballs and terrified out of her mind by the prospect of more war. Now I know Hugo is hardly the world's greatest advert for alcoholic refreshment, but I needed a drink.

CHAPTER FOUR

I was glad to be dropped back at the noise and heat of the Corona. Eden was standing outside with a group of others as though he hadn't moved since I'd left. People were trundling around getting ready to go somewhere and I sensed a bit of a story coming on. They like to give you something to get your teeth into on the first day. We'd all been gripped by a website called 'Where is Raed?' where this Iraqi bloke talks about his life in the suburbs of Baghdad somewhere. We called him, or actually I think he called himself, the Baghdad Blogger. It was a news story 'lite', something to liven up the grimness of war, so everyone had got very into him and most of us were putting out feelers that might lead us to a face-to-face interview. No big deal, just a jokey feature to cheer up the readers. Today he'd told us that Iraqi radio DJs weren't allowed to call the band 'Bush' by its name because of its less musical namesake. They have to spell it out. 'Another track from Bee You Ess Aitch.' Tamsin would be pleased if I got to him first.

'We're being dragged off to a children's ward. Want to come?' Eden asked me, running a hand through his hair.

I looked at him with a question.

'You know – first day, injured babies, horrors of war?'

'Hmmm,' I said.

'They want to show us the carnage we've wreaked. Come on, Faithy!' He rolled up his notebook and put his pen in his shirt pocket.

'Might,' I said, and dumped all my protective stuff at my feet. There was a pale blue bus with bits of lined paper Sellotaped to the window. A government-approved outing. The CNN signs took up the first few rows and behind them the BBC. Pip would be pissed off. The BBC hates to be second to CNN. They see CNN as half-witted propagandising sensationalist drivel and themselves as the very font of truth and knowledge. They feel enraged (perhaps defiant?) when they're lumped together with CNN or, worse, belittled by them. Both, of course, are somewhere between the two descriptions above (though anyone would surely concede that the CNN people have bigger hair. One only has to remember Flip Spiceland, the surreally named CNN weatherman with the orange tan.)

'Give us a fag, Eff Zed,' McCaughrean shouted at me, waddling towards the bus with a can of beer. 'Hair of the dog,' he grinned, holding it up jauntily. His eyes were puffy and watering.

'Buy your own,' I said, giving him one.

The TV people were taking their places with their endless stuff. Incredible palaver it is to provide the public with pictures of really horrible things happening. (The decision on exactly how horrible is taken by a million people from the cameraman himself to the executive producer of the particular news show in London or New York. 'Let's go for quite horrible since it's going out after ten.' 'Dunno, Ed. We did moderately horrible for the six o'clock. People are going to want a bit more.')

We all had various pieces of accreditation clattering round our necks and everyone was excited. There is always a bit of a school trip atmosphere on these outings. Anticipatory mania, jostling, shouting, arguing. Don actually started singing 'Ten Green Bottles' until Grant hit him with an old copy of *Newsweek*. The teacher figures, naturally, are the locals. The driver (big moustache, gold watch), Mahmoud the fixer (young, baseball cap, eyes firmly focused on a future in the Florida Keys) and Ayesha the translator (hair so thick and glossy that she might be the subject of a fairy tale and who was actually holding a copy of the Ba'athist paper *Thawra*), most of them provided by the Iraqi Ministry of Information and therefore little real help. At least, that's the myth. People like Pip Deakin are always sneeringly dismissive of quotes or leads from MI employees, but actually I've often found them pretty useful (though admittedly whenever I ask anyone what they think about the war, they always start going on about the barbecues they've had to cancel and the termite and caterpillar infestations they're anticipating when the repellent shortages get acute. Nice bits of colour maybe, but not exactly the address of Saddam's bunker). Anyway, on trips like this one, clouds of dust spewing up around the city, the locals accompanying us tend to get a bit downhearted.

I dug Eden in the ribs. 'Shit! That little girl's got a grenade launcher!' I hissed, pointing at a barefooted, tousle-headed creature in the street below.

''S a Hoover, Faith,' he sighed.

'Oh yeah,' I admitted. Well, people were dragging very odd things around. There was an old bloke with a fridge balanced on top of an old pram.

'He's forgotten the baby!' McCaughrean shouted out in glee.

These idiotic twittering children, the Iraqis must be thinking, are responsible for showing the world what is happening to us. Oh, great.

29

They had the radio on at the front of the bus and there was a deeply odd moment when the music stopped and the volume seemed to have been turned up. The Americans had somehow scrambled themselves on to the airways and someone shouted, 'This is the day you have all been waiting for,' first in English, then in Arabic. Was it? I wondered. In my case, actually, they turned out to be right. I suppose. Or the day I'd always dreaded.

They had to take us a special and ridiculously circuitous route round Baghdad so that we didn't see any of the actual damage caused by the bombardment. We were suddenly in a surreal situation where we could have been on a tour bus looking at a slightly shabby, very hot, historic, yet modernised city like Cairo or Damascus. It was a bit like going to lunch at Nur's in its seeming banality, but that's what is always so weird about war. Not the war itself, but the apparent lack of it. And yet, five minutes later we went along the river down Sadoun Street and saw a couple of men holding rocket-propelled grenade launchers (not Hoovers this time) and wearing red and white checked headscarves. Weirdly, they seemed totally unmenacing. They flashed us the V sign. I could see now how Nur and Hugo were able to remain pretty much oblivious to the horrors around them. They really were basically avoidable unless you were a journalist. Or, of course, someone living in the wrong place. At the wrong time.

'God, that is really a hideous piece of artwork,' I said, pointing at a big spiky sculpture of lots of people screaming. Ayesha came to tell me it was by Dr Ala Bashir. I remembered reading something about how he was Saddam's surgeon and may be the man chosen to remodel him for exile. Perhaps he would go for a more Janet Jackson look.

Everyone was doing pieces about his body doubles. Was it or was it not Saddam himself rallying his people out in the suburbs? Not that it much mattered.

'Look! No war!' Eden commented, blowing his smoke in the direction of the bus window, out of which could be seen, as he so rightly pronounced, no war. On the other hand they were taking us to see innocent victims of the carnage perpetrated by the imperialist pigs, so – all a bit confusing.

This (i.e. confusing) was a position Iraqi officials continued to hold right until the man with the purple beret, the one who told us every day how Iraq was winning (Mohammed Saeed al-Sahhaf, he was called, for your information), ran away to Egypt to have sex with belly dancers. Today he'd told the people who made it to his press conference (the rest of us had to make do with photocopied sheets) that the Americans had not been able to attack Baghdad because of the brilliance of the Iraqi air defences. Uh-huh.

As if to emphasise the whole school trip thing, Don started singing again. 'The wheels on the bus go round and round . . .' McCaughrean sang until Grant tried to kill him. 'Ouch! Fuck off, Bradford. I'm just trying to cheer everyone up a bit.'

'Well, don't,' Grant told him. 'I am already intensely happy.'

He wasn't lying either. This was exactly his kind of story. The tabloids, and that's him, were going to love a big children's hospital piece. They could start a campaign and outsell everyone else by daring to splash with 'really rather disturbing' front page photograph of horribly (but not fatally) injured baby. Grant was jiggling his knees up and down.

'Oh, right.' Don coughed, adjusting his enormous expanse of flesh for maximum (though minimal) comfort.

Don leapt out first when we got there. 'Come on, Zanetti, you slag,' he shouted. 'You won't get a camel's arsehole of a story in here, you know.'

'Thanks, Don,' I said, and scrambled after him.

We all stumbled off the bus, stretched our legs and tried desperately to get a feel for a place we would later have to describe succinctly. Perhaps Saddam Hussein has always been a canny manipulator of the media and therefore slapped up all these absurd billboards of himself absolutely everywhere such that it is hard even to notice anything else. Or maybe he was being considerate. Just wanted to make sure his opponents had plenty to do when he was finally overthrown. Hours of fun would later be had tearing these stupid pictures down, plugging them with bullet holes and beating them with shoes (weird, eh?). And I would be changed forever. Later.

A doctor was standing waiting for us on the steps of the hospital, her hair blowing about in the hot wind as though a helicopter was landing near her. There was a fair amount of shouting. There were several hypodermic needles on the ground and a few bloodied gurneys standing outside some swing doors. (I hate the word gurney. Reminds me of executions in America where they strap people to them before they kill them.) On one of them, as well as a spreading bloodstain, there was also a clump of black hair. We seemed to have been taken to the A and E entrance and people were being rushed in on stretchers, bleeding dramatically. A veiled mother and a mustachioed father ran alongside their child, praying, comforting, pleading. I couldn't tell what had happened to him. Shrapnel, maybe. The nurse who came out to them was already in tears.

The jubilant expectation of the bus subsided fairly immediately and everyone lurched straight into work mode, a lot of the camera crews setting up right there to get shots of the outside hysteria and chaos. The doctor turned towards us, squinting in the sun. She waved in an instruction to follow her. A lot of people didn't, but Eden, smiling, ready for the flirt; Don, equipment beating his enormous body as he moved; Grant shining with anticipation and I, wary, tired, climbed up the steps to shake her hand, solemn now.

'Faith Zanetti,' I said, trying to straighten my leather jacket (my dad's old leather jacket, battered and worn by both our wars) to look a bit more respectful. Because I was. Respectful. People like this always

32

chasten me. Here we are watching and here they are doing something. She led us inside with a strained smile. She didn't have to tell us that she held us responsible for the start of war with which her hospital was not equipped to cope. She could tell we were appalled by the not equippedness. 'It's worse down at the Al Kindi,' she said. A hospital in the working class Al Nahda district, apparently.

Why is telling you where things are worse useful? It's like being ill and yet being aware that somebody else is iller. It doesn't actually make you feel any better. So the Al Kindi's worse, is it? Hmmm, well, suddenly this place looks like a hospital in Beverly Hills. Yup.

'Fuck me,' McCaughrean said, putting his hand to his mouth. The hospital stank.

Eden walked along with Dr Sharif, looking earnestly into her face. She was blank and professional, not responding to his attempt at seduction. Pathological. He does it with everyone of both sexes. I mean, obviously with the women he is partly trying to get laid and with the men he's not, but he needs everyone to love him. Everyone. That's why he likes me. Because I refuse to fully succumb. Pathological. I do it with everyone of both sexes.

'And once they've been stabilised?' he was saying. Dr Sharif pointed towards a shabby ward, black robes swishing around in front of our eyes as mothers fetched and carried for their sick children. Sick, in this case. We hadn't got as far as the war wounded yet.

I can't read Arabic but I could tell what the posters all over the thickly gloss-painted walls were all about. It used to be the same in Russia. Not that the standard of care and training isn't pretty impressive, just that they don't have the supplies they need. So the whole place is full of signs about how to keep yourself clean (i.e. they won't be doing it) and healthy (i.e. don't get ill, we haven't got the drugs to cure you). A bit like that time Edwina Currie advised the elderly to wrap up warm for winter. Well, that's the NHS down the tubes then. My favourite Soviet one was, 'Meat is bad for you.' There was, of course, a major meat shortage at the time. These posters showed happy people with a solid black wedge of hair and very red lips. 'Drink liquids', 'Eat food'. That kind of message.

I had a friend at school whose house was covered with Second World War posters. One of them showed a meek-looking orphan and read, 'Collect bones for glue. Now!' And, of course, the 'Careless Talk Costs Lives' campaign, with couples in bed and a German soldier peeking out from behind the wardrobe. Anyway, my favourite was a whole series of pictures and advice about how to live every aspect of your life. 'If you see a neighbour spit, let the warden know of it. On this matter please be firm, handkerchiefs will stop that germ.' 'Do not wear your coat in bed, keep it for outdoors instead. It is chillier out there and you will need the extra wear.' Sinister really. What to do after Armageddon.

Now normally I can cope with this sort of thing. I can. That's not to say I like it. It's grim and upsetting, but it's possible to achieve a level of detachment that makes it bearable again after a drink and a cigarette. After all, it's almost patronising to get too upset, to intrude on genuine grief. It's their tragedy, not mine, and who am I to be weeping and wailing about the horrors of the world when I am not experiencing them directly? That's a feature writer's area.

Some men helped us on with green smocks, face masks, gauzy hair nets and shoe coverings. Then we walked down a bare and quiet hall like a prison corridor. The only thing on the wall was a framed portrait of Saddam Hussein grinning like the maniac he is (was?). Dr Sharif opened a door and we went into a small room where an older woman in a black abaya was sitting on a metal chair. We were shown through some curtains and to a bed on wheels with a kind of hoop built over it.

And this boy was burnt. I mean really badly burnt. It seemed unbelievable that he was still alive. A woman stood next to him actually screaming. There weren't enough staff here to start dealing with her grief as well as his burns. Eden turned round to me, relaying information from Dr Sharif.

'It's not as painful as it looks,' he said.

Oh good. Because let me tell you . . .

'They don't feel that much pain because of the damage to the nerves.'

I thought about this and began to feel sick.

'That's his grandmother. Mother, father, four sisters, three brothers, some cousins, everyone – dead,' he whispered, reverent, awed.

It doesn't matter how many times you hear these horrors, it's always terrible. Most of us have been bereaved, so the base feeling is just about knowable, but the idea of having everyone you know completely obliterated in one go is something nobody can describe. Accept that it's horrible and move away. I once heard a rabbi giving a talk about the meaning of the Holocaust. He stressed that we mustn't forget it but admitted that there was no way of understanding or dealing with it. We must, he said, simply bear witness. Is that perhaps what we were doing here? Well, maybe, but it didn't feel as dignified or as grand as that. In fact, I felt distinctly parasitical. I coughed.

In a non-specific way, nothing looked clean enough. It's not that there were pools of festering fluids on the floor or rats scuttling about. It was just hot and didn't smell enough of bleach. The equipment was old, with its once-white paint flaking off to show the rusting steel underneath. You didn't have to look in the supply cabinets to know that they would be more or less empty. A few glass vials of something nobody needs, couple of rags. That sort of thing.

The boy had lost both hands. Lost. Silly way of putting it. He won't be finding them again. One stump was bandaged and the other one was being bathed in something by a young man in pressed jeans. The patient was unconscious but sort of twitching. The yellow smell of iodine, blood and sweat was overpowering. We were clearly in the way, but Dr Sharif demonstrated her exhibit with a certain amount of pride.

The message was clear. LOOK WHAT YOU HAVE DONE. And I felt ashamed.

'Shit,' I said, and I turned away. 'Shit.' I was finding it hard to breathe and stepped out of the cubicle, just some dirty green curtains really, and into the main corridor. Lots of men stood smoking out here now, their hair and moustaches dyed an unnatural black. Some in jellabas, some in western clothes (if you call thin snakeskin belts with gold buckles and matching maroon loafers western).

There are two hair looks for Iraqi men. The short back and sides with glossy moustache like Saddam Hussein or the cleanshaven face and head combination like Uday Hussein. Huge quantities of aftershave are required for either. The reek of all the different perfumes was not helping with the nausea. I lit a cigarette myself and tried to calm down. I must have had my face in my hands because it was Joshua Klein who pulled them gently away.

CHAPTER FIVE

I don't like being touched. A matey slap on the back, a clearly sexual caress – fine. Anything in between gives me the creeps. This was one of those occasions. I jerked my hands away and glowered at the perpetrator. He was standing too close to me. No prizes for guessing his nationality. As American as apple pie and the right to bear arms. Clean teeth, minty confidence, white nails, sharp cuffs, flashes of gold at the wrist and fingers. There is a line in the Jack Nicholson film *As Good As It Gets* where he says that there are plenty of people who have had lives full of trips to the lake and noodle salad, 'Just no one in this car.' But Josh Klein smelt as though he was one of the people who had had such a life.

'Back off,' I said and he smiled, but he didn't back off.

'Hello. Joshua Klein. Who are you?' he asked.

Ah. Nur and Hugo's friend. What had Hugo said? 'A bit of an arse-hole.'

Klein introduced himself as though he had bumped into me at a church fete. I looked at his face and thought, hmmm. Cute. I tore all my burns unit clothes off and draped them over an empty metal trolley, suddenly feeling silly.

I love this moment. The lurch of interest. You know. Sometimes when you meet the waiter's eye and can't help smiling.

I remember once working in the offices of some American television company in Moscow, trying to earn money to keep myself and my new Russian husband in vodka, and I had to arrive at 5.30 a.m. to relieve the night shift. I used to walk across the Smolenskiy Bridge in the pitch dark, the river frozen solid beneath me, my breath crystallising as I trudged through the uncleared snow. I banged on the window of a kiosk and woke up a drunk boy with a gun who sold me cigarettes. Then I would go behind the Ukraine Hotel, one of Stalin's dark wedding cake buildings, to the post office which steamed with yellow light. Misha would open the door, and heat and light poured out into the black dawn as he handed me the day's papers.

One morning I hugged them to my chest and stomped across the eight-lane road to the office (there were hardly any cars then. Now that road is a 24-hour-a-day traffic jam). I pushed the double steel doors open and smelt the ink from the clattering Reuters, AP and TASS machines and flicked on the fluorescent strip lights. A boy I hadn't seen before raised his sleepy head and looked at me – big green jumper, dark floppy hair, black shiny eyes. Hmmm. Cute, I thought, and beamed at him.

'Want to go for a drink later?' I asked him.

'Sure,' he grinned. There was a fling, but that was the best bit of it.

Joshua Klein watched me thinking, Hmmm, cute, and he smiled at me and nodded. The twinkle in his green eyes and the slight upwards twitch at the edge of his mouth said, 'It's not me that's cute, sweetheart. It's you.' He didn't say it though. I wish I had properly noted that at the time. I always thought I knew what he was thinking, judging by the passion in his touch and the adoration in his eyes. He never said it though. Not without a gun to his head. But that was all to come.

'Faith Zanetti,' I said, and grabbed his hand, shaking it extremely vigorously. 'Faith Cleopatra Zanetti.'

I have never told anybody my middle name before. Would you? With this man though, I wanted to go in big. Now I'm not someone who finds it hard to make an impression normally (if nothing else, everyone always remembers my hair, a kind of blonde Afro), but this time I wanted to be sure.

Joshua Klein threw back his head and laughed. I laughed with him, more quietly. He looked carefully into my face for the truth, his face less than three inches away. He saw, and he was right, that I was not lying.

'No!'

'Really.' I winked and smiled so broadly my face hurt.

'Stupid name,' he said, shaking his head, still laughing.

'Tell me about it,' I agreed.

He was a lot older than me. Probably fifty-ish, I thought, though I could have been a decade out. But he moved like a young man and his hair wasn't yet completely grey – salt and peppered. Really though, it was his inexplicable enthusiasm for life that made it hard to guess. All his lines are laugh lines and his eyes laugh even when he doesn't. They are as alert as they must have been when he was a little boy, glancing round at everything, boring into everyone, bright green sprinkled with gold, with a look in them which I find shocking. Found shocking.

'You can't go around *looking* at people like that!' I said. 'It's disgusting.'

He laughed again, lots of white American teeth.

'Like what?' he asked, looking at me like that again. It was hard to interpret exactly, but it was about sex. It was about doing all kinds of rude things and I wanted him to do them. You know the Woody Allen thing. Is sex dirty? Only if you're doing it right.

He was glittering with flirtation, as though he was playing an exciting game and was just about to win. It was extremely infectious.

'Like that,' I said, fidgeting for my cigarettes. 'Yes. That. Exactly like that.'

'Stop me,' he said, and took my lighter out of my hands, lighting my cigarette for me and looking at me exactly like that as he did it. A challenge of some kind?

I wanted to tear his silk tie and his cufflinks off him and eat him.

We were both laughing when a nurse, her kholed eyes blazing, stormed out of one of the nearby rooms, slamming the door behind us.

'SSSSSHHHHHHHHH!' she hissed, consumed with anger.

Joshua Klein apologised in Arabic until she smiled and blushed a bit. As the nurse sidled off, embarrassed and pleased, Dr Sharif swept out of Jamal's cubicle and saw Joshua. She hauled herself up and straightened her white coat a little.

'Professor Klein.' She nodded, and carried on along the corridor, her stethoscope swinging round her neck.

'Not just a pretty face,' I said and he raised his eyebrows at me, complicit, knowing. Us against the world already and I'd only known him eight seconds.

'Come on, baby, let's get out of here,' he said, and I followed him through the little groups of growling men and out into the sun. Late afternoon. Baby? Baby. Nobody has ever dared call me baby before. I like it.

'Wow,' he said to the breathtaking heat. Really. Like having a hot towel stuffed down your throat. And then he looked down at me, briefly concerned. 'Feeling better?'

And me? I couldn't even remember what he was talking about.

Oh, yes. I'd been upset, thrown off by the burnt boy.

'Better? Oh. Yes. Fine. Thanks.' I paused. I knew what I wanted to do and I knew what I should do. Unusually, I went for the latter. 'Listen.

I should wait for the others. I need to get back to the hotel. I'm staying at the Corona.'

He shrugged. 'Me too,' he said.

I left him standing in the street and ran back, breathless, quite glad to have escaped really, to find the others hanging around on the steps of the hospital. We hadn't heard a bomb for ages which was almost more worrying than hearing them.

McCaughrean was fiddling with his lenses. 'God, that was gross. Poor fucking kid. Think I got the shot when he opened his eyes though. No good with their eyes shut.'

'Well done, Don,' I said.

He was sweating. Big patches on his shirt under his arms and under his enormous flabby breasts. 'Hot as an A-rab's armpit,' he muttered to himself. Eden was behind Don, smoking. He looked suddenly clumsy. He rubbed his hands through his hair. Half an hour ago that gesture might have reminded me of occasions when his hands had been in my hair. Now it looked a bit gauche. Fiddling with yourself like a child. Forty-one seemed stupidly young, somehow.

'Grant's still in there with Jamal. They're going to go mad for it. Where'd you go?'

Where did I go? Oh, that's right. I was . . . I couldn't breathe. It was . . . too awful.

'Needed a piss,' I said, trying to think of something that sounded vaguely feasible.

I slung my jacket over my shoulder carelessly and skipped back towards the bus, my cowboy boots noisy on the concrete.

I still felt the twinkle of Joshua Klein on me. I needed to say his name. I needed to get a fucking grip. That's what I needed.

'How old do you think Joshua Klein is?' I asked Eden, squinting at a flash in the sky that might have been a plane. He was right behind me.

'Who? Never heard of him,' Eden answered.

41

I slightly wished I hadn't either, to be honest. Shouldn't get involved. Nope. Definitely shouldn't.

Not that should or ought have ever figured particularly large in my mind. Not in that sense anyway. I mean, obviously everyone should be really nice to each other and not drop bombs and cut each other's hands off. That would be good, and I've seen enough of it to feel sure. But in the sense of shouldn't drink too much or shouldn't sleep with him – well, why not? Hey, we'll all be dead soon (some sooner than others, of course) and all our shoulds and oughts won't amount to a whole hill of beans in this crazy world. Or whatever the quote is. *Casablanca.*

Everyone was chastened in the mini bus. No songs, no shouting, very little jostling. Before wars start most of us have some kind of pub bore 'view' about it. The Americans should attack. They should have waited for the UN resolution. They should keep their noses out of other people's business. There was a good cartoon in the *New Yorker* of all the different ribbons you ought to be able to wear on your lapel. 'Anti war', 'In favour of war but sick of hearing from spouse about how my younger self would despise the person I have become', 'In favour of swift decisive military action but unable to bring myself to call it war'. Something for everyone.

But once the fighting begins and the bodies start piling up, views of any kind become almost embarrassing. Killing people is disgusting and no amount of apparent justification can make a corpse stink less (justification like the Ba'ath Party has executed more than three million Iraqis in three decades). And it's all so grotesquely inevitable. Protest in your student union as much as you like but people are going to carry on doing it until the end of time. Which, I've got to say, is beginning to seem distinctly more imminent.

So we all sat there smoking quietly as our tatty bus trundled through the back streets of Baghdad. Al-Zawra Park, usually full of footballers and families and couples nearly holding hands, was completely empty, the lawns looking as though they were just waiting for a bomb to land in the middle of them. A barefoot shoeshine boy was still taking his chances and there were a couple of old blokes smoking nargilahs at a coffee shop. Could almost have been any Middle Eastern city – closed shops that probably sell fizzy drinks and cigarettes, their corrugated iron awnings down, dusty neon signs, honking cars, crumbling ruins. Perhaps the ruins of Mesopotamia itself. Though it mostly feels newer. A lot of Baghdad has a seriously seventies thing going. Bad bridges and weird square things that wish they were high-rises but only manage ten floors. I know what it looks like – the set for *Thunderbirds*.

At one point Eden actually put his head in his hands. I could hear explosions now and my stomach seemed to melt. I wondered if it was something I had eaten (not, come to think of it, that I had eaten anything for some time) and then I realised – I was nervous.

Irritating. Everyone knows that journalists on a job are by and large safe – or they can be if they want to be. It looks more dangerous than it is. Normal life goes on alongside wars. I found I was having to tell myself this. Must take a Valium. Or two.

I chewed the inside of my mouth all the way to the Corona and worried about Joshua Klein. I'd forgotten to mention to him that Nur and Hugo had wanted me to meet him. It seemed inappropriate somehow, bringing anyone else into it. And something was bothering me about the Jamal story. I went to my room and drank a warm vodka from the broken mini bar. Out of a plastic cup. Gross. I flicked the computer on to see what the Baghdad Blogger was up to but he was less spirited than usual. He felt sorry, he said, for anyone who had ever had an ideal and fought for it. Well, me too, but why was he only just getting disillusioned now? I could have told him years ago that idealism was a big mistake. It was nice, though, in what I imagine might be a patronising and sort of colonial way, to have the voice of an ordinary Iraqi to listen to. He brought some perspective to it all with his ranting and raving. I found him almost comforting. I put a couple of calls in to the local news agencies to see if he might be a mate of anyone's. A serious girl with a frown in her voice said she'd get back to me if she heard anything. Hmmm. Not exactly a scoop.

I was slumped in front of the computer when a message came under my door on that thin hotel paper stamped with the big crown logo. It was from Klein. This is one of the great things about staying in a press pack hotel. It's like being at boarding school (not, of course, that I was ever at boarding school). You can't get away from each other. You bump into people you long to see and people you dread at every corner. A long-lost lover you thought had died in Kosovo can step out of the lift when you least expect it and messages under the door or bleeping on your phone are as illicit and exciting as Valentine's cards when you're thirteen. Listen to me – if you are in a relationship with a foreign correspondent who covers crises and stays in big hotels then he or she is sleeping around. Take whatever action you like, but know that this is true. No exceptions.

The message made me smile. 'Don't file on Jamal before you talk to me. I want to talk to you. I liked talking to you, Faith Cleopatra Zanetti. And I want to do more than talk. JFK.'

Hmm. Cool initials. Americans are funny with their initials. I once had a friend called Anne Catherine Hyem. In England her by-line was Anne Hyem. When she went to work at the *Washington Post* she changed it as a joke to A. Catherine Hyem. They loved it. She won a Pulitzer, actually. Not because of that, of course, but it might have helped . . . I called the desk downstairs (they, too, were pretending there was no war on) and asked them to post a message to Klein.

'I'm free,' I got them to write, and I lay down on my bed to smoke. I knew it was him when the phone rang.

'What are you wearing?' he asked.

'Fuck off,' I said and he laughed. What is one supposed to say to that?

44

I guess the required answer is 'Stockings and suspenders' or 'Chanel No.5' or something. I have never played these games before. Not that it mightn't be quite fun. I wanted to retract my fuck off and see if having phone sex might be fun. 'A lace negligee and a smile,' I should have said. Damn it.

'Meet me downstairs. I know a place,' he said. 'Bye, baby.' And he hung up. I stood up and paced a bit.

'Bye, baby,' I repeated with a sneer, trying to mock it. I went into the bathroom and looked in the mirror. This is when normal women put lipstick on, brush their hair, have a shower, change their pants. I looked down at my T-shirt. There was coffee on it. I took it off and put a shirt on. Now I looked like I was making too much effort. I put a cleaner white T-shirt on. Hair. Is there really anything I could possibly do with this hair? I tried to drag a brush through it and it bushed out even more and made me look like a clown. I put it in a ponytail. I realised what I was doing. 'Fuck it,' I said to myself and I smiled, picked my jacket up and rode the lift downstairs.

Something about this guy made me believe that he wouldn't be where he said he'd be. I expected to be stood up, avoided, disappeared on. So when he was standing by the lifts in a crisp outfit holding a trilby hat, I laughed.

'Looking good,' I said, and he nodded graciously, putting his arm out to link with mine.

Okey dokey. If it rained he'd probably throw his coat over a puddle.

'I think we'll walk,' he said. 'Come on.' So we did. The first command I think I have ever obeyed. Unfortuantely for both of us, not the last.

CHAPTER SIX

My elbow in his as though we were dining at a stately home and he was taking me through to the table, we swung out of the revolving doors. He glanced over at a heap of polystyrene casing from a television set or a fridge, perhaps wondering if something might not be lurking behind it. Now I know this is ludicrous, but I felt as though I was going on a date. I don't think I've ever been on one before because the whole thing was completely new. Normally I am drunk and he is drunk and we go to bed. This was a meeting designed that we might get to know each other better and then make a decision as to whether or not to go to bed. Stone cold sober. Is this really what people do?

JFK strode along, a head and shoulders taller than me, as though his country needed him. He talked, about the war, about Nur and Hugo (I would leave asking him about Dad until later). He described Hugo as 'a prick'. I didn't bother to tell him the animosity was mutual.

I felt so secure and, Jesus, happy with my arm in his that I couldn't believe anyone had ever disliked him. For what? He was magnificent and funny. Regal and silly. Good combination. Also, I detest people who want to tell you what other people think of you. There was someone I worked with on a left-wing thing years ago who was always desperate to tell me what people were saying about me in the canteen. It always tells you more about the person who's snitching than anything else. I didn't want to join them. Quite apart from the fact that it took pretty much all my concentration not to swoon away like an Elizabethan heroine because my arm was touching Josh's. Hopeless.

Along the river a bit he turned abruptly down a stinking alleyway where a one-eyed cat raised its back at us. The alley smelt like a sewer and already felt a very long way from either the hotel or the bombardments. Medieval. People write books and essays about what it must have been like in London in the Middle Ages. The stench, the brutality, the disease, the fear of death. A bit like this basically.

He led me through an entrance with an old sign swinging on a rusty bracket above the door, a sworl of Arabic announcing a business of some kind, I supposed. We went through a curtain of red and white plastic ribbons and emerged in a long narrow room with a sparkling marble floor and low brass ceiling fans whirring above pretty mosaic tables. Two waiters in gleaming white rushed forward to meet us, fawning and flapping and pulling us both forward to a table, sitting us down and flicking starched napkins over our laps.

Joshua Klein shook hands with them in turn, batting away their servility and putting us all on an equal footing. The very way in which his actions said, 'Stop, stop. I'm not the king. Please. You are my friends,' made it blindingly clear that actually he was the king. Only the insecure need to be fussed over – like spouses of the famous who are aware that their status is borrowed. Anyone secure is unfailingly nice to everyone – they can afford to be. Compare Saddam Hussein with Tony Blair for example . . .

The manager, ecstatic at Joshua's arrival, came running out of the kitchen, sweat beading on his bald forehead, his stomach wobbling under a tight shirt, his black bow tie choking him. Joshua stood up to greet him and was smothered with grateful kisses on both cheeks.

'Mr Klein, how wonderful. *Hlan wasahlan. Hlan wasahlan.* Terrible, terrible times, *al hum del Allah.* So glad to have you with us. And the beautiful lady?' he said, turning to me and kissing my hand.

The beautiful lady was embarrassed not to be wearing the heavens' embroidered cloths. I should have been seventeen, swathed in silk, droplets of gold hanging over my forehead and from my ears and wrists. I should have smelt of attar of roses. In fact, though, I was sweating, hungover, dirty and wearing, as ever, jeans, a T-shirt that didn't completely cover my tummy, dusty cowboy boots and my leather jacket. I shook my jacket off and one of the waiters whisked it away from me. I patted my hair.

'My dear friend, Faith Cleopatra Zanetti, a journalist from England,' Joshua said, nodding between myself and the maître d' as though he were introducing Marilyn Monroe to President Kennedy (which perhaps he did).

'Such an honour,' the bald man said, and shuffled away to get some menus. No wonder he was happy to see us. We were the only people in there. And this had to be the only man in Baghdad mad enough to open his restaurant today. Had to be.

'How do you know I'm a journalist?' I asked. I had wondered how he had been so sure I was even going to file on Jamal.

'Faith Zanetti,' he said, twinkling his fairy dust over me. 'Nobody in any other line of work would go out dressed like that.'

'Like what?' I smirked, trying to emulate his stare, to show him the things I wanted to do to him in the dark. I threw my arms out and looked defensively at my outfit as though it was my best dress and I'd put it on specially. I had, in fact, thought longer than ever before in my life about how I looked before coming out. Can't say it showed though.

'Like that.' He laughed and leaned over the table towards me to show me, with a smile, what he'd like to see me wearing. Not much. By the time the menus came we were giggling like teenagers who think they have invented sexual attraction. I haven't felt naughty for years, if ever. When I was little, there were no rules to break. If you're allowed to do it, why bother? I've always been able to do pretty much what I want. This, though, was like bunking off school.

Joshua ordered us what turned out to be dead rat in green slime with chips. And, more importantly, a bottle of champagne. The maître d' nearly died with joy. So rare (and, in fact, illegal) was this kind of order that he had to dust down the bottle with a big white cloth and it took him ten minutes to find the right glasses. Drinking tepid champagne in a hidden cave on the first day of the bombardments was, I think, the most delicious thing I have ever done. (Not, though, the most delicious thing I was ever going to do.) I pushed the rat around in the sauce a bit and ignored it.

'Well. Cheers, Faith Cleopatra Zanetti. It is nice to have met you,' Joshua said, clinking glasses with me, the sharp bubbles dancing about under our lips. Our hands touched briefly and we looked up to check that we'd both noticed, that we'd both felt the thing . . . Ha! So this is what being sixteen was supposed to have been like.

'It's nice to have met you too,' I said and we both laughed.

'I feel like a kid,' he said.

'Me too,' I nodded. 'Me too.'

'Well, that's different. You practically are a kid.'

'Hardly.'

We paused, both looking down at our glasses.

'So,' I said, sitting up straight and coughing, pretending that we were going to have a normal conversation and not think about each other's mouths and what they might taste like and what unkeepable promises we might make with them. 'What is it that you do?'

He raised his eyebrows and took a big healthy bite out of the side of his rat. He wiped his mouth with the back of his hand.

'Weapons,' he said, reaching out for the champagne bottle, glistening in its silver bucket. A waiter nearly slipped and injured himself in his frenzy to get there first. 'I'm a weapons inspector. You got any weapons, Faith C. Zanetti?' I liked my new name. Might change my own by-line, come to think of it.

Youbetcha, I wanted to say.

'Just some caesium 137,' I told him. 'Nothing that could take out more than a couple of thousand. Here, look, it's in my pocket.'

Hang on, though. What was he doing at the hospital then? Everyone was talking to him as though he was some kind of aid worker. Not that he had the scowl of an NGO.

'Hiding weapons of mass destruction at the Al-Yermouk then, are they?' I wondered, wanting to suck the sauce off his fingers for him.

'No, that's just a . . . well, you know. They need stuff, right? I'm guessing you met Jamal. Need to talk to you about that. Poor kid. I'm trying to get a friend over from DC to do a skin graft. He's going to have to hurry up, though,' he said, shaking his head, not looking at me like that for the briefest of seconds. He patted the mobile phone in his pocket, perhaps waiting for his friend to confirm he was coming or something.

'Not good for Bush to have civilian casualties so quickly,' I muttered, moronically uninterested. I found it very difficult, if I looked at him, to remember what we were supposed to be talking about. The waiters buzzed around us, nearly intrusive, almost helpful.

'Faith Cleopatra Zanetti,' Joshua Klein said, his tone completely changing. From orgasmic to avuncular in the flash of a silver fork. He stared into my face as serious as cancer. 'Jamal was injured in a gas explosion in his home. If the hospital has been instructed to tell you otherwise, then they are lying. Saddam is not bad at propaganda and people are still scared enough to obey him.'

At the mention of Saddam, the maître d' who was pretending to polish glasses over by the bar dropped one.

I knew he was telling the truth. It was obvious when you came to think about it. The Americans weren't going to fuck up on the first day. And the trip to see Jamal was all too well-organised. The bus, the accreditation, Dr Sharif. No way. I flattered myself into thinking that maybe that had been my problem in Jamal's cubicle. Overcome by the stench of spin.

I shuffled in my seat and emptied my glass too quickly. I suddenly felt about fifteen in a bad way, trying to explain to the headmaster why I was just such a totally crap person and what plans I had for rectifying the situation. None.

'Shit,' I said, keeping my eyes down. I needed to tell the others. I wanted to protect Eden from filing a load of bollocks, Iraqi lies, along with pictures of a poor kid whose appalling agony was going to be used for the war effort. I should go. Should. What I wanted to do was stay here and drink all afternoon, leaning across the table to talk to the first person who had ever made me feel truly comfortable just as I am. Or uncomfortable perhaps. I couldn't quite tell which.

I looked up at Klein and he smiled.

'I really should go and tell the others,' I said, starting to stand up.

'Sit down,' he said, still smiling, kind but firm. I sat back down.

'God . . . you are very . . .' I raised my hands in an effort to explain what I meant. 'Sticky.' I tried to leave but I was stuck in some invisible glue he had around him. He laughed.

'Sticky? Sticky. OK,' he said.

A grip needed to be got. I stood up and stayed up.

'I should go. Thanks for lunch,' I said and took a last sip of champagne. 'Sorry to be so . . . I'd like to stay but I . . . perhaps another time.'

'Sure,' he said, indulging me. 'Another time.'

I walked towards the door.

Oops. Forgot my fags.

'Forgot my fags,' I said when I got back to the table. I picked them up and looked at Joshua Klein and he looked at me like that. We both smiled.

'Maybe see you later,' I said.

'I'd like that,' he agreed.

Outside, confused by the street, by being alone again having been so intensely not alone, I waved an old man in a Lada Samara down and made him take me back to Jamal.

'America,' the bloke said, and spat out of the window. OK, well, that's clear. He had prayer beads on his rear-view mirror and his whole car smelt of a tannery. Yup. That's festering meat and sharp chemicals.

The potted palms by the steel swing doors looked sad in the face of the hospital's enormous problems. My protective clothing was still where I'd left it earlier that afternoon and I put it all back on. Grant was, staggeringly, still there. Was there no detail this guy didn't want in his piece? The translator had long since calmed Granny down and she was describing the planes and the bang and the glass and the rubble descending on everything. Allah this, Allah that. Allah who, frankly, seemed to have let her down in very dramatic fashion. The boy's other arm was bandaged now and he looked more peaceful. Or was he dead?

No, I could see his chest rise and fall, pathetic really in the face of this kind of injury. He was so tiny and the damage was so huge.

I shuffled around trying to look as though I was waiting my turn.

They have these charts at the bottom of the metal beds, (re. Carry On Matron etc.) clipped on so that the nurses know who's had what and what's wrong with them and why. It was in Arabic, sure, but the time of admission scribbled in the top-left hand corner was pretty clear. Before the bombardments had started. Klein was, unsurprisingly, right. And lots of other things too . . .

Grant and probably Eden would go with the story if I didn't say something sharpish. And was that really so bad? After all, didn't the Iraqi people deserve some sympathy? I mean, even if this particular child wasn't a victim of the war, there were others who were. The whole of Baghdad was going to be obliterated, for Christ's sake. Plus which it was going to look pretty bloody churlish of me to do a piece about Iraqi misinformation when there were plenty of genuine civilian casualties practically littering the streets. Or there would be. I couldn't decide and didn't quite know why. My main worry about my silence was that maybe I wanted to share a secret with Joshua Klein. Hmm. Not good. I do not do emotional involvement. If you're fourteen and writing in your diary about how nobody truly understands you, it's one thing . . .

I waited for Grant to leave (and he had a real bounce in his step, the bastard) and got the translator to ask Granny for the address. Professionally, of course, the best thing to do would be to let the others run their stories and then have mine in the day after. Then they'd look like Saddam-sympathising idiots whose newspapers print any old lies the MI feeds us. On the other hand, that would be a vile, duplicitous, mean and dishonest thing to do. I ought to tell them.

I'd asked Lada to wait and I'd taken another flob out of his window as a 'yes'. The heat had lifted now and the calls to prayer had started across Baghdad. A nicer sound than air-raid sirens though not completely dissimilar. Someone, it might have been Nur actually, once sent me a big plastic clock shaped like a mosque that sings 'Allah'u Akbar' at you whenever it's time to pray. Lada grumbled to himself all the way back down the dusty streets but didn't refuse the cash. Back at the Corona, I shot up in the mirrored lift, fished around in my washbag and took a couple of Valium. I stood briefly on my balcony and watched the black long-necked birds wheel around before going to bed. Little white water birds flew around near the banks of bulrushes. Two F-18s came roaring past and dived at the Board of Youth and Sports. One of them spiked downwards and a rocket burst out of its pod and plunged into the building. Then it lunged upwards and there was this huge whoosh from the trees on the riverbank just down Abu Nawas Street. It was a heat-seeking missile and it swooped up in a white vapour trail, chasing the nearest American jet which was already long gone.

Inside now, sick of the sodding conflict, I sat on the edge of my bed and I suppose I must have lain down.

I dreamt I went into a municipal swimming pool that was completely frozen over. Stuck in the ice were hundreds of frozen corpses, one of which was my father. A nurse told me that the bullet wounds would be barely visible by the time the body thawed. She pulled an enormous lever that turned on the heating and, as the ice melted, the people toppled over one by one.

I woke up gasping for breath. My room was pitch dark and the phone was ringing. From the balcony doors I could see fires far away across the city. I put the receiver to my ear.

'Zanetti? Where the fuck have you been?' It was Tamsin on the desk in London.

'Hey, Tamsin. What do you mean? I've been here. Baghdad. You know. War. Destruction.'

'Jesus, Zanetti. We've been trying to get you all fucking day. Do you know what fucking time it is?'

I looked at the red glow of the radio alarm clock by my bed.

'Shit,' I said. It was 3.30a.m.

'We thought you were dead. The early editions of all the other papers have got great stuff about a kid with his arms blown off. Faith, we are the only ones without a splash on that. We've used fucking wire footage of the bombardments and an AP shot. You better have a fucking bril-liant fucking excuse.' Tamsin was beside herself with rage. Her job was, of course, on the line. The competition had wiped the floor with us on the first day of the war. Wire copy on the front page. Very, very bad.

And my fault. Valium and champagne, apparently, don't mix. Or rather, they do.

'No! No! Tamsin. Calm down. It's OK. It's not true. The kid was hurt in a gas explosion. Misinformation at the hospital. I've got the real story. They'll all look like idiots tomorrow. I swear.' I swore. I flicked the lights on and glanced around the room, trying to get my bearings properly. I put the television on. It was that amazing Pentagon spokeswoman with the weird suits saying something that was being translated into Arabic. She was wearing a lemon-yellow jacket with large purple triangles on it. I mean, what?

'No. Not tomorrow, Faith Zanetti. Second edition today. File within an hour and a half or you're fired,' Tamsin said.

I sighed deeply.

'Faith? Do you understand me?'

'Yes, Tamsin. I understand you. It is not a subtle point that you're making.'

'Subtlety has never been my forte,' she snapped and hung up.

Oh bollocks, I thought. The bombings seemed to have been stepped up since I passed out and there was no way I could file without actually going to check out Jamal's house, wherever the fuck it was. I tried to call all kinds of official numbers to get something from the gas board but nobody, unsurprisingly, was answering tonight.

Still dopey, I ran down to the lobby where Karim from the front desk was alone, sweeping up a smashed glass – a lot of nervous people about. He pointed me in the direction of an idle *New York Times* allocated driver, Samy, fast asleep in an armchair with a copy of Egyptian *Marie Claire* spread across his chest. When I spoke he sat bolt upright and stroked his moustache.

'Can you take me here?' I asked, showing him the address.

'Now?' he wondered, looking at me with Minstrel eyes as though I were a madwoman. The air outside smelt of burning. We always get the crazies trying to go on trips before dawn, he seemed to be saying. 'Why do you want to go there?' Samy, who once spent six months in Canada, wanted to know. 'They're not bombing there.'

He didn't feel safe using the Sinak Bridge near the hotel so the journey, bouncing along in the back seat of his Audi (he wouldn't let a woman sit up front, even a woman like me who, presumably, barely counted as a representative of my sex), took twice as long as it otherwise might have done. We went past where the gold souk ought to have been and down by a few of those restaurants where in happier times you could pick your fish from the tank and watch it gutted, sliced and grilled. Past the pristine, sausage-serving Nabil where the UN crowd used to go.

We passed by the Al Jihad district where most of the Ba'ath Party families live, or lived. The windows of these grand white houses, all newly built, were taped up and there were no cars in the drives, or toys in the yard. No lights on anywhere. Perhaps the families might be in the cellar? I shivered.

The idea of running down into the cellar with tins of beans is so old-fashioned, somehow. I can only think about it in black and white. Boys with Brylcreem in their hair and little girls in white socks and neat dresses. Women drawing seams up the back of their bare legs with eye pencils and longing to get knocked up by a GI. Strange and hideous that people are still cowering underground now, hearing planes and sirens, grabbing the children and trying to pretend it's a game. 'No, no, darling. Just a precaution.'

Being there near them does not make it more imaginable, any more than seeing someone with their arms blown off tells you what it must be like. It is not possible to put myself in their shoes. I'm going home when the war's over.

Jamal lived in a scuzzy neighbourhood a few miles south of the ritzy one. Not quite as grim as the notorious Saddam City but not a nice

place by any stretch of the imagination. Dawn was lighting up the edges
of the black sky now and the stars were going out one by one. The
people here, up fighting for life already, looked much more worried
about food and water than being bombed. Things were going on at a
frantic pace, old sandals kicking up the dust. A little boy in just trainers
and underpants was tugging at the rope round the neck of a moth-eaten
goat. An old man was loading a donkey with bags full of rags, Saddam
Hussein watching him through the early gloom from four different billboards.

It was not difficult to find Jamal's house. Samy only had to ask twice.
That's because his house was now an enormous hole in the ground. A
few people huddled around it, some of them pulling stuff out of the
rubble and some just crying. I watched for a bit from the car and then
got out and walked over to them. I couldn't have been more conspicuous, not only as a white, blonde woman stepping out of the dawn, but
in jeans and a leather jacket, dirty, with tangled hair and a cigarette in
my hand. They stopped talking and rummaging to stare at me. Samy
translated.

As I expected, nobody had seen any American planes. 'Lah, lah,' they
all mumbled, shaking their heads. I went up to one man eating a breakfast of sunflower seeds with gnarly hands who looked mad enough to
want to chat. He chewed the brown mush in his mouth thoughtfully,
nodding keenly as he spoke and occasionally scratching at his wrist.
Samy translated. 'He says Jamal's father was a secret consort of Uday
Hussein. The Americans smuggled a bomb into the house disguised as
a gas cooker and hoped to kill him.' Uh-huh. About as mad as he looked
then.

Leaving him to his insane babbling, I moved a couple of steps in the
dust over to my left where a dapper bloke with a waxed moustache, who
Samy said claimed to be a surgeon, said authoritatively, sagely, that it
was much more likely that Uday had killed Jamal's father himself. You

never know quite how much gets lost in the translation, but I know a nutter when I see one. There are always people (I imagine Hugo Greene is probably one of them) who think it is impossible, and unconscionable, to cover a country without speaking the language. They are ludicrously overestimating the requirements of the average newspaper story. Ask them what they think and then write it down, wildly inaccurate and barking as it is.

I've always thought it was weird that vox pops are supposed to give your articles credibility. You know, no piece is complete without a few random comments from salt-of-the-earth folk you come across in the field ('in the field' is supposed, I think, to make us sound more intrepid, though it usually means 'at the airport' or 'in the bar' or, the fail-safe classic, 'in the taxi'). What nobody ever tells the reading or viewing public is that most of the people hanging around the scene of a disaster, natural or otherwise, are absolute fucking psychopaths, both stupid and entirely unhinged. If they weren't they would be safe in their houses, getting on with their business.

Then a young woman with bright lipstick and a shiny headscarf started shouting. 'None of these people knew the Husseins, you lunatics,' she yelled (according to Samy). Ah, that sounded more like it. The ring of truth. Most importantly, though, I could smell gas.

'Can you smell that?' I asked Samy, sniffing suspiciously, wondering if I was perhaps imagining it. He put his nose to the air, fiddling with the prayer beads in his left hand.

'Yes. Definitely gas.'

'Ask the sane woman (what was she doing here anyway?) if she thinks this could have been the result of a gas explosion,' I told him.

She said, and this is Samy's translation, 'Of course. They say they're coming to fix the leak today. They won't though, not with you people bombing us. Everyone has switched off the gas in their houses.' She looked at me. 'You should put your cigarette out.' It was true, nobody else was smoking which, in the Middle East, is highly unusual. She was a convincing witness.

Part of me wanted Joshua to be wrong, to be lying. I quite wanted an excuse to stop my heart pounding and my stomach swooping. I hated his certainty – certainty that made me feel so uncertain about every-thing. He has a self-confidence that makes mine seem shallow and false. Which, let's face it . . .

I shrugged at Samy. I'd seen enough. In order to meet Tamsin's dead-line I filed to copy over the phone from the car. I like filing to copy. 'Hello, copy?' they say, men and women sitting at their computer screens in Wapping or Canary Wharf twenty-four hours a day, taking down stories straight from the horses' mouths. Whatever hellhole you're in, whatever's happening, you can phone London and a cosy voice welcomes you as though they had just made a cup of tea and were gossiping about page three girls and footballers. Tamsin, who had been working for sixteen straight hours by this time, called back to congratulate me.

'Thanks, Zanetti,' she said, and hung up. You just get such a warm bloody glow from the praise they shower on you.

Driving back to the Corona, I noticed that the city had gone quiet. It was already seven-ish. People had come out on to the streets again and the panic seemed to have receded. A lull, apparently, in the attack. I wanted to watch the news. Weirdly, but not unusually, it's the only way to find out what's going on. And I don't mean watching the Koran readings. In Iraq, prisoners can earn parole by learning the Koran. No, seriously.

It's all very well looking up at the sky and trying to work out which buildings are burning and which aren't, but the only people who really know what's happening are in Washington. Or perhaps the journalists at CentCom in Qatar know too – news straight from Washington. Samy said he didn't think it would ever be over. 'Saddam Hussein will be back.' He nodded, smoking my cigarettes and fixing the road with his stare. (There's a vox pop for you. Something for a longer more reflective piece, perhaps in the first person – a Saturday special maybe.)

The skies were just brightening with day now and Joshua Klein was presiding over the lobby, pristine and grand, as though he had the world pretty much under control. People get up early in a war. Well, to be fair, I imagined he probably got up early every day, like all powerful people. But even the drunken slobs are up at dawn when they're working. You can sleep when you're dead.

It's claustrophobic, this communal living. Stay in the same hotel as someone and you'll see them a few times a day whether you like it, whether you are ready for it, or not. Klein was alone there, apart from a young western bloke who looked like a peace campaigner or something. The human shield type – dreadlocks, black T-shirt, ripped combat trousers. He was cross but Klein looked calm. I stomped towards them across the marble and just caught the young man saying 'Hypocrite!' before he stormed off. Joshua smiled at me as though an angel had just walked into his view. Someone had been out to a street vendor and bought pitas and eggs which were laid out on a table in the coffee area.

'So?' he asked, but his face said, 'You're beautiful. I might kiss you.' We both laughed.

'Gas,' I admitted, though I don't know why it was an admission really. I didn't want to look into his eyes in case I couldn't look away again.

'Thank you, Faith. I appreciate it,' he said, and he reached out to touch my face and then retracted his hand before it got there. This was a man with 'issues'. Not issues like Eden or the other men I spend my life with. Their issues are existential angst, inability to deal with all the carnage and evil they've seen, all the bereavement they've suffered – without a fuck of a lot to drink, at any rate. Joshua Klein seemed to be tearing himself to pieces with indecision over a flirtation that had so far been going on for less than twelve hours. I mean, where I come from, you look at someone like that, you ask them if they'd like to sleep with

61

you and then you do, or you don't do it. This business was not something I'm trained to deal with.

And why was he thanking me for Jamal, for fuck's sake? I was the one on the receiving end of the favour, wasn't I? Well, wasn't I?

'No problem,' I said, smiling. 'Sorry. What are we talking about?'

'Dunno,' he admitted and threw his hands up. 'Hey! Look at this.' He tried to find something in his newspaper. Back into flippant mode. 'They found this guy in Norway called Saddam Hussein. And he's Kurdish. Been getting crank calls from people who find his name in the phone book. Here, listen. "When my father chose the name twenty years ago, we didn't know what we now know about Saddam. The president was a respected man, even among Kurds. It wasn't shameful to be called Saddam then." He hopes shortly to become Dastanse Rasol Hussein. "It's no fun being called Saddam Hussein these days."'

I laughed and he looked at me in a pre-coital way. When I was little, Evie always used to tell me that I shouldn't say everything I think every time I think it. I have throughout my life entirely failed to follow this advice. I know that if people aren't saying something it is because they don't want to say it. However, I want to hear it anyhow. You're not in the mood to talk about this? You get in the mood. So, yet again, I failed to shut the hell up like a normal person.

'Are you really thinking what you look like you're thinking?' I asked Joshua Klein. 'It's disgusting.'

'Not disgusting. Beautiful. Are you really thinking what you look like you're thinking?' he said. Very political. Always answer a question with a question.

'Yes,' I nodded. 'It's disgusting.'

I turned away to light the cigarette I'd been holding. God, but this guy was a pain in the arse. And when I turned back round, Joshua Klein had gone. At least, he was halfway across the lobby, flashing me a smile and throwing me a wave. When he doesn't want to talk any more, he really doesn't want to talk any more. And he hadn't admitted a thing. Though I had. It's this thing he does. Engages you completely so that you feel glued to him and then he walks away, ripping the very skin off your body. And I'd known him for half a day.

My father's sudden absence had exactly this effect, I recognised. I hadn't felt it since. Or, that is, I had felt it for so long that I had forgotten what its opposite was like. I used to live mostly with Dad's girlfriend Evie (must call her) and we watched the news to find out what was happening wherever he was. Then, sometimes unexpectedly, he would come home and the flat would explode in colour and light. There would be presents from the ends of the earth (cotton from the deep South, sand roses from the Namibian desert, silk from China), and I stayed up late while Dad and Evie drank wine, and we laughed and laughed and laughed. A few days later, as suddenly as he had come, he would go again and Evie and I fell flat on our faces. We sat together on the sofa eating takeaway pizzas and watching *Dallas*, but there was a hole in my heart and nothing seemed funny any more. Then, one day, his jacket and his watch and his short-wave radio and his electric razor came home without him in a plastic bag. The hole, it turned out, was to be permanent. Day after day after day of tomorrows, all without promise.

'Coffee, Zanetti?' Eden Jones asked me, trundling up with a pile of press releases under his arm. 'You missed a good one. The bloke in the purple beret said there had been no American planes over Baghdad last night. He's brilliant.'

'God. Why are they briefing us at the crack of dawn?' I wondered.

'I suppose there might not be another chance.' He smiled. 'Blogger's funny today too. Fun fact of the day – when were Iraqis last allowed to express a free opinion about government policy? Nineteen sixty-two.'

'Jesus. Coffee would be great.' I sighed. 'Have you found out who it is yet?'

'Uh-uh,' he shook his head.

I sat down with Carly while Eden went to organise coffee. Weird thing about trying to cover a war is that you spend a lot of time confined to the hotel, or out on tour buses. I didn't feel I'd seen Baghdad at all. I don't mean 'seen' like gone round the sites, but normally you do a fair amount of skulking in weird bars and meeting the friends of people you vaguely know in London. I lit a cigarette.

Carly is emaciatedly thin. When you're seeing a lot of her it's easy to forget. But sometimes the light will catch her in a certain way and she looks just skeletal. She is haggard and raddled and exhausted. She pulled her compact out of her back pocket and reapplied her bright red lipstick. I noticed that it had begun, over the years I'd known her, to seep into the cracks around her mouth.

'Saw you with Klein,' she said, trying to get comfortable with only a lobby chair and her bony arse to help her. There was an empty bottle of water in front of us on one of the little brass tables they have dotted about as though a hotel in central Baghdad is just the kind of place you might pop into for refreshment at any moment. We both stared at it. Water, eh? Wonder who's been drinking that.

'Old men and young girls. It's a sorry story,' she said. She shook her head like some old voodoo priestess.

'A: not a story. B: I'm hardly a young girl.'

Carly made her hands into a W. 'Whatever,' she said with a gravelly laugh. 'He'll never leave his wife.'

'Carly, you're a psychopath.' I dragged on my cigarette and looked over at Pip Deakin having a huge row with his producer near the lift. The words prima donna were being used. 'I'm not fucking him. If I was I wouldn't want him to leave anyone. That's if he's even got a wife.'

She did the W sign again and looked generally challenging.

'Oh, fuck off, Posner,' I said. 'Read my lips. NOTHING HAPPENED.'

'Really? Nothing? Not a little kiss?'

'Nope.'

'Did you want to?'

'Yes.'

'Did he?'

'Yes.'

'So?'

'So we didn't,' I snapped. Annoying now.

'Exactly. Weird. That's what they do.'

'What is what they do? What is wrong with you?'

'Nothing's wrong with me. I'm telling you that it's a big mistake to get involved with a guy like that. If you'd slept with him it'd be one thing. He's going to to and fro until you're seasick, honey. It's not sex he wants.'

'Please,' I sighed. 'What else is there?'

'Here's my advice. Don't stick around to find out. Leave it alone. I've seen it all before.'

'Great, Carly. Thanks.'

Ditching both her and Eden I stomped off to my room and spent all day ignoring the war and reading the Baghdad Blogger. He was actually on good form. A superb source of rumours. Apparently all the top Ba'ath Party officials had had their phone numbers changed because the Americans had somehow hacked into their phone lines so that every time they picked up the receiver they were told in Arabic not to offer any resistance to the attack and not to use chemical weapons. Could it possibly be true? I was beginning to think this bloke was one of the hangers-out in the lobby – it was obvious he knew some or all of us. He had that tone of voice of someone who worked in or for the press. Also he was writing in American English though he claimed to be Iraqi. I did a piece about it which Tamsin predictably described as 'light'. It was supposed to be light. The whole paper is 'light'.

Really, though, I was just thinking about Klein. So I did another adolescent thing to add to all the ones that seemed to have been racking up lately and phoned Nur, our only mutual friend. You know, the old 'I fancy your mate' routine. The trouble with this technique, notoriously, is that you end up getting very close to the middle man who is endlessly disappointing for not being the quarry, and the middleman is, of course, annoyed at being only the middleman. And so on.

'Darling? You're OK?' Nur purred at me.

'I'm fine. Fine. I just wanted to tell you I met your friend, Joshua Klein,' I said, lighting a cigarette and pacing a bit.

'Ah,' she said. Ah? I waited for more. Not forthcoming.

'What? I thought you wanted me to meet him?' I nearly whined.

'Yes,' she said. Well, this was fun.

'I like him,' I offered. Never one to hold back on the gushing when necessary.

'Yes,' she went on.

'What did you say he does for a living?' I wondered, feeling the need to check his version.

'I didn't, darling. Something awfully grand . . . So, you are OK?'

I gave up. 'Yes. I told you. Fine. You OK? Hugo?' I put my cigarette out. She obviously wasn't in the mood for a chat.

'Yes. We are thinking of . . . well, I'll tell you in person. Would you like to have a drink with us?'

OK, that's better.

'Yes, that would be lovely. Whenever's good for you.'

'Why don't you come over this evening? I'll make whisky sours,' she said and we hung up. If there's anything I loathe it's caginess. Spit it out, for Christ's sake. Though we must be bugged, so if it was important, best not spit it out, I suppose. Still, all very irritating. If you've got something to say, either say it or stop giving me little signs that there are things you're not saying. Makes me want to punch a person.

I'd been up half the night and I must have fallen asleep after I'd filed, feet up on the smoked-glass coffee table, also hideously decorated with the Corona logo. There were explosions far away across the city and I could see the blackness of oil fires on the horizon. Baghdad smelt of burning tonight, but it wasn't all putrid. There was a sweetness of honeyed tobacco and ordinary bonfires as well as the other kind of stink of carnage. A cigarette burning in the ashtray, I shut my eyes, I was being taken for interrogation, perhaps by Iraqis, perhaps by the Taliban. I knew I had to pledge my support or be killed. The interrogator was a woman, familiar, older but definitely malign. She wanted to catch me out, to win the argument, to prove that she was right. I was flanked by two other prisoners who had been tortured. Middle-aged men, intellectuals perhaps. The kind of people who could have been the fathers of school friends. To make her point, the woman ordered her flunkies to shoot the men in the head. They slumped bleeding to the floor of this hot, overlit concrete cellar. Though I was covered in their blood, I had to pretend not to notice. But I failed to look enough like a supporter and when she shot me my head exploded.

People say you never die in your own dreams but that is not true.

CHAPTER SEVEN

I am sick of my own subconscious. What kind of dream is that? Why can't I be flying over fjords or something? I woke up sweating to a buzz from reception telling me that a car was here for me. The explosions weren't constant and sounded a long way away. The air from the balcony was thick and sweet and the air conditioning downstairs made me shiver. I kept my head down. Didn't want to meet anyone I knew.

I was faintly aware that I should be gazing out of the car window for little splashes of colour to add to my pieces but I couldn't be arsed. I shut my eyes and leant against a strip of fawn leather. The chauffeur seemed to be a Kylie Minogue fiend.

When we got there I came over all gloomy. I hadn't enjoyed myself last time, let's face it, and now the place had a sinister look to it: isolated, darkening skies, inappropriate grandeur. The sprinklers were off and the lawn had died. It looked like a house nobody lived in, bought by a sheik for holidays and abandoned to the ghosts or whatever. Nur opened the door, grey in the evening light and showing her age.

'Faithy, Faithy, Faithy,' Hugo shouted behind her, all mock bluster and enthusiasm. He was pissed. The house was too hot and the servants had gone, probably run away to their families somewhere safer. True to her promise, though, Nur had made whisky sours and had the very jug in her hand. I kicked my boots off and chose a pair of white Moroccan slippers from a pile.

'Come through, come through,' she said, smiling too broadly.

I went through but there was no getting away from the fact that I had to manoeuvre my way around a huge mound of very expensive suitcases.

'Going somewhere nice?' I asked, but nobody laughed at my joke.

'Paris. London. Not sure where we'll end up,' Nur said in a sugary way, arranging herself coquettishly on the sofa, having handed the drink situation over to Hugo. She was trying to pretend they were doing a grand European tour rather than running away.

I sat down with the drink I'd been given, ice already melted, and leant forward on to my knees. 'How's your brother?' I asked.

Nur opened her painted lips to speak, but Hugo butted in.

'Hush, hush,' he drooled, as though we were in an episode of *'Allo 'Allo* or something and it was all a huge adventure.

'Didn't you used to hope he'd . . . you know . . . ?' I asked, pretending not to have noticed I was on shaky ground.

'We have our hopes,' Nur said. 'He's in Paris.' She looked up at Hugo and he nodded, barely perceptibly, but enough to expose her lie. Not to totally belittle their ambition, but there are plenty of people waiting in the wings, all from big influential families, all with their country's best interests at heart. I doubted any of them stood much of a chance to be anything other than part of some kind of American-led interim government that would have to organise elections and then be abolished.

'So, I met Klein,' I told them again. I was feeling combative. As I said, I hate caginess.

Hugo coughed and then sat down. 'Bit of an arsehole.' He smiled.

'Yes, you said,' I acknowledged. 'He's not, though.'

'Ah, working his charm.' Hugo laughed and I felt affronted. Just because somebody is charming does not immediately make them duplicitous. Or just because somebody is able to use their charm to their advantage does not mean that it can't sometimes be sincere and real. Does it?

'Why would he want to do that, Hugo?' I asked, frankly hating him now. Hugo, not Joshua.

'Pretty girl like you,' he mumbled and Nur laughed falsely. I got the impression that she would never appreciate other 'girls' being described as pretty.

'Hardly,' I said. 'Anyway, why's he here at the moment? Thought the inspections were over.'

'Oh, the Yanks always like to check their facts. He's with the government,' Hugo said, but they were both plainly lying about something. 'As a matter of fact, he can be a bloody useful source.'

Government. OK. Well, not necessarily that sinister.

'Yes,' I nodded. 'I see.'

'Very knowledgeable,' Nur agreed.

'You said he knew Dad.' I sipped my drink and already wanted another one though I hadn't finished this. There was a vast painting of some unicorns hanging above the mantelpiece, in a gold frame. Nur's first husband was a really tasteless bastard.

'Did I?' Hugo looked surprised. 'Yes, maybe. Ask him.'

'I will,' I said, and held my glass out, desperate for anything that would take the edge off this nightmare. Though I hate cocktails.

I was elated when Tamsin phoned me from the desk.

'Zanetti,' she said. I made an apologetic face to Nur and Hugo. 'Anything?'

'No,' I said and she hung up. I pretended I needed to get back to the hotel as a matter of urgency. Which I did, but only to get away from these freaks. Even Baghdad looked normal compared to them. I was much drunker than I wanted to be.

I sat down in front of CNN and took my boots off. What is with their intonation? Who is their audience that they need to talk like that? It's like a spoof of a news channel, I thought, a British comedian painted orange and buried under a huge wig doing silly voices.

Things were blurred. I was dozy and desperate to sober up. I hardly noticed that it was night-time. I couldn't remember the last time I'd eaten and I was thinking of seeing if room service was working in wartime conditions when a note came under the door. I stood around and stared at it for a bit, all innocent on the carpet.

It said, 'I have been thinking about ways in which we can be close. I think that you will like them. Isn't it amazing the effect that this thing has on one's mind and body? J.' I lay back and tried very hard not to think of ways in which we could be close. I failed. I didn't want to admit the effects on mind and body and nor did I want to think about what he must mean at his end. Or, rather, I did. I was half tempted to nip upstairs and take him up on what looked a lot like an offer. On the other hand, I was stalled by what Carly had said and what Nur and Hugo had suggested – that he was up to no good in some way. What was it? He would to and fro until I was seasick. I strongly suspected that if I went banging on the door in my negligee (would have to borrow one) he would turf me out, saying he had work to do.

Dazed, I walked out to the balcony and the whole world seemed to be burning. It was orange and black and alight, and although I knew it would all fall into perspective in the morning, while the attack was going on, it might have been the apocalypse itself. I had no idea what time it was. Bombs fell like rolling thunder and I could hear the quick crackle of artillery fire from out in the suburbs and the whine of the high-altitude jets followed by the squeal of their descending missiles. And the night so dark in what had become a fairly complete blackout.

I stumbled along to Carly's room and found her sage and sharp as ever. More than could be said for me.

'He's a mind fuck,' she said when I showed her the note. 'Should be doing it, not going on about it.'

'It's sweet,' I said.

'Tell me that again in a month,' she hissed.

What does she know?

I sat there watching her drink warm white wine out of the bottle. She says she is on the white wine diet. You don't eat at all and you just drink white wine. Then, if you get really hungry, you have a glass of red. Well, she is certainly very thin. She was miserable because she'd filed a 'below average' piece, as she put it. She'd been on the phone to her stepson, if that's what he was, who had been kicked out of school for dealing dope that lunchtime and was now home alone. Going back to London didn't even occur to her. We are not much good at parenting, those of us who have tried. They don't include me. Wouldn't dream of it. I am deeply unimpressed by the job done on me, and yet sort of sympathetic to the shambling perpetrators. I mean, to do it properly you have to give up your whole life, licence revoked. It's not your turn any more, you are just a facilitator of theirs. My dad couldn't drag himself away from all this, and I don't feel I ever really knew Mum.

We're in touch now, since I called her from Jerusalem. After all, you only get one life, I thought, so I called her. Even went to see her in London before a funeral I had to go to. It's too late though, isn't it? All these emotional reunions people have on television with mothers who had them adopted. There's a lot of catharsis in it, but you can't get the time back, or really forgive them for the birthdays and Christmases and school concerts when they weren't there. All the grazed knees they never gave a toss about. Evie came to school as parental representative in my case (guardian, is it?). She used to sweep into parents' evenings in some fur she'd been wearing for a shoot earlier in the day and explain that although she might only be my father's girlfriend she would have to do. Afterwards her only comment would be, 'Assholes.' My teachers tended to be unenthused about my general respect for authority. Well, I was unenthused about their respect for me.

Eden came into Carly's room, looking for me. He was excited.

'Hey! Check this out. Allied Central Command have got an actual list, a LIST, of things they're not allowed to talk to the press about. Guess what they're called.' He was delighted.

'Give up,' I said, throwing my arms out.

'Pooh traps,' he said, gravely. 'Seriously. Pooh traps. Can you believe it? Market bombings, civilian casualties in general, depleted uranium. You name it, they won't tell you about it.'

'Jesus,' I said. Carly just raised her eyebrows. I felt myself sobering up a bit. It was a nice story and his desk was pleased with him. I thought he was behaving like someone who had just been given a gold star by the teacher.

'Well, aren't you impressed, Faith Zanetti?' he asked me, lounging on one of the twin beds with his hands behind his head as though he had just had an extraordinarily satisfying sexual experience and had had his performance praised. I raised my eyebrows at him and the explosions began again.

'Shit!' Eden said, standing up. 'Shall we go up on the roof?'

We all scrambled for the door and followed him up the service staircase and on to a flimsy metal ladder out into the night, Carly being exaggeratedly agile in case anybody noticed she was now rolling drunk. Hey, who wasn't? There were already a few people up here – Pip Deakin, for one, and his crew. They were just slavering to be used but Pip refused to put his videophone down in his pretence at being a unilateral roving reporter out in the desert trying to get killed. He liked to give the impression that where he was going, no crew would dare follow. Like, to the bar. Grant Bradford looked plain scared, and Don plain pissed. I noticed he was only wearing one shoe.

'McCaughrean, you're only wearing one shoe,' I said, and he peered at me through the dark, bleary and belligerent.

'What? Is there some kind of fucking law suddenly? Two shoes at all times of the day and night or a machete up the arse?' he slobbered.

'Just saying, Don. Just saying.' I laughed. He put his camera up to his face in a huff.

'Tripod,' he muttered, and staggered back towards the door, turning sideways to squeeze himself through. 'Don't touch my stuff,' he shouted. 'Poofs!'

It was beautiful out here. A warm night with a breeze off the river. Stars needling low over our heads, billions and billions of them, clouds of them in the thick black sky. And the silver flash of warplanes. It was hard to imagine some nervous, shaven-headed boy with his oxygen mask over his mouth and a gear stick in his hand actually piloting those things. They came in so fast and so low and left a landscape of fire behind them.

The satanic black fog of the oil fires was invisible in the dark, but the city seemed as medieval as it really is, trying to fend off an enemy as hi-tech as aliens in a Hollywood film.

'Put it out, Faith,' Eden said, nodding down at my cigarette. Normally I liked having someone to look out for me, but right now I was just annoyed.

'Listen, Mr Jones. I am thirty-four years old. I have smoked cigarettes on enough rooftops in enough war zones to know whether or not I am endangering anyone's life. You can't seriously think that they are about to start bombarding the hotel. They've got a war to win, for God's sake,' I said, putting my cigarette out as my argument trailed off.

It was too late though.

Carly had fallen. At first it looked as though she might have slipped in the dark. She was, after all, extremely drunk. Eden and I stepped forward to help her up, shuffling a bit towards the edge of the roof where there wasn't a railing. I tried to lift her under the shoulder and my hand met a warm wet patch.

'I'm hit,' she said, groaning.

'Jesus. By what?' I wondered out loud, pulling her towards the door into the hotel. A B-52 buzzed slowly past us and dropped a bomb. The world seemed to be ending.

'Sniper,' Eden said, quietly, helping me move her. 'We'll get you to a hospital,' he told her, sounding calm and as though we really might. 'Hey, can someone get a driver! Carly's been shot!' he shouted suddenly, making it real.

Everyone seemed to shuffle about hurriedly, but the noise of the bombs and the burning put us all into an awful slow motion. Pip was now doing a live piece to camera in the pitch dark.

'A colleague of mine appears to have been hit,' he said. 'Oh God.' And he clicked his fingers at the crew to close the bird so that it would look as though his grief had prevented him from going on. That and the incredible danger.

But Carly had been shot and she wouldn't lie still.

'No, I can't do it,' she said, holding her shoulder and coughing ominously.

I knelt down next to her and tried to sound encouraging. A siren wailed in the hot street below.

'Of course you can,' I told her, pushing her hair out of her face. 'Of course you can. You're going to be fine.'

She wasn't going to be fine. I've been here before and I could see the glaze over her eyes and the appalling pallor that people get, kind of waxy.

'Don't bullshit me, Zanetti, you bitch. I can feel it in my chest,' she said, looking pleadingly at me.

'Carly, Carly,' I said, wanting to cry but not wanting her to see it. 'It looks bad, love. It does.'

She smiled at me, weakly. She had blood in her mouth.

'Get out of my way then,' she said, and with amazing strength she pushed me backwards on to my arse. Then she hauled herself up in her tatty jeans and soaked shirt with something like a choking scream and she ran, stumbling, into the darkness towards the fires blazing across the city. Twenty floors she fell.

Into a garden with palm trees in it and bright red gaudy flowers, it turned out.

It was getting light by the time the aftermath was over. One of the para-medics, Omar, said he had never seen anything like it. 'Mind-blowing,' were the words he used. He was as staggered as though an angel had lowered her to the ground. In fact, that may be what he believed. It is incredible to survive even a three- or four-floor jump. But to be shot and to dive twenty floors, well, it was unprecedented. We didn't know if she would survive much longer than she already had, but I sort of thought she might if she'd come this far. It was amazing, and typical of Carly. Always trying to kill herself – alcohol, war zones, fucked-up men – and always living. There had been hysterical hotel staff sobbing and wailing, phone calls and the ambulance, frantic television and radio pieces about the press hotel coming under fire – probably, it turned out, by a jittery civilian. Or not, as the case may be.

A bloke from Japanese television was the first to interview me, standing outside in the garden where she'd fallen. He had a fearless look in his eyes and was obviously glued to the career path. Like, this isn't real to me, I just need to do the job so I can get the promotion. The lights hurt my eyes actually and I told him, not that he or his producer were so much as faintly interested, that I had been smoking and had perhaps attracted the attention of a sniper. The CNN and BBC interviews went on forever because they're always live and they have so much air time to fill. Largely unwatched apparently. Pip asked me how I would feel if it had been me. What the fuck kind of question is that? 'In pain, Pip,' I said, not completely able to disguise my contempt.

Afterwards, I felt sick and dizzy and dazed. Eden seemed to have taken control of the situation and of me, and I followed him around as his shirt got more and more sweaty and crumpled and his face became more angular and shattered, his walk slower. 'Can't take much more of this,' he kept saying to himself. He would though. At about half four he took me up to my room.

'Get some sleep, Faithy,' he said. 'Try and get some sleep.'

He might as well have told me to write out the periodic table. I lay on my bed in my clothes and stared at the ceiling. I scrabbled for another cigarette while I still had one in my mouth. I called Evie but got the ansamachine. I had wanted Eden to stay really, to lie down next to me and hold my hand. But he would have started telling me about how I block people out and am emotionally stunted or something and I didn't think I could handle any adolescent psychoanalysis at the moment, so he loped away, one hand in his hair, his shirt rumpled, the slump of his shoulders exhausted. I opened a can of Coke from the mini bar but the sweet burbling smell of it made me retch and I tipped it down the bathroom sink. I lay back down on the bed. I got up again. Sometimes even the lights and wailings of misery and upheaval are better than the asthmatic gasping of being alone.

I can't say I was sorry to find Joshua Klein down in the lobby with everyone else, presumably doing something related to what had happened to Carly. We were 'special friends' already and we smiled to acknowledge. This has never happened to me before. Perhaps we all belong to somebody whether we know it or not. It was starting to feel a bit like that. Where have you been all my life? I thought I'd never find you.

'Hey, Klein. Do you know which hospital she ended up at?' I asked, tapping him on the shoulder. Immediately everything I had thought, Carly's suspicions, Hugo's aggression, evaporated. Here was a lovely man and that was all there was to it. I trusted him and I felt safe as soon as his eyes met mine.

'I can find out,' he said. 'Sit down.' There were lots of little huddles of smelly westerners and perfumed Iraqis, drinking dark coffee and talking urgently. The television lights from outside on the lawn gave everything an ominous green glow.

'I got your note,' I said.

'And?' he asked, twinkling with bad behaviour.

'I liked it,' I told him.

'I thought you would,' he said.

I felt I should be busy with something important. Instead, though, I grinned like a six-year-old and sat down, comforted, I thought then, by the presence of greatness. That's what he was like. The story was exploding at my feet and I was going to drink coffee with a green-eyed old man who smiled as if he knew me better than I know myself. I should get out of here.

'Got to go,' I said, fishing for the personality that might protect me, regretting having been pleased to see him. I was sinking here. I felt weak. In a good way. 'War.'

He laughed and leaned forward to scrutinise me. He seemed amused that I thought war was safer than a coffee with him. Well, I was right. I wanted to break the tension. I thought maybe I would try and make this a normal relationship where people fancy each other and have sex.

Somehow this 'thing', if that's what one dinner and some intense little moments amounted to, had escalated out of all control, become a big deal of some kind. I didn't like it.

So, I very nearly said, 'Listen, can we stop dancing around and flirting. I can't stand it. If you want to have sex, let's go upstairs.' Then perhaps we could relax. Didn't though. Just couldn't quite do it. What if he didn't want to? What a thing to think. If he doesn't want to, Faith, he will say he doesn't want to and you will smile and thank him for being nice about it and then be friends. What have you got to lose? Everything.

I stood up to walk away.

'Shut up and sit down,' he said. So I did. He could leave whenever he wanted to. I wasn't allowed. And I liked that too. When you spend your whole life being powerful it is nice to hand the baton to someone else from time to time.

In the glare of his attention everything I knew slipped away from me. My clothes, my job, my packet of cigarettes felt like affectations, things I had somehow created to protect myself from Joshua Klein, and it wasn't working.

'You like covering war?' he asked. And he seemed really to want to know. Always excited, asking, telling. This was not a difficult or a particularly interesting question. If Don McCaughrean, or maybe one of the young ones, cowering there in their flak jackets and asking terrified questions about chemical weapons, had asked me the same thing, I'd have said, 'Yes.' Or perhaps, 'No.' Or even, 'Fuck off.' But here, under a tacky lamp in a tacky hotel (the Americans wouldn't let anyone stay at the Sheraton because it was in a target zone) with this man leaning in too close to me, and Carly in pieces in hospital, I started wondering if I liked it or not. My job, that is. Instead of thinking about what had just happened. His shirt was crisp like someone playing a barrister in a film and he wore two rings. A wedding ring and a dark gold signet ring on his little finger. Family heirloom-type thing. So, preppy. Yale? Harvard? A long, long time ago.

'Sorry? What? Oh, yes . . . I . . . um . . . yes. Yes, I suppose I do like it. Well, like isn't the right word, but it's . . . exciting. It's . . . well, it's not going into the office every day and coming home on the six fifteen with a newspaper under your arm,' I said.

A German camera crew clattered past us, trailing leads and poles for lighting umbrellas. The correspondent was ageing and probably refused to be shot without pink reflectors. Even here.

'Saddam's been kissing children out by the big mosque,' someone shouted.

What? At this time of night. The man must be a psychopath.

I watched them, pretending I didn't want to look into Joshua Klein's eyes. He was laughing at my stupid answer, or was it my astonishing wit? He seemed charmed. By my girlish silliness, by my embarrassment. He looked as though he might be about to kiss me. And I should say that girlish silliness is not something I'm known for. I lit a cigarette and waved at the receptionist, Karim, who leant down to hear my whisper. I needed a drink urgently and if you don't ask for things, you don't get them. It is an English cultural thing not to ask for too much. It just means you don't get much.

'Do you think there's any hope of a vodka?' I asked and I put my feet up on the coffee table. I felt that whatever I did I would probably still look like Sophia Loren to Joshua. He seemed to fancy me in a way I'd never encountered before. There are all those songs. 'You make me feel like a natural woman.' Who's that by? Anyway, I was aware of not being the first person in the world to feel like a goddess in the presence of . . . a god? Hmmm. Dunno. Listen, I know I'm not ugly but I also know that men will sleep with anyone who is not physically deformed or some-thing. I've got a good figure, I'm blonde, I always have a tan. People don't refuse without a good reason – but that is not the same as being completely drenched with desire. And that's how Joshua and I felt that second dawn of the war. Or at least, I thought we did. That was back when I still knew what I thought.

'I'll see what I can do for you, madam,' the boy grinned and skittered off across the marble.

Joshua Klein smiled again, captivated by me like my father was when I wore a yellow dress with a white lace collar decorated with multi-coloured teapots. When I turned eight and it didn't fit any more (I'd always hated it anyway) he was stricken, as though the reality of human mortality had only just occurred to him. Or perhaps not quite in that way, since Klein was definitely looking at, and thinking about, my tits.

My vodka arrived, a tiny little sip of the stuff in the bottom of an enormous mug.

'Thank you so much,' I said, smiling and drinking it.

Joshua stopped Karim in his tracks under the whirring ceiling fan spinning with flies. 'Hey! Come back here!' He grinned and the boy returned, meek and cautious. 'What's your name?' Joshua asked him, actually tugging at the boy's sleeve as though begging for another sweet from his mother.

'Karim,' he said, blushing slightly under his wispy facial hair. He was clearly aiming for a very serious moustache and beard one day, when he was properly grown up and had a gun and a Mercedes.

'Karim,' Joshua said, leaping up and fishing around in his pockets. 'That was a nice thing you did for the lady. Been working here long?'

It was quite a performance on Joshua's part. He gazed, charmed, at the boy exactly as he'd been gazing at me two seconds before. He smiled, at one stage he even winked, he pressed his hand in sympathy on the boy's shoulder. Hey, as far as I could see the presidency was in the bag.

Karim had been working at the Corona for two weeks, he said, since his engineering college was closed down by fear of impending war.

'And your family?' Klein asked. Banal question, but the way he said it made him sound genuinely concerned. How do you do that?

82

Karim's mother was a hairdresser in a boutique over at the Sheraton and his dad had been killed in a car crash during the Gulf War. He has two sisters, both at home.

'My brother drives a cab in Manhattan. I'd like to go there,' Karim confessed.

Confession is what this man elicits. I smoked and watched, leaning back in the mustard velour of my seat. Perhaps I should have worn my cleaner T-shirt today. Though Joshua Klein behaved always as though I was in a pink silk negligee bordered with black lace. Evie's got one. It smells of lavender.

'You know what? I'll be over in Manhattan next week. You want me to take a letter for your brother?' Joshua offered, and Karim wrote down Klein's room number and smiled in bewildered gratitude. Not as bewildered or as grateful as his next smile would be. A smile that was the result of a twenty-dollar tip. I was insulted now on Joshua's behalf that Carly and that weirdo couple had been mean about him. Yes, he's a big personality and maybe they can't handle that. I have a similar problem. But he's honest and beautiful and I like him.

'Thank you, sir.' Karim bowed.

'Nice boy,' Joshua said, looking for something like a five-year-old looking for a beetle under a stone, all enthusiasm and energy. 'Nice boy.'

He found it. His card.

'That's my mobile number. Easiest way to reach me. We'll have dinner,' he told me, and swept away, leaving a huge hole in me somewhere. It occurred to me to wonder what he was playing at. Carly would probably have an answer. She would say something about him suddenly feeling he was in too deep and having to back away before he completely lost control. I could imagine her snorting about old men needing to be in control at all times, not to slip up, not to get emotionally involved. Then I realised I was just describing myself. It's just that his slip-up was

83

making love (does anyone still call it that?). Personally I can do that without getting involved. It's the other stuff that bothers me. Right now it was all I could do not to reach out my hand and say, 'Don't leave me!' What I actually said, I think, was, 'You'll be lucky,' but Joshua Klein had already gone. I blinked a few times, breathed out and looked at the card. American government, apparently. No department. No title. Just an imposing crest. Just like Nur had said. Interesting. And perfectly benign.

Eden had been on the lawn giving interviews. Apparently he'd seen me talking to Klein. He was grey and anxious from the terrible night that was now ending.

'Don't you realise we're a couple?' he asked me, sitting down and drinking Joshua's untouched coffee.

Well, no, I hadn't actually, since as far as I was aware he was having it off with Ayesha, the interpreter. This had only dawned on me lately. I had been busy with my own stuff. But I'd seen the way he'd smiled at her on the bus on the way to the hospital that day. He always picks them out like that.

'Don't know what you mean,' I said, unable to stop myself smiling.

'Yes you do.' Eden nodded, grimly. 'He's too old, Faith. He'll never know you like I do.'

'Oh please.' I laughed and put my cigarette out in an ashtray with the hanging gardens of Babylon on it. 'I'm getting bored of saying this to people, but NOTHING'S HAPPENED!'

Eden looked down at his hands.

'That serious, uh?' he said, ending the conversation. I was not in the mood for his shrinky business. Time for bed.

CHAPTER EIGHT

I woke up a few hours later at about nine. The sky was full of planes and I could hear the frenzy of news production going on in the corridor outside my room. Even here the metallic popcorn popping sound of ammunition dumps exploding was audible and there was a grinding noise coming from the low-flying A-10 Warthogs, firing four thousand bullets a minute. I found my cleaner jeans under the bed and lit a cigarette. The phone rang.

'Hon?'

'Evie! Hello,' I said, reaching across the rumpled sheets for the ashtray.

'Oh, Jesus, honey. I was so worried about you. You're not in that hotel where the girl was shot on the roof?' she asked, pacing, I assumed, up and down the corridor of her flat in Richmond, Victorian tiles under her Agent Provocateur slippers, a golden glow of wealthy light over her sharp black bob.

'I am, but I'm fine. It was just one snipe. She's alive. Still critical, but . . . I don't think they're going to hit the hotel. Evie, I wanted to tell you about this dream I had the other day . . .' I started to say. When I had bad dreams she would stroke my hair and sing 'Daddy's Gonna Buy You A Mocking Bird'. It always seemed sad the way she sang it. Perhaps because he wasn't there.

'Pumpkin? You're cracking up. I'm glad you're OK. Call me when you get home,' she said, and hung up. Her voice assumed I'd be home soon, not needing to know more.

She hated me for going to wars, for doing what Dad did. She faked a distance that might protect her if anything happened. Refused to find out too much about where I was and what I was doing. I didn't blame her. I would have done the same in her position, but I couldn't help it. It's an addiction. Nobody's here on some kind of altruistic mission from God, to tell the truth about the world to the world. We're here because the desk sent us, because it's exciting, it's . . . well, fun. Almost.

After a big assignment you sit at home in London and your heart sinks. Mine does. I watch television and eat takeaways and feel edgy when I switch on the news, feeling I should be in all those place I'm watching. Nervous about who is there and whether they're doing a better job than me. Just before I came out here they sent me to Oxford to do a thing about students drinking too much. I ask you. I sat around outside a pub called the King's Arms with people whose surnames were the names of supermarkets and household items. They were all mildly pissed and majorly bored and one of them – Rufus his name was – said, 'People say we have an alcohol problem in Oxford. It's no problem! There's plenty of it.'

Ha ha. I thought I might kill someone. Them. Myself. Now I know it doesn't sound very nice of me to be glad when a war is about to start but . . . you know how it is. Suddenly everyone is clamouring to get to Baghdad or at least somewhere near it. Even people who are absolutely terrified and have no intention of going even if the desk asks them to have to put in a request, just to look keen. People's careers are made on this stuff. All the big names in news made their names being extra brave and authoritative during a war. Don't go, don't have a career in news. At least, not until the next time. Pip Deakin's trying to get spotted by an American network though he'd never admit it. Fat chance. He's ten years too old and ten times too pompous.

I went down to the lobby, still shaky from the horrors of Carly jumping. 'Zanetti, you fucking bitch,' Eden spat at me, standing up from an armchair. He had been sitting with Grant Bradford who was white as a sheet and sort of quivering. I genuinely couldn't think why. There were about ten Iraqi soldiers striding about importantly and spreading malaise. Amazing that they wear aftershave with their uniforms. You've got to give credit where it's due.

'S'your problem, Jones? I didn't even do anything, I told you already, and anyway I'm sick of you trying to claim me the whole time,' I said and threw myself down into a chair to join them. Now he felt stupid standing up. He sat back down and rolled his shirtsleeves up. Nice shirt. Did I give it to him?

'What?' he asked.

'No, I mean it. You think you can play every fucking role there is in my life? Like I don't need anything else? What are you, God?'

'What are you talking about?' He stared, putting his cigarette out in his espresso cup.

'I was answering your allegations as to my being a bitch,' I said, getting confused now myself.

'I'm talking about the Jamal story, you stupid cow. Why didn't you tell us? Did you know about the gas before we ran our stories?'

I glanced down too quickly. He knew me too well.

'You fucking cow, Zanetti. Bradford here's been sacked,' he told me. Triumphant.

Grant Bradford, cocky, arsy, atomic-haired Grant Bradford burst into tears.

'I have to give her two grand a month,' he sobbed. 'What am I going to do?'

Well, they all had those problems. Don, Grant, Pip – all of them. You can't have a family and a war addiction. It isn't possible.

As he said this all the background humming that is the life of a hotel simply stopped. The fans stopped whirring, the computers stopped buzzing, the lights went out. A hundred journalists swore in unison as their laptops crashed, the little lights on their camera batteries went off, their mini bars shuddered to a halt. Power cut again. I was losing friends here and the oddest thing about it was that I didn't care. An edge of me hated them and their banal little lives, panicking about their jobs and alimony, Eden feeling like he'd got a right to shout at me. Joshua, I thought, would not shout at me.

I wondered if Carly was conscious. How much pain she was in. Whether or not they would be able to save her. 'They'. 'They' have a hell of a lot to do in the world.

'Shit,' I said.

'What?' Eden asked.

'Grant, mate. I'm really sorry. Listen, they can't afford to lose you. You know that. They know that. Let's go out and get something that will wipe the other tabs off the face of the planet. Come on!' I put my hand on his knee and he looked up at me meekly. I hated to see him look meek. What was it George Bush said? He had always assumed 'the meek shall inherit the earth' was some kind of mistranslation from the Aramaic. I know what he means actually. Meekness has never seemed like much of a virtue to me. Bradford knew I was right though. The Brits were supposed to be arriving today, a fact that his paper was hardly likely to be able to ignore. Eden joined in.

'They couldn't do without you, Bradford. Nobody can rewrite the wires like you can.' He smiled, shaking his cigarettes for reassurance that there were still some in there. There weren't. He crushed the pack.

'Really?' Grant asked us.

'Really.' We nodded, gravely.

Well, honestly. I broke the story, they got it wrong. Why did I have to be responsible for the whole sodding career of Grant Bradford? I didn't, is the answer.

He did look crushed though. Horrible to see someone so cocky brought so low. And worrying to see how much our jobs matter to us. I mean, really, what the hell else could he possibly do? He'd have to go on a course and learn how to programme computers or something. Or do that desperate thing of trying to start his own newspaper or magazine. I don't know. We're not qualified for much.

In the end, thank God, I didn't have to play a personal part in saving Grant's career from the edge of the abyss. We were right about his paper's inescapable reliance on him (what were they going to do? Suddenly put the showbiz correspondent on a plane?) and he ended up having to pay some poor driver a thousand dollars to drive him out to Um Qasr to meet the British land troops who were supposed to be arriving near there. No guarantee of his job back but could he just help them out a bit? It was in the bag, though. Royal Tank Regiment, he said. He was going to join a column of Challenger 2 tanks and he said something about the Desert Rats. He loves all that. Um Qasr is a place that was reported as having fallen every day for weeks before it actually did. The Allies were big on trying to create self-fulfilling prophesies. Uprisings and mutinies against Saddam, whole towns surrendering. A policy not completely without success, oddly.

You could see Grant's mood lifting at the thought of our brave boys slapping up their mess tents in the hot sand for bacon butties and good, wholesome, war-winning shepherd's pie. Not to mention the possibility that their chemical weapons gear wouldn't work or their guns would jam in a sandstorm and all those other career-ending issues for a defence or a prime minister. By the time Grant set off in his jeep with a nervous-looking driver, his freckles were positively glowing with excitement.

Eden took a sip of mint tea and rested his elbows on his knees. Karim brought a tray over for me – vodka in a teacup. He knows where his tips are coming from, this boy. I winked at him and sat back.

'So,' Eden asked, rubbing a palm against the grain of his jeans. 'Where's your friend?'

'No friend of mine,' I snapped, putting my cigarette out, not wanting to talk to Eden Jones about Joshua Klein any more. There was nothing to say. 'I'm tired, Eden. Bad day. Bad night.'

'Bad life.' Eden laughed.

'Exactly.'

We shared a glance of complicity and I was relieved to feel safe in my cynicism again. Ludicrous that I should have thought, should have hoped . . . I don't know. Something. It has slipped away from me now as all those little glimmers of positivity always do in life. Slip away. Run away. In any case, try arguing that the world is a violent hellhole and you won't find many people contradicting you. Eden and I cling together in that knowledge. Fuck the suggestion that there might be more to it than that. You know what? Fuck it.

Hotel staff were running around with tangled armfuls of wires trying to get a generator working. It didn't look hopeful. Eden and I had both got our armour up and running and I couldn't even imagine a time when we'd had real snipe-free conversations. We were relieved, I think, when Pip Deakin came hurtling in from the street in a cloud of dust to tell us that there were Abrams tanks making forays into the city. He yelled to his crew who were scattered about the lobby.

'Seriously, I saw them coming over the bridge by the whatsname! You know, the Jumhuriya.' He was hysterical.

'Bollocks,' I said. How could they just drive into Baghdad? The sheer

. . . what's the word? Chutzpah. I mean, say what you like about the Americans but they aren't half arrogant. It's so staggering in its audacity somehow that it's impressive. You know, you've almost got to hand it to people like Bush who rant about abortion and every human life counting at the same time as signing death warrants on minors. So here they were. A few days into the start of the offensive (or do they believe it's somehow defensive? Probably) and they're already riding around Baghdad in their big green war machines. Already! It seemed as though we were only just beginning to get a handle on covering all this and a new phase was underway. I thought of Nur and Hugo and wondered if they'd got on a flight yet.

Mahmoud, the young westernised bloke who'd taken us to the hospital, agreed to drive me and Eden to the Jumhuriya Bridge where Pip said he'd seen the tanks. Even Mahmoud was sort of excited, fiddling with his palm pilot. If they could wrap the whole thing up this quickly he'd be mixing tequilas on the beach before you could say Donald Rumsfeld (quite a long time in his case).

The Abrams were crouching there like those lumpy dinosaurs, swivelling their guns to and fro. I think when people watch wars at home they imagine that they are seeing what we are seeing. Of course, the cameraman chooses what they see. In reality it all looks much, much odder than that. Odd because of the backdrop of normality. Tanks and guns on a very ordinary-looking bridge in a very ordinary-looking place with washing strung out on balconies, a few boats on the gleaming river and birds wheeling about in the sky. The machinery of death tends to look so out of place you feel you might be imagining it.

A Warthog looped over the tanks and the façade of the Ministry of Planning across the river shattered. The astonishing thing was that nobody was even firing at them. Well, I say nobody – the odd shot rang out and we put our heads down but it was hardly what anybody would call a firefight, let alone anything that could be described as 'anti-tank' anything. Some rocket fire arced into the air towards them. Half-hearted and ineffectual.

We pulled up on the pavement on one side of the bridge and listened to the rumble. As the first Abrams rolled by I saw a notice in English and Arabic taped to the back of it: 'If you can read this sign, you're closer to Allah than you think.' The barrels of their guns had names spray-painted on to them. Assassin, Carnage, Cold Steel, Crazy Train, Rebel, and even, get this, Got Oil?

Ha ha. Jesus, the gall of it all. I was dying to see what the Blogger was going to say about this. Were they actually occupying Baghdad now, or what? It had been a South African reporter who found him. He was a fixer for Iraq's main TV station and someone saw him fiddling around with his website. I said I'd do a weekend piece about it but haven't even made the calls.

It was all we could do to stop ourselves waving at the Americans, the sense of victory was so overpowering. And I wasn't even on their side. Not, obviously, that I was on Saddam Hussein's side either. Basically a horrid bloke with a horrid regime and horrid raping torturing sons who would without any doubt be better off dead.

Eden pointed to a nude painted on the side of one of the tanks.

I suppose it's the self-congratulatoriness of the Americans and Brits deciding what's right and wrong and what to do about it all by themselves. As though there really is a right and wrong. As though the world is a moral place where things can be set straight. Can they really? Seems doubtful. Or perhaps Utopian. So, we obliterate all the regimes that are vile and replace them with lovely ones and at some distant point in the future everything will be perfect? Hmmm. Sounds familiar. Ah, yes. Communism.

Well, we counted the tanks (seven) since that is apparently what we are supposed to do and Mahmoud took us home again. 'Crazy,' he said.

Basically it seemed like the American army had swung into positions encircling the city and then started these amazing forays. Trouble with the Iraqis was that they were perfectly happy to fight but they weren't in any kind of military formations, unlike the slick perfection of the Americans. You could see Iraqi soldiers' heads peeping out of foxholes all over Baghdad, dug about every ten yards. Units of the Republican Guard, Saddam's elite, with their little red triangles on their sleeves, had been hanging around at every junction. But they weren't doing a whole hell of a lot now. We saw some Ba'ath Party militiamen chugging around in motorbike sidecars with guns mounted on top and some blokes in balaclavas standing on the back of a pick-up with bazookas and Kalashnikovs. And yet, here were the Abrams tanks and nowhere was the fighting.

When we got back, the buzz of air conditioners and ceiling fans told us that the electricity generator was working.

'Cool,' Eden said and he looked around for familiar faces. He wanted to get away from me.

Someone had gone out to one of the few restaurants that was still open in the city and come back with big foil trays of Iraqi delicacies, including that mazgouf fish that people pretty much try and shove down your throat wherever you go along the river. Or they did. The press and all the fixers and translators were crowding round some tables that the hotel had set up. There were white starchy tablecloths with metal clips, and there was kind of a party atmosphere as everyone screeched about the Abrams and stuffed falafel and little cheesy samosa things into their faces.

'Here, I'll get us a plate,' Eden said. I watched him push forward to pick up two paper plates and two plastic forks and start loading them up with food.

Don McCaughrean was sitting dangerously on the edge of one of the tables, smoking and eating straight off the serving plates. Not cute. He was shouting and dribbling.

'They took us out to see a burnt-out Abrams in the suburbs last night, the stupid bastards. Couldn't think of a way of getting us there without us seeing all their fucking burnt-out army vehicles though, could they? So they're all on top naffing about and cheering like they've won,' he said, holding up a demolished chicken leg for emphasis. He looked up at me and away again. Was he pissed off about Grant getting sacked too? But he'd already been reinstated, for God's sake. This was absurd. It was extremely unclear to whom exactly Don was talking. It is very often hard to tell with McCaughrean whether he is very very drunk or not. 'But the tank they're saying they captured is pointing out of Baghdad and it's got a fucking tow bar on the back of it! I mean, they can't honestly think that someone of my experience is going to believe . . .'

And I tried to tune him out. 'First Marine Expeditionary Force' was the last thing I heard him say before my brain switched him off. Easier said than done with McCaughrean.

I rested my cigarette in one of those stand-up ashtrays with sand in it and wriggled out of my jacket. Was it really so seriously underway so soon? Maybe there honestly wouldn't be many casualties at all. At least, not civilian ones. As though killing soldiers is all right. Boys who have been terrorised and choked with propaganda. The Iraqi ones too . . . No, OK, boring to make politically correct jokes, attacking America. After all, where would we be without them? We being the world, not the English. I wondered what Joshua would think.

I went upstairs to pace about and worry about writing something. My computer looked friendly compared to everything else I had to deal with. Emails uneventful apart from an insane request from Tamsin on the desk to try and find out exactly where Uday and Qusay Hussein were. Uh-huh. Okey dokey. It's like asking for a little piece about where Saddam's gone. 'You know, just a couple of hundred words. OK, Faith?' 'Ooh, certainly. No problem. He's just here behind the wardrobe.' And the Blogger was disappointing. Too concerned about his electricity generator and bottles of mineral water to be a decent vox pop about the tanks. I also find him slightly embarrassing in his desperate effort to sound up on things western. 'For all your efforts I salute you with a hearty FUCK YOU.' The English is perfect and yet completely wrong. Like that bit in *My Fair Lady* when Eliza is accused of being foreign because her English is too good. Or those ancient Indian men you meet in Delhi who say things like, 'Not my cup of tea, my old chum.' Also the lustre had gone now that we knew he was this fixer with toss all else to do but write his memoirs.

I smoked four cigarettes in a row and listened to the phone ringing. Took a deep breath and kicked my heels up on to the bedside table before I picked it up.

'Hi,' said Joshua Klein. 'It's me.'

'Hi. I knew it would be,' I said, knowing he could hear the smile in my voice. 'It's lovely to hear you.' Well, I don't know how you do hard to get.

'Faith Zanetti,' he said and sighed.

'Mmmm hmmm. That's me.'

'Well, you're wonderful.'

'Thank you. You too.'

'Do you feel weak? I do.'

'I do.'

The sky was getting dusky. At first we had tried to count the hours it takes a B-52 to get here from London. Six. Now though there were too many different things in the sky to be sure.

Klein was silent.

'What?' I asked.

'I want to . . . to tell you that your friend is in the Al Yermouk. Where we met the first time . . . and to read you a poem,' he said.

'Umm. That would be . . . lovely,' I told him, smiling. 'But you'll have to come here and do it.' I hung up.

I opened the door so that he wouldn't have to knock and lay down, blissfully defeated. What was I doing? I don't know. Maybe that's Baghdad for you. The bombs, you know. They skew your thinking.

'Is it too late?' he asked, smiling, his sparkle of energy almost offensive. He strode in with coffee on a tray which he put down on the little round table in front of the television. The television, I noticed, was on. Al Jazeera on mute, showing us the damage to Baghdad so far and some corpses piled up at some morgues.

'For what? To fulfil my childhood ambition of being an actress? For Carly not to be in intensive car in sodding Iraq? To get a life? Yes.'

Klein laughed. 'How're you holding up?'

'I'm not. Look. See? I'm down,' I said, leaning up on an elbow nonetheless.

'Best place to be sometimes,' he said, pouring out coffee black as oil. 'Sorry about your friend. I meant to say it downstairs, but . . .'

'Not your fault,' I said. 'Mine. She might be OK.'

He brought me my coffee in a cup and saucer, carrying it carefully, looking awkward with a small delicate thing in his big hands. The presidential manner had been put aside. He seemed older. Sager. I wondered if he might actually be as old as seventy though his thick hair was still dark. He swivelled his signet ring round his little finger and looked down at me. We both smiled.

'Thanks,' I said.

'What do you think?' he asked.

'About what?'

'The glasses. On or off?' He took them off, smiled, put them back on again.

'Good either way,' I said. Well, it was true.

He peeled me a tangerine from his pocket and put a piece into my mouth. Then he sat down on what passes for an armchair in these hotels and watched me drink my coffee like a nurse watching an invalid. Weird how he makes me helpless. I feel like somebody else entirely. He had a book in his pocket.

'Listen to this,' he said. 'It's about you.'

Totally confident but not declaiming, he read out a Louis McNeice poem called 'Postscript to Iceland', looking up to make sure I was listening and to check my reaction every other line. I have never been read a poem before. Very odd. Quite nice. Hard to call. There is a verse about the poet sitting alone, insomniac, in his flat, waiting for the phone to ring or for 'Unknown angels at the door'. I wanted to interrupt him and tell him that really it's about him – the unknown angel at the door. I didn't though. He was reading too beautifully. Like coals glowing in a fire, safe things I've never known. The poem ends with a kind of portent of death, of gun butts rapping on the door and the idea, I think, that one should make the most of the time before that happens. Or was that just what I hoped it meant? I don't know now, and I daren't look it up and read it now for fear of just breaking down entirely. Was that the fear that seemed to be holding Klein back? Maybe.

We sat there for a couple of seconds after he finished and I sighed. He put the book back in his pocket. There were no lights on and a breeze from outside was making the long net curtains flutter into the room from the balcony doors. Everything was fuzzy and grey. Cars honked a million miles away.

'Are you sad about your friend? These things happen. It's a war,' he said, looking straight at me with eyes that made everything OK. It was like trying to talk to God. No, that's not it. Because he made life seem basically benign and broadly pretty funny.

'Well, she might be OK, you know,' I said again, crossing my boots at the bottom of the bed and glowering at the ceiling. 'These things happen. Well, they happened to my friend and it makes me hate the whole fucking world.'

'I can understand that,' Joshua Klein said, still looking at me, laughing at me. I could feel it. He didn't understand though. He said it like a priest or a shrink or something. As though he could sympathise with how I felt but really I was wrong about everything.

'It's all shit,' I added, to emphasise my point.

'You don't believe that, baby,' he said, very quietly, and I wished he would just take my clothes off and do it. If I could taste him it might all go away. 'You know you don't believe that.' He smiled, and oh, sod it, I didn't know what I believed. Of course I didn't believe it was all just pointless shit. Life, that is. I spend an awful lot of time saying that's what I think, but really . . .

Well, really, I love standing on roofs watching the fireworks, flying into a new place in the middle of all the chaos and the nightmare. I love the taste of vodka and the smell of the desert and I am devastated when someone I know dies. If you're devastated you care, right?

'No,' I whispered. 'I don't.' And it was such a relief to admit it. I felt as though I had told my biggest secret (apart from my middle name, that is) and it was OK. I was allowed to smile and to enjoy the thrill of it all, to miss people and to hope that . . . to hope.

I sat up and grinned at Joshua Klein so happily that my cheeks hurt. We stood up and took a step towards each other. I put my head on his shoulder, where his left lapel would be, tears streaming down my face as I shut my eyes and smiled and the butterflies swooped in my stomach (in Russian the expression is 'scrabbling kittens'. A better description of the feeling, I think). He put one hand in the small of my back and with the other he held the back of my neck.

'You need a bath,' he said, staying where he was.

I laughed and moved in closer to him. Not that anywhere would be close enough.

'I'm so tired, Josh,' I whispered.

'Of course you are, baby,' he said.

The knocks on the door were like the gun butts of the poem.

'Hey! Zanetti!' Eden said, walking in. 'Just came to see if you needed—'

He stopped and looked at us as we moved apart. He was holding a can of Coke that must have been for me.

I lit a cigarette, lighting the room with the scratch of my match.

'The weapons inspector,' Eden said.

Joshua threw his arms up with a smile. 'You got me,' he said, and came forward to shake Eden's hand hard, with both of his. 'This girl can't seem to take her hands off me.'

I drew my breath in and very nearly punched Klein in the head.

'Hey. I wanted to ask you something,' he said to Eden, putting his arm round his shoulders and leading him out into the corridor. But he leant back in to speak to me. 'I think we'd better call this a day, Faith. OK? I know you understand.' He closed my door behind them and before they were out of earshot I heard Eden laugh. Smitten. Of course.

I suppose I must have passed out, partly in confusion. I dreamt about my dad again. It is the worst dream I have ever had. He was going to be executed, in some sort of hospital, by lethal injection. I had to fill in some forms at a booth and there were five minutes to go. I decided that I would just have to bear it and it would then be over and we could start the mourning and the funeral arrangements. He would suffer briefly and it would be done. Then suddenly I galvanised myself. I can't let it happen! There must be something I can do! I screamed at the functionary behind the glass and told her it was a mistake. I tried to get someone official on the phone to call it off. In the end they said I could talk to him. He wouldn't be able to talk to me, but they would lift the sheet from his face and put the phone to his ear. I had made it worse. Far from being over quickly I was now making him suffer more. She handed me the receiver and I had to speak. I didn't want to break his heart wailing, 'Daddy! Daddy!' so I just made out I'd see him soon and

99

made some awful joke. Then they did it and the families had to walk with their gurney to take it out for the funeral. People following corpses in white sheets wept through the hospital. I couldn't find my dad. A nurse took me to the right stretcher and the sheet over his face was dotted with blood.

I woke up choking with tears and ran around flicking all the lights on. Someone had pushed a message under my door. A real message on a piece of paper. Not a hotel-issue thing. I refused to acknowledge the lurch in my stomach. An invitation to dinner? Just a little 'I love you'. Shut up, Faith. Don't you know nice things don't happen?

Dear Faith,

I have enjoyed our brief acquaintance more than I can say. I have been completely consumed by you, in fact, and have thought about nothing else for the short time that I have known you. This has never happened to me before. I have spent too much time working hard and being extremely careful. I hope you will under-stand that we must cool this thing down before it gets out of control. I leave for Basra today and I am sure that when I return we will be able to put our mutual attraction behind us and get on with the jobs we both have to do.

Yours,

Joshua Klein

It was typed. The signature included. I put my hand over my throat and sat down on the bed, waiting for my defensive torpor to sweep over me. I don't do rejection. There is a switch that turns on a protective feeling of very thick blankness. Takes a couple of seconds though. There we go. WHAT? Last time I saw him, it was all poetry and embrace. What is with this shit? As soon as Carly was able to speak I would be pouncing on her about this. How many hours had I known him now? 'Out of control.' Clearly an undesirable thing from his point of view. Odd. Very odd. I mean, we haven't even had sex. What is going on? He is behaving like some sort of chivalric knight who is having an affair with the queen but fancies the princess. Or something. Why couldn't he calm down about 'it', whatever the hell it is. And, more to the point, why couldn't I?

CHAPTER NINE

No amount of calling the Al Yermouk was going to help. Nobody knew or could tell me in English whether Carly was in a fit state for visitors. There was only one thing for it.

I liked being a broken-hearted wreck, or I liked the idea of it. The war didn't seem to matter, I was all wrapped up in my blanket of misery, smoking and staring out of the taxi windows at people and places that didn't exist as far as my crushed ego was concerned. Precious, like having a terrible hangover. So, perhaps not technically broken-hearted then.

At the hospital there was still a queue of journalists waiting in the corridors to interview Jamal and his family, to hassle the doctors, to try and get them to admit that they'd lied. Obviously, nobody was seeing anyone or saying anything. They all snarled at me when I walked past. Ha! Idiots. Most of them were standing there in flak jackets. It makes them feel important. Which is odd because it actually makes them look pathetic. None of the Iraqis were wearing them. The Iraqis were getting on with the business of opening their shops, looting the museums and robbing each other.

I stood in a long hot queue of people waiting for news about their relatives and then had a surreal conversation with an old man who had dyed hair and tache. I mimed falling off a roof in the end. It did the trick.

'Aiwa,' he eventually nodded and drew me a very complicated map of the hospital.

Carly was in a big room upstairs by herself, attached to some super hi-tech equipment. She was in a body cast, tubes up her nose, lines in both hands, green as a fish and thinner even than usual.

'Hey. I'm in the Ba'athist section. Surviving Hussein family members and Americans only. You look awful,' she said to me.

'You can fucking talk,' I said, smiling, and sat down. A nurse poked his head round the door and left again. The blinds were pulled down and apart from the lack of cards and flowers, the place looked really normal.

'Faith, you've got to do something for me,' Carly croaked. She wasn't croaking because of her condition. It's just how she talks.

'What?' I asked, all earnest and eager. 'Anything.'

'Give me a fucking cigarette,' she said, her dry lips almost straining towards my jacket pocket. In the end we compromised and shared one. A drag for me, a drag for her and so on. All administered by me because her hands weren't moving properly. One of them because of a cast. The other one just wasn't moving. Years of physio loomed.

'How's the old man?' she asked me, nearly smiling.

'Bloody hell, Carly. You're half dead and you're interested in my love life.' I laughed, elbows on my knees, next to her on a metal chair.

'It's got to be more interesting than the nurse's,' she said.

'I wouldn't bet on it. Look at this,' I told her, pulling the note out of my jacket pocket like a schoolgirl with a Valentine's card.

'Oooooh, shit,' she said, appreciatively. 'No sex yet then?'

'How can you tell that? How do you know that?' I snatched the note back to scrutinise it for evidence. 'No, no sex yet. What is wrong with this dude?'

'It's bad news, Faith. Very bad news.' She shook her head.

'Oh, spit it out, Posner,' I told her.

'He's in love,' she announced.

'Please. He thinks I am and he's letting me down gently. If anything. Which really pisses me off, I have to say.'

'How old are you, Faith Zanetti? Thirteen? If he didn't give a shit he wouldn't be doing all this "cool this thing down" crap. Let's face it, what thing? He doesn't mean the sex, now does he? So, what's he talking about? Presumptuous to talk about your feelings – ergo he's talking about his. Men hate being in love. It makes them weak and they get all nervous. Honey, I've seen this a million times over.'

I looked back at the note. Almost convincing.

'Mutual attraction,' I mocked, quoting the vicious message. I couldn't look at it without feeling his beautifully aimed shard of coldness searing through me. 'Mutual fucking attraction. What's with the vocabulary?'

'He's probably trying to be formal. You know, get things back on his own turf. Business, power,' Carly said. 'Light another fag, Zanetti, eh?'

I didn't feel like fighting her. This time we had one each, me holding them both. Idiotic.

'Every time we nearly have sex he runs away and says something mean,' I said, actually whining now. He shows up at my room with poems and oranges and then he sends me terse little notes dumping me. He's fucked up. But the worst thing is I'm totally sucked in,' I told her, pacing around to emphasise my misery, flicking the blind up for a look at the car park, lines of cars baking in the morning sun.

'Of course you are. That's how it works. He adores you, then he hates you. Then he adores you again. It would send anyone insane. It's the whole point. I mean, if you were just having a proper thing with him, it would be no big deal. He's making a monster. Basically, Faithy, he's shit scared.'

Suddenly someone shouted something down the corridor and the whole hospital could be heard praying.

'God, I hate it in here,' Carly said. 'Nutters.'

'What's he scared of? Sex? I'm not going to bite him for fuck's sake.' I thought about it. 'No. That's a lie. I am going to. But not hard enough to cause lasting damage.'

Carly laughed and then shut her eyes. I thought my time was probably up.

'Sorry, no grapes,' I said. 'I could bring you a pack of Saddam Hussein playing cards.'

'That would be great,' Carly told me and then she was asleep. Or unconscious. Or something. The nurse came in and started fussing over her.

'She is a miracle,' he said, and he was right.

Not that she'd helped me much. In fact, she'd made me more confused. I wanted to hate Klein for being a twisted bastard, but now I was starting to feel a bit sorry for him. All this confusion. Hell, I knew what I wanted. It was becoming a matter of some urgency actually.

When I got back to the hotel I lay down on the floor with my cheek to the cheap vinyl and thought about crying. This was someone, I knew, who could help me to my feet. Nobody else. But the tears wouldn't come, not even when I sang Joni Mitchell songs to myself. I phoned Don's room. I almost wanted him to be out on a job so that I could feel even more alone and abandoned and crap.

'Don McCaughrean, photographer extraordinaire,' he announced boozily.

'Don. You are a tosser,' I said.

'Ah, the delectable Faith Zanetti. My favourite virtue.'

'Grace.'

'Whatever.'

'Don, can you come up?'

'No.'

'Oh, go on.'

'OK. Give me ten seconds.'

He arrived in a cigarette and a half, breathless and wheezing at my door.

'This had better be an emergency, Eff Zed. I've got worlds to change.' The heat seemed to pound through the hotel from outside.

'Yeah, well, change mine then,' I said, and I showed him the note from Joshua Klein. His first reaction made me want to kick him.

'What about Eden?' he said.

'What about Eden? Eden Jones who fucks every blousy translator he can lay his hands on? You mean that Eden?'

'Zanetti, if you think it's for any reason other than that he can't have you then you're dimmer than your editor.'

'Leave it out, McCaughrean, you moron. What do you think?'

'I think this is from someone you have fucked who doesn't like you and is trying to let you down gently. Sounds married or otherwise engaged and is crippled with embarrassment at having involved himself with a tart like you. Plus which he's probably as fucked off with you as the rest of us for screwing Bradford over and making him lose his job.'

'Listen, lard arse, they gave it right back to him in three seconds.'

'Yeah. Not his reputation though.'

'Ugh. I didn't invite you up here to tread me further into the fucking dirt. I just wanted a male opinion, but you are clearly too bitter and messed up for comment. Want a vodka?'

'What do you think?'

'I think you do.'

'Then what are you asking for?'

We sat on the bed together, gazing at the balcony doors, and we drank six vodka miniatures each, clinking tiny bottles each time. We didn't speak, unless you count Don's burps which were loud and vile.

When the fridge was empty he hauled himself sweatily to standing and mopped his forehead with the back of his hand. He was red and bloated.

'Listen, Eff Zed, if you're in need of a shag or anything . . .'

'Get out, Don. Go and take some pictures of dead people or something.'

'All right. All right. Don't get your knickers in a twist. I'm only offering.'

'Sweet of you. Out.' I had to lie on the floor again, but this time just to reach my cigarettes from under the bed.

Basra, Basra, Basra.

Suddenly it sounded beautiful and romantic. Basra. He was there. Maybe thinking about me and what he'd had to give up (Carly's theory). Maybe relieved to be shot of this intense mad bitch who'd started hounding him (Don's). Either way he was there and it felt like a billion miles away. Not only that but I couldn't bring myself to believe the truth of the situation, that he was doing his probably pretty boring job and meeting lots of boring or mad or dangerous people. I pictured him holed up in some kind of harem with heavenly ladies a decade younger than me popping grapes into his mouth and anointing him from head to toe with aromatic oils while he regaled them with hilarious anecdotes. I was, hopelessly, in agony. Couldn't think about anything else and could barely breathe. I'd already wasted a whole day thinking about him and now my head hurt.

Incredibly, I managed to file an embarrassingly cobbled together piece about the Al Yermouk based purely on my visit to Carly and some cuts off the internet. That and a progress of the war piece which was slapped into shape from Reuters and AP in the kind of way that gets journalists sacked from the *New York Times*. Speaking of which, God, we all felt sorry for that bloke. You know, the one that got sacked for making up a few quotes and pretending to have gone to Maryland when he couldn't be arsed. Honestly, there wouldn't be a single British journalist with a job if those were sacking offences. Everyone took a sharp intake of breath at work the day that story broke.

Anyway, I was still sitting in my room (mini bar restocked with a paper bag of miniatures that a Swiss journalist had brought from the plane and was selling, I mean selling, in the lobby) and my head hurt. Come to think of it, my head hurt a lot.

Suddenly I couldn't remember when my head last hadn't hurt. I switched the computer on to test my reading ability and it all looked blurry. I shut my eyes, tried to touch the tip of my nose with my index finger (a doctor's coordination test someone once taught me) and missed. Then I coughed and my head definitely hurt more. It crossed my mind that I might have a brain tumour. And then it crossed my mind again and again and again. I knew an American girl once, twenty-nine, much younger than me, who had a brain tumour. A string of doctors told her she was toast and she eventually found one willing to try and remove it. She had to be wide awake for the operation (which involved, obviously, sawing through her skull) so that they didn't touch nerve endings they weren't supposed to touch. I think she actually had to read out loud for the hours of the operation. Anyway, they hacked it out and she forgot all nouns for a year. She's fine now. Makes arts documentaries for a Canadian network. My point is, it happens.

I took too many Valium and passed out in my clothes.

I couldn't tell how long I slept but it felt like years. Dreamless, dark sleep, undisturbed by the destruction outside. My head was killing me. It seemed like afternoon out there but I was too dizzy and dishevelled to be sure. Six o' clock. Well, it couldn't be six in the morning. I felt I needed to hold my head in my hands to control the pain. By the time I dragged myself through the lobby, past Eden Jones who pretended

ANNA BLUNDY

not to notice me and towards the taxi ranks (hugely diminished since the city started going up in flames), I was hyperventilating so much with terror that I thought I might actually pass out. I could feel the location of the tumour, just behind my right eye. Part of me knew I was a lunatic, and part of me wanted an immediate diagnosis. I could fight this thing if only I knew exactly what I was fighting. I got into a taxi, registering the panic in the air as night fell. What had I been doing for twenty-four hours? Everyone tried to hunker down at night when the bombardments were at their worst. I could hear the pounding from the suburbs.

At the hospital I was already beginning to feel a bit silly. Would there really be anyone with the time to give me a brain scan? Did they have the equipment? Maybe I should just try and get on a flight home. Carly must have seen a neurologist, right? I decided to pop up and get a recommendation. My vision was definitely not right.

'Have you got nothing better to do, Zanetti?' she croaked at me as I came through the doors. She had a bit more colour in her cheeks and her lipstick was back on which had to be a good sign.

'Posner, don't laugh, but I think I've got a brain tumour.'

'You haven't got a fucking brain tumour,' she cackled.

'How the fuck do you know? I might,' I said, defensive. I poured myself some water from her plastic jug.

'You haven't.'

'Well, aren't you a genius. Hey, they could use you at the world's top brain department. Why waste all this money on MRIs and CAT scans and what-have-you when we could just ask Carly Posner to take a cursory glance at someone and the diagnosis would be in the bag?'

'You want a diagnosis, Faith Zanetti?' she offered.

'Maybe,' I said, feeling actually quite ludicrous now. The water had already made a vast improvement.

'Give me a fag and shut the door then,' she said.

110

They had taken a cast off her hand some time since I saw her last so she held it herself, smiling blissfully on her first deep inhalation.

'You didn't bring any booze, did you?' she asked.

'Carly, I came to see a neurologist, not to bring on your early expiration.'

'Fair point.' She nodded. 'So. Here goes.'

I sat down and dragged another chair over so that I could put my feet up.

'Psychosomatic cancer.' Hmm. Brilliant. I hate psychosomatic. My dad used to say that my car sickness was psychosomatic as though this just completely dismissed it. OK, so maybe the causes were psychological (fear at driving three hours in a smoke-filled car to go and see some people dying in a nursing home) but the vomit was real. Often all over him, in fact.

'Faith Zanetti is in love.'

'Hello?' I said.

'That's my diagnosis. You are so pathetically unself-aware that you don't even know it. You don't recognise the feeling because you've never had it before and it scares the crap out of you just as it scares your friend Joshua Klein. You have transferred this fear to the scariest thing you can name – brain tumour, i.e. death – and that has allowed you to go out of your mind with fear which is what you wanted to do in the first place because positive emotions mean you've got to get a real life and stop pissing about being ironic. That, Miss Zanetti, is my diagnosis.'

I sighed and lit another cigarette. 'You, Miss Posner, are full of shit. You sound like Eden Jones. Psychoanalyst to the stupid.'

She laughed and one of her machines beeped. 'Don't make me laugh, they'll come in and confiscate the fags. Give us another.'

I did as I was told and as I sat there two things happened. The first thing was that my head stopped hurting. In fact, there was no denying that I felt miraculously fine. The second was that I had a thought about Eden Jones and I needed to put it to him. I stood up.

'I've got to talk to Eden,' I said and started walking towards the door. A big explosion shook the room. It sounded quite near.

'Jesus,' Carly said.

'You're OK. They're not going to hit a hospital,' I told her.

'Not that, you idiot. The state of you. Go on,' she said, and blew me a kiss that smeared the palm of her hand with lipstick.

Outside I could already see the flames from the explosion we'd heard. The air smelt sort of sweet, like bonfire night. A man ran past me shouting for Allah and holding his robes up to his knees. There was only one taxi waiting, a slash of Arabic on its neon sign.

'Hotel Corona,' I said, and slumped into the back seat. It's my job to chat but, sod it, I didn't want to and that would have to do as an excuse.

Don was in the lobby, lying on his back and blowing smoke rings to the ceiling. His stomach wobbled with every breath.

'Hey, McCaughrean. Seen Jones?' I asked, kicking the sofa he was on. The fluorescent airport lighting was beginning to get me down.

'Thought you had a new boyfriend,' he said, not even turning his head to look at me.

'Yeah, well, I thought I'd try and find Eden and rub his nose in it,' I said.

Don seemed to find this reasonably convincing.

'Oh right,' he said, facing me now though not sitting up. 'He's in his room. Just went to interview the Blogger and he should be writing it up now. I did the pictures. Boring as shite.'

'Thank you, Donald.' I bowed and walked towards the lift.

I stood on a strip of orange carpet and knocked on Eden's door.

'Fuck off,' he shouted from inside.

'Open the door,' I shouted back.

He came and opened the door.

'Sorry, I thought you were Don. He keeps telling me what I should put in the piece. Twat. Haven't seen you for ages. Where've you been?'

I walked into his room. Ayesha must have moved in because there was a satiny nightie on the bed and all sorts of pink potions in the bathroom. He sat down near his computer.

'My room mostly,' I told him.

'Oh, Faith. Why didn't you call? Are you OK?'

'Brain tumour notwithstanding, yes,' I said.

'You haven't got a brain tumour.' He laughed, spinning round in the office chair he must have pilfered from somewhere.

'That's what Carly said,' I told him, sitting on the bed but feeling like an intruder.

'Hey. You've seen her? How is she?' He looked concerned which I found irritating. Sanctimonious bastard.

'Fine,' I told him. 'Self-righteous, but otherwise fine.'

'What's wrong with you, Zanetti?' Eden asked, opening a bottle of Lebanese wine he must have got from Ayesha. He used his Swiss Army knife which irritated me too. All these handy tools. We had to swig it from the bottle though.

'She broke the tooth glasses when I said I didn't want to marry her.' He smiled.

'Hmmm. Actually, Eden, I sort of wanted to talk to you about that,' I started, shifting my legs around and reaching out for the bottle.

'Faith, darling. Are you proposing?' he asked with a sneer.

'No,' I said and took a big swig. 'I'm not . . . but . . . Eden . . . do you love me?'

He laughed and rolled his shirtsleeves up. His eyes dulled and then he sighed very deeply.

'Yes, Faith, I do,' he said, looking straight at me.

'Is it awful?' I asked him.

He laughed again and then he put his head in his hands, rubbed his hair and looked back up at me. 'Yes. It is. Sometimes I think I'm dying. Sometimes, when we get together, I feel I'm King of the Universe. I rarely think about much else. Every song I hear applies to me. It's fucking appalling.'

I smiled at him.

'Sorry,' I said. 'I never knew.'

I stood up and walked over to his chair. I knelt at his feet and put my head in his lap. He put his fingers through my hair.

'It's OK, Faith. There's an upside. It gives me a reason for living. When it's bad, that's what I say to myself. My reason for living. And let's face it, we all need one.'

'Yes,' I said. 'We do.'

It had always seemed like a joke, this thing with Eden. To me at any rate. Not that I wasn't fond of him, but I'd never really let myself slip up too violently. Not with someone as unreliable as him. Not with anyone until now. It had only occurred to me, talking to Carly, that he might actually love me.

I kissed the back of his hand and stood up, walking out, shutting the door very gently behind me. Then I leant against it and let the tears stream down my face. Joshua Klein, you absolute bastard.

In the relative safety of my crappy room I passed out and dreamt I was falling into a miserable little pond full of tangled weeds. I was stuck in a pocket of oxygen, a cave far beneath the surface, and there was no way out.

CHAPTER TEN

People who have a normal life can have pathetic little meaningless flings with strangers and then never see them again. Us, we live right on top of each other all the time, creeping from room to room, gossiping, working, drinking. There was no escape. Carly had been so exactly right. 'Mind fuck', not that it's a phrase I would ever use personally. I had a friend who said that at her university this had been the name of the bar's most popular cocktail.

I was getting seriously disturbed by my dreams and was crouching downstairs, pale and unkempt (not that I have ever knowingly been kempt). Eden Jones was sitting there reading 'Why the intifada failed in Iraq since the Gulf War: prospects for democracy'. What an irresponsibly sensationalist title. There was no avoiding people at the Corona. Klein, mountain-fresh as ever, as though no note had been written, no Basra had ever been to, said good morning, swivelling the ring on his little finger, and he sat down next to me at one of the tables near the depleting breakfast buffet (down to a couple of rolls and a ladleful of broad beans in brown sauce). 'Want a story?' he whispered, his breath on my cheek and the closeness of him making my head swim. His hair looked greyer than it had a few days ago.

'What kind of question is that?' I said, loudly, not entering into his clandestine hissing. Murmuring. Words so soft it was almost a kiss. 'I got your note, arsehole. What did you think I was going to do? Sit begging outside your room or something?' I felt my eyes blazing at him. 'Listen. If you think we're having some kind of affair, we're not. OK? Don't start dumping me before you've even fucked me.'

He looked at me blankly, like a cashier in a bank looking at a customer paying in a cheque. The most boring, inconsequential, vapid relationship in the world. Though actually, I noticed, he didn't look at me. Not really. I thought he said something.

'What?' I shouted.

'I prefer to call it making passionate love,' he said, completely unembarrassed, challenging my sordidness rather than defending his purity.

'Do you.' I smirked. 'Do you indeed. Well, why the fuck do you need a name for it at all?'

'Faith. I was conflicted,' he said. What the hell was he talking about?

'Conflicted?' I laughed. 'Conflicted, my arse.'

He looked right at me, showing me my own shallowness and doubts. Exposing me for the idiot that I am.

'Anyway,' I said, sighing, all shouted out. I smiled at him now and he smiled back, some of the gold dust back in his eyes. 'What happened to Basra?'

'I'm back,' he said, looking at me like that again. Back because of me? I didn't even want to acknowledge the things this made me feel. Things about sex and violence and maybe even . . . His shirt was blue and white-striped today. Well turned out enough to be perfect and beautiful. Not flashy enough to be vain. He smelt of the sea and he reached out and took a coil of my hair in his hand. I brushed him off and stood up.

'Klein? Fuck you,' I said. The trouble was, I knew he'd got me. Otherwise I wouldn't have been angry. I would have laughed at him and made him crumple.

The scarred woman (Shirleen, is it?) and her friend, eating some kind of slosh at the next group of sofas, turned round to stare, mouths full of food open in surprise. Journalists, on the whole, don't do very much arguing.

'No. I mean it,' I said, still too loud, smiling for whatever audience there might be. 'Why do you want to give me a story? Think you're going to get a fuck out of it, or what?'

Joshua Klein reached across the table and grabbed my wrist. Whatever he said now I would believe. Because when he took my arm I felt as though a part of me I never knew I'd been missing had been returned to me.

'Listen, Faith Cleopatra Zanetti. I'm sorry, OK? My life is very complicated right now and I was . . . I was tempted. I find you very attractive. I wanted more than I can have. I don't want there to be hard feelings. Is that so terrible? I'm a weapons inspector. I told you that. I found something. I thought I would share it with you instead of with the rest of the pack. Because of what we have. Because of what we can never have.' He was staring into my face and the truth burned out of his eyes. He wasn't smiling now.

'OK,' I whispered. 'OK.' I'd have gone anywhere.

'I have a car,' he said. 'Let's go.'

He put his arm through mine and led me out of the revolving doors.

I expected a shabby old car and a chain-smoking driver, prayer beads on the rear-view mirror and Egyptian pop on the radio. Instead I got a beige jeep and Joshua Klein as the driver. It was air-conditioned and had blacked-out windows and Iraqi plates. Almost a military vehicle, almost a Range Rover. In any case very, very odd. Not a rentacar. Not, surely, his own.

'Where d'you get the car?' I asked and he laughed and turned to flash a look at me.

'Why? You want one?' he said, making me reach out for a handle as he skidded round a corner and into a side street where a mangy dog leapt out of the way. We passed the Al Safeer Hotel on Abu Nawas Street where the hacks sometimes used to stay. A cinder-block wall had been slapped up where the hotel's big ground-floor windows had been. A bit further on I could see that the Air Defence Ministry had been completely flattened. Two huge holes had been punched into it by cruise missiles and now it was just a mess of grey concrete slabs.

'You know, one day Saddam had all his ministers in for a meeting and the Justice Minister made the mistake of looking at his watch. Saddam saw this and he said, "Do you have some place you would rather be?" At the end of the meeting, he forced the Justice Minister to sit in the same chair for twenty-four hours.'

We sat in silence for half a minute after that, both with our own Saddam thoughts. Then he crackled into life again.

'Listen to this. Don't you love this?' he asked, pushing a button on the stereo system. ·

I did love it.

'Yes. I do. I absolutely love it,' I said, after a couple of seconds listening to it, already almost in tears for some reason.

'It's *La Traviata*. "Sempre Libera". Maria Callas. I wanted to play it to you when I saw you,' he said.

'Thank you,' was the best I could do at being moved. I don't know how to do all this.

It was hard to imagine something more dangerous than driving out to look at evidence of weapons of mass destruction in the middle of an actual war with no military escort and no permission from anyone from whom one might need to ask for permission. We cruised through this city that was being bombed and where anarchy was about to be let loose and yet I have never felt safer.

'Hold on tight,' Klein said, so I sat back in air-conditioned splendour and lit a cigarette, smiling at the smoked glass and the dusty streets thundering by outside. The *Traviata* aria we'd been listening to before, finished, and he switched the music off. The silence was edgy. I noticed a couple of camels wandering about in the palms by the roadside, abandoned maybe.

'So, tell me about yourself.' He grinned, driving too fast, knowing the way too well. Not many maps in here. Not many guns either. I wasn't sure if that was good or bad.

'I love Elvis and I drink too much,' I said, not about to enter into some mawkish kind of maundering about my life. No thanks.

He looked grave now but he didn't say anything. I wanted to throw my arms round his neck.

'Hmm. Your dad always said you would do amazing things,' he said. 'Tell me about some of them.'

I took a second to make sure my voice didn't betray what my throat and heart and stomach were doing.

'Nur and Hugo said you knew him. I don't want to talk about it. You'll just have me down as someone with an Electra complex or a neglected little girl or fuck knows what.'

Klein laughed. 'Don't be silly,' he said, and he reached over to touch my legs. It could have seemed sleazy, but all I can say is that it didn't. 'I had a couple of drinks with him. That's all. He wasn't a friend. Good guy.'

'So they say.' I nodded. 'No, he was. Well, I liked him. I find the hero journalist thing tedious though.'

'The worst,' he agreed.

'I mean, nobody makes you do it, right?'

'Right.'

119

'We were always so impressed by the places he'd been and everything. I think I might have preferred it if he'd been at home with me,' I said, coming as close I ever had done at maundering on.

'He'd probably have been a real pain in the arse,' Klein said.

I laughed. 'Yes, probably.' Klein had a nice irreverence. 'I think the trouble I've always had is being someone who's father was basically murdered. It informs your whole life in ways that you can't quite grasp hold of. Because everyone's parents die in the end, right? Yours?'

'Dead,' he agreed.

'So in a way it shouldn't be such a huge deal. But murder, because it wasn't a huge firefight, it was a well-aimed snipe, is different. Why? I don't know.'

'I don't know,' he said, and put his hand between my thighs. I leant on his shoulder. It didn't seem to impair his driving any. And he'd done it again. Drawn me out and offered nothing. Or everything.

'Hey,' I said, not moving my head. Not wanting ever to move anything. 'Why'd you send that horrible note?'

'I don't know. I don't know what to say to you, Faith.'

'What kind of thing might you say if you did say something?'

'Umm. Wow, maybe.'

I laughed. 'Wow. Cool. That would have been much better than "fuck off I hate you".'

'I don't think that's quite what the letter said.'

'Near enough.'

'I wanted to try and get a grip on myself.'

'Get a grip on me,' I suggested.

'Try and stop me.' He smiled, looking down, and kissing the top of my head.

We had driven out of the city, past Nur's house where I had gone that first day, and I had barely registered the group of soldiers by the side of the road before they started waving their weapons at us and pulling us over. I froze my body and mind. A way I have of obliterating fear. Fear comes later, when it's over, when you're trying to digest everything. Long after you've told your brain that everything's OK, your body is still reacting to terror.

In this particular instance, on a dusty violent roadside outside Baghdad, during a war, it was entirely unnecessary. They weren't pulling us over. They were waving to Joshua to remind him where to stop. He seemed to nod to himself in recognition as he wrenched the wheel over to the right. We didn't bounce out of the car and put our arms round everyone, but Joshua definitely knew these people, or had made some arrangement with them. I stood as still as possible, ready to take the lead from whoever had it. It reminded me of all the other military experiences I've ever had. The slight tension, the shifting around of authority. I spent a lot of time with the Israeli army about a year ago and it was all just like this.

So, who took the lead? Klein, of course. He shook hands with each young soldier in turn, nervous-looking men with red and white checked scarves round their necks. Their guns were slung across their chests now and none of them looked at me. We walked in the gritty sand past a bending palm to a sort of trailer. The secret, whatever it was, was in here. I looked back at the soldiers who were more concerned now with guarding Klein's ritzy car than with us. Joshua pushed the door open and we climbed up the steps. He flicked the lights on inside and it was immediately obvious that this was some kind of mobile lab. Microscopes on the work surfaces, big fridges everywhere, racks of test tubes and a sterile smell. I had an idea what Klein was about to say.

'Chemical weapons,' he stated, with the grave certainty of a child pointing out of a car window unable to stop itself saying, 'Sheep'.

Now I couldn't actually see any chemical weapons, as such, but it wasn't an unconvincing claim. I can't deny being excited. This was the story we were all trying to break. I never quite grasped why this had become the crux of the war. There was a feeling at the time that if we could prove that Saddam Hussein has 'weapons of mass destruction' (already an irritating way of putting it) then it is okay to bomb Iraq. That and linking him to Al Qaida. Why couldn't we just bomb him for being a vile dictator? And why did we have to prove he'd got weapons of mass destruction for the second time? We know he's got them, don't we? Ask a Kurd. I mean, like, he's USED them, right? People (the general public, readers of *The Chronicle*, those ones who write you letters in green biro about God, who volunteer to be in documentaries and who see aliens in their back garden) get all kind of he-that-is-without-sin-may-cast-the-first-stone-ish about America going to war. Why? The fact that America is unpleasantly flawed doesn't mean it isn't in a position to tell slime buckets like Saddam Hussein where to get off. I mean, where would you prefer your daughters to grow up? Chicago or Tikrit? That's right.

Anyway, we'd all been briefed to follow every lead that might provide proof of Saddam's chemical stockpile. And I'd found it. Or, that is, Joshua Klein had shown it to me. And I loved him. Oops. No, not that bit.

'Where?' I asked, glancing around, patting the packet of cigarettes in my jacket pocket. Being in a confined space with this man was a pain in the arse. I had to clamp my hands to my sides not to reach out and tear his clothes off him. And every time that thought flicked through my mind he smiled at me, thinking the same.

'Your . . . button . . .' he said, looking at my cleavage. Echencrure. The only word I remember from school French lessons. The 'V' or cleavage of your shirt or jacket.

I looked down. Yup. Undone. I did it up.

'These weapons?' I asked, pissed off now.

It seemed to bore Klein to talk business. 'This is a mobile biological weapons and warfare laboratory. It's been cleaned up and dumped here,

122

I guess so that we won't find whatever compound it's attached to. Within a week or two, when the regime's over and the looting starts, it will get ripped apart. Mainly for the fridges. I was at Yale with one of the guys who's been doing this stuff his whole life. Met him at a conference before the last Gulf War. He actually told me about it, openly. Proud of himself, I suppose. This one looks as though it's for smallpox.'

He gave me a detailed guided tour, told me to take notes. This is for this, this is for that, this is how it all works. 'Air compressor, refrigerator, fermentor, dryer. Identical to the one seized near Erbil.' He did a brief lecture about how smallpox might be disseminated (for example using missiles and rockets with biological agents in them) and then he said, 'Oh God,' and took my face in his hands.

'We are just going to be friends,' he said, his lips brushing mine.

'OK,' I said. 'Friends.'

And I think it was here, under the fluorescent lights of a mobile chemical weapons laboratory, just outside the squat blue chemical toilet, fifteen kilometres outside Baghdad on the road to Karbala, near the destroyed fields of date palms, that I really fell in love.

'Conflicted,' I said, breathless, dishevelled.

He laughed and one of the soldiers banged on the door. Guilty as teenagers behind the bike shed we stumbled out of the unit into the glaring road, straightening our clothes, not quite holding hands. Something had happened in there. And yet nothing had.

Then a very loud 'boom' sent us flying to the floor, eating sand, trying to think of ways to be flatter. One of the boys who had been guarding Joshua's car was thrown backwards as though by a water cannon or something, hurtling through the air, his feet not touching the ground, flames shooting from his clothes, screaming in burning agony. The others hadn't been so near the car and were, I think, lying in the sand like us, hissing in Arabic. The sky was so white and the attack was so bright that it was impossible to tell what was happening.

123

'Give me your shirt,' Klein yelled at me. 'Take your shirt off.'

'Dirty bastard,' I shouted back, unable to stop the quip, inappropriate and crazed though it was.

'Jesus, Faith. Your shirt!'

Well, he didn't need to get all arsy about it. I was already taking it off, wriggling in the dust to try not to raise my body enough to be a target. Joshua's car, the petrol tank already exploded by the whatever it was, was burning madly at the side of the road. Opposite it, I could see now through the smoke and the smell and the flames, was a big green tank. Later I would note that it had 'Apocalypse' painted on the back. I chucked my shirt to Klein who held it up, waving it as conspicuously as he could. I really badly wanted to move from where we were. In front of us the car was burning, behind us the lab was also on fire. The dead boy had been thrown into the scrub by the explosion.

I have had rifle butts in my face before but I do not like it when I am lying down. In my bra.

'Listen, sweetheart. Do I look armed to you?' I asked a handsome black boy in a big green helmet, his dog tag swinging out over his bullet-proof vest.

'Get up, lady,' he told me, terrified, shaking from the horror of having fired, of having perhaps, he didn't know yet, killed some of his own people. That's how it must have looked now.

I got up, hands behind my head, blood dripping down my face, dirt in my hair, torn jeans, a bra, for fuck's sake (and I don't have any nice ones), my leather jacket lying in the road.

Klein was already up.

'Why did you blow up my car?' he was asking a bewildered Yank, but he was smiling and holding out his presidential hand to be shaken.

I think the shaven-headed boy carrying an M249 machine gun actually said, 'Sorry, sir.'

The few other cars on the road were screeching to a halt at the Americans' makeshift road block (a tank). The American boy's less bewildered colleagues were taking our Iraqi boys into custody. That was the easy bit. Iraqi? Armed? Come with me. I thought they looked mildly relieved to be prisoners of war rather than dead people. The torture scandals were yet to come.

'Joshua!' He ignored me. 'Joshua? My shirt, for Christ's sake.'

Standing there in clouds of acrid smoke, my evidence on fire behind me, Joshua looked lustfully at me and laughed.

'Really,' I said, not amused. Not funny. Naked here. 'My shirt.'

We rattled back to town on the back of a Toyota pick-up that Klein just pulled over with a regal wave of his hand and a hundred dollar bill. My shirt was gone, trampled, burnt. My jacket didn't zip up.

Here's the scene: Baghdad nervously getting on with its life, windows taped up, neon signs grey and lifeless, Saddam posters beginning to look passé, squat sand-coloured buildings, low-hanging wires draped over all the streets, tracer fire and explosions visible in flashes through the smoke from all the raging fires. We are crouching, exposed in the blistering heat on the back of this truck, having paid the driver months' worth of wages to risk his life for us, the sky full of sparkling planes and Joshua Klein chooses this moment for his strange confession.

'I'm married,' he said. 'It's not good. Was never good.'

Well, I knew. I had seen the evidence on his hand. And Carly had guessed. Funny to announce it, though. The word 'married' makes me imagine the actual wedding – champagne and kisses and promises. Change of gear into flippant mode.

'Yes,' I said. 'I assumed. What's wrong with it? Nice. Pipe, slippers, delicious stew bubbling on the stove.'

He dug me in the ribs. 'It's not like that,' he said, amused by the idea.

'No? Ugh, poor you,' I said, before he could say anything else. It was not the kind of conversation I normally have when my mouth tastes of the blood that is dripping down my face. More for leaning over a bar in Covent Garden than sitting with our arses on the ridged metal of a pick-up. I have never had much time for the institution of marriage. I managed under a year and I've rarely come across anyone with anything good to say about it. The best most people do is, 'Well, for the children . . .'

When I was in my late twenties everyone I knew was desperately looking for someone, pretty much anyone, to marry as though it was a rule. I know women are programmed to want to reproduce around then and I get that (nearly did it myself once) but the idea that you have to promise the rest of your life to someone in order to do it seems to me completely absurd. How could anyone get on with anyone for a decade, let alone a lifetime? Nobody wants to sleep with the same sodding person for forty years. Do they?

But then I got worried. Considered the fact that many people do. Was Klein being faithful to this woman? Had he been so far? Suddenly I was jealous. Jealous of all the people he'd kissed, all the girls at school and women at work dragged into the stationery cupboard. All the steamy hotel rooms and parked cars that there must have been. Surely. I mean, who could resist him?

I ploughed on with the tone I'd started with.

'So, you say, "I think I'll have a cup of tea now." And the other one says, "Why do you want a cup of tea? You've just had a cup of tea. You drink too much tea anyway."'

He laughed. 'Right.' He nodded. 'Right.' He paused and sighed.

'Someone once told me that the secret of a successful marriage is just being nice to each other. It's as difficult as that,' I said.

'Maybe. I wouldn't know.' He glanced round to twinkle his eyes at me and we were silent.

Joshua Klein spent the whole journey holding my hand. We were both smiling.

Having managed to get neither killed nor arrested all the way back to the hotel, Joshua then did an astonishing job of fending off all the brutal-faced aftershave-smelling thugs from the Ministry of Information (or secret police?) who hang around smoking ominously and then of letting me slip back up to my room.

'I'll see you later, baby,' he said, smiling, and he touched the small of my back.

I spent the rest of the day and nearly all night on the phone to graphics, trying to describe the mobile lab in enough detail for them to do one of those really complicated diagrams to go with my piece. With arrows and little drawings of test tubes. I wouldn't have put it past them to put a skull and crossbones in there somewhere. They were bafflingly concerned to get the measurements right. Still, someone would be pleased in the morning. Not my colleagues here whom I'd beaten to the scoop, that's for sure. Tony Blair mostly. Attack on Iraq justified! All because of me. I did not feel proud. Well, I felt proud of my scoop, pleased it was me and not Eden or anyone. But I wasn't crazy about the implications, not that that's any of my business. Can't be responsible for the way people inter-pret the facts. Can we? The Blogger was laughing about the tanks being a 'show of force' rather than an invasion. Like, what's the difference?

Of course we were supposed to file from the ministry itself but since it didn't seem to exist any more, nobody was about to stop us doing it from here. The noise outside was incredible and I was just wondering whether or not to sleep in my flak jacket when McCaughrean lurched into my room without knocking. Pissed out of his mind and covered in bits of plaster, he had apparently been at a ritzy restaurant (open?!) downtown when it had been bombed just in case of the presence of senior Ba'ath party members (probable). But Don was grinning all over his face and it wasn't just the pictures he'd got (glamorous women with lustrous hair and glossy lipstick looking as normal as anything apart from the fact that they are bleeding, staggering from piles of rubble. The point being – they're just like us, you know).

'I'm in love!' he shouted, wobbling down on to the edge of my bed. The television, showing local stuff about the evil infidels (mustn't miss the live Koran reading at nine) was blaring out from its hinge on the ceiling. I switched it off in shock and awe.

'No!' I said, offering him a cigarette. 'Who is she?'

'Faithy,' he said, red-faced, puffy-eyed, a wreck of a person. An explosion rocked the city outside. 'She's beautiful, she's as delicate as a china doll.'

Oh, lord.

'Uh-huh,' I said, sucking my own smoke in and putting my feet up on the Perspex coffee table.

'Irochka. Russian student . . . Came up to talk to me, said I was handsome . . . she was with an Iraqi friend who runs a Pepsi bottling franchise . . .' He smiled in unadulterated bliss and sank back on to my bed, passing out with a loud burp.

I hardly had time to wonder what to do when Eden Jones (Eden Jones. I had forgotten about him. Amazing. I'd met someone who made me forget about Eden Jones. About time too) banged on my door, shouting as he came in.

'Zanetti! Have you seen Don? We were down at that place with the pink fountains and the cunts bombed us. He disappeared . . .'

Eden stopped babbling as I nodded over to the bed where McCaughrean snored, belly and face shuddering with every exhalation.

Relieved, Eden stepped towards me in a protective gesture, as though he was about to take my face in his hands, to thank me or something. Anyway, he slipped and banged into the coffee table, knocking the full ashtray to the floor.

'Fuck. Sorry,' he said, and knelt to tidy up.

'Don't worry about it,' I said, genuinely wanting both these idiots to leave.

When they did, McCaughrean roused by a wet flannel on the face, I lay clothed on the bobbly beadspread and drifted off into the dawn. I dreamt I was running along a beach and a horse was running towards me, black and wild. We reached each other and stopped, me barefoot in the surf, and the horse put its soft muzzle to my face.

CHAPTER ELEVEN

Thank God, I thought. I was watching some CNN footage of one of the shockingly boring Qatar press briefings and the serious-faced man who never answers any questions was announcing that proof had been found of Saddam Hussein's biological weapons capabilities. I was wandering around in my pants looking for my deodorant and I allowed myself a celebratory cigarette, shaking the last pack out of the block I'd bought duty free. Well, hey, OK, I'd have smoked it anyway. Thing is, I had been vaguely worried about my story, in case Klein had been wrong and we both just wanted to believe it too much. But now that there was other evidence I could relax. As far as one can relax in a city going up in smoke.

I stared at the screen to watch Dave Thingey from the competition right-wing broadsheet put his hand up and stumble to his feet as someone passed him the mike.

'Dave Thingey, right-wing broadsheet,' he said. 'What proof exactly?'

I was already pulling my jeans on and wasn't concentrating as hard as all that, but then Vince (serious American spin man) said, 'Reports in the early edition of today's London *Chronicle* suggest that a mobile smallpox laboratory has been found at the roadside outside . . .' Blah blah blah. Oh God. The rest of the world picked up my scoop. So, I'm the breaking story, am I? Okey dokey.

I took a Valium and worried about it. Much as it's fun to be alone with the story, a bit of corroboration would have been nice. I put my cigarette out in the enormous crystal ashtray and phoned Joshua Klein's room. I soon wished I hadn't. Perhaps if I hadn't it would all have been different. He would still be alive now.

'?' was the muffled answer I got.

'Joshua? It's me. Faith,' I said, pacing up and down the static carpet with the phone clenched between shoulder and ear.

'He's not here,' a girl's sullen voice said. She sounded young, American, possibly stoned or something. I wasn't going to let the panic rise. I should write notes to myself when I'm actually with him. Because the second he slips out of my sight this doubt attacks me. What is he playing at? OK, dignity.

'I wonder if I could leave a message,' I said formally – special tone for press offices and other obstructive institutions like horrible slags who might be sleeping with the man I . . . Well, you know.

She didn't answer but I heard another voice behind her, a bloke this time.

'Jesus fuck, Nita,' he said. 'What are you doing? Let's get out of here.'

Was he being robbed, for Christ's sake? Now? Here? It was hardly credible.

I paced a bit and then found myself lunging for the door. I was going to try and catch them. Not so much a decision as a reaction, and, let's face it, more to a girl picking up his phone than to anything else. You want the object of your desire to be a lonely hermit, no friends or family or exes to take up so much as a sliver of him. I wanted him all to myself. And, if he was in fact being robbed, I could be a hero.

I shoved myself through the fire door and took the stairs four at a time, clinging to the banister and swinging out on the corners. It smelt of piss and cigarettes back here. I arrived in the lobby through a back entrance, flushed and feeling like a fool.

But in my pathetic display of intrepidness – Faith Zanetti, a force for good – I did catch them. I hurtled down, ready to intercept and confront them, to pin them to the floor and insist they hand over Klein's watch and cufflinks or whatever. I am very practised at this. 'Hand over the goods, snake breath,' I would shout, sitting on their backs and cuffing them. Not that theft from Baghdad hotel rooms during wars by young westerners can be that common an affair. The point being that I had intended to use all my sitting on criminals prowess to retrieve Klein's stolen property and make him forever grateful to me. However, just as I was about to approach the couple (OK, so I didn't actually catch them as such, but I could have done), Klein himself came out of the other lift on his way about his world-saving business. Or at least I assume it was the guilty couple, tumbling out of the lift, glancing around shiftily. The bloke was the same human shield/aid worker type who had been talking to Joshua a couple of days ago, who had called him a hypocrite. Hey, who isn't? He wore combat trousers and his black hair was matted into dreadlocks. I noticed this time that he must be very young. Knackered looking, but barely twenty. The girl was in a dirty Middle Eastern style sack thing, made in Greenwich Village or at least bought there. I was nearly choking to death from my run down the stairs and my heart was pounding with the defensive lurch of horror that I'd got when this girl picked up the phone. Oh, please, don't be his lover. Don't be.

Joshua went up behind them and put a hand on each of their

shoulders. They spun round, angry and embarrassed, and Klein smiled benignly.

Karim was collecting coffee cups from the brass tables. There was hardly anybody else about. Just a couple of the mustachioed thugs who were supposed to be stopping us doing our jobs. Even in the air conditioning the heat was pounding through the lobby doors and the metallic taste of war was on my tongue.

'Going through my stuff again, huh?' he asked them, perfectly happy. Now this was very, very weird.

'No,' the dreadlocked one said, petulantly, as though he was denying taking an extra biscuit from the jar.

I ran up to them, confused.

'Hey,' I said in sweaty greeting (no air conditioning on the stairs). 'I called your room and this girl picked up,' I told Klein, not that I could possibly have proved this.

'Ooh. The worst.' He smiled, catching me with his fairy dust.

'Did not,' she said, and glowered at me. I thought she might be about to spit. Her nose, eyebrow and lip were pierced. What a fashion. They don't get much less alluring than that. Karim was standing there, cups and saucers balanced all the way up his arm, staring at these two freaks. Fairly conservative, the Iraqis.

'Faith Zanetti, meet Daniel and Anita,' Klein said. 'They have come to Baghdad to protest the American attack.'

Daniel piped up. 'I'm going to devote the rest of my life to protesting against you,' he snarled, grabbing Anita's arm and making his way towards the main entrance ten yards away. They made an extremely odd scene in the foyer of a five-star hotel.

Just before the boy stormed out, he turned round to shout, 'And the name's Ziggy.' Uh-huh.

Klein shouted back, 'Be careful, Ziggy. Please.'

I looked into his face for an explanation.

'Kids,' he said, forgetting them already, touching my fingers with his. 'God, you look great.' And to my shame, I forgot them too. For the time being.

Over by reception (a portrait of the great leader smiling down from above the clocks) a pretty Russian girl in a red mini skirt was asking for McCaughrean's room number. Bloody hell, I said, shaking my head in absolute amazement. Good for him, though. I mean, he needs something nice to happen to him for a change. It crossed my mind that she might be some sort of spy or assassin, but of course this was ludicrous. I mean, why shouldn't she find Don attractive? Well, because he's grotesque, for one . . .

My inner dialogue was interrupted by Eden Jones who positively leapt out of the lifts in unadulterated glee.

'I'm embedded!' he squealed, grinning all over his face.

'Congratulations,' Joshua said.

'Since when?' I asked.

'Thanks. Since just now. Whatsisname broke his leg jumping down off the tank and I'm getting transferred over there. Oooooh! LOVE being embedded.' He was almost jumping up and down.

'Good for you then,' I said with less grace than might have been appropriate. Felt like embedding an axe in his head. What is he? Fourteen? It's all very well liking tanks and guns and soldiers if you are Christopher Robin or someone, but Eden's old enough to know that they are for killing people with and that the whole thing is grim. Still, he'd write good pieces about it. He always does.

'What about Ayesha?' I asked, rummaging for my cigarettes. Klein pulled them out of my jacket pocket for me, lit one with my lighter, put it between my lips and put the packet and lighter back where they came from. Eden raised his eyebrows and buried his chin in his neck in a 'What the fuck?' kind of expression. I smiled, victorious. Now normally if I asked about a girlfriend of Eden Jones's I would be sniping meanly. This time I honestly wondered if she'd mind him going out into the field, if he wanted me to pass a note to her or something.

'Oh, she managed to get herself on a plane to Jordan yesterday,' he mumbled, unconcerned. 'Embedded!' He punched the air with his fist and I rolled my eyes. I couldn't remember what I had ever seen in this man, handsome though he may be.

'I better go see what the damage is,' Klein said, with a sigh. He was wearing gold cufflinks.

A sandstorm was starting. The sky had turned a swirling yellow.

An artificial night had fallen over the city. I flicked my computer on to learn that the Blogger's snot had gone red from the sand. Great. What a piece of information. I never even asked Eden how the interview with him had gone. We'd all lost interest. Those big blue hearts, a memorial to the Iran–Iraq war, cast ominous shadows across the street. Not that they weren't ominous before. The memorials in Baghdad are ghastly. Nobody is satisfied with just the names of the fallen or an eternal flame. There's a bunker that the Americans bombed 'by accident' last time, packed full of women and children, and they've preserved it, along with bits of burnt skin and charred possessions. The guide who will show you round if you ask her lost eight of her nine children in the 'bunker-buster' bombing.

The sky, already filled with smoke from the fires started by the bombardments and then the thicker, blacker smoke of the oil fires, was now completely obscured by the choking sand blowing in from the desert. It felt apocalyptic somehow that it should be raining sand, as though it were raining frogs or locusts or blood or something. I left Eden to celebrate and went outside to choke in the atmosphere. It was like being on another planet.

In a daze, I realised that I had walked all the way over to the river.

There was a low mist of sand on the water and when I turned back to the hotel I could see the yellow glow of the lobby. A low boom made the ground rumble under my feet. Something was wrong. Suddenly, over at the Corona, there was more milling about than was normal and the blurred movement of the people I could see looked frantic and disjointed.

I ran back, getting a mouthful. A car, its headlights dim in the thick atmosphere, swerved to miss me. People were crying – Shirleen with the ruined face, even Pip Deakin and Don who, rather than taking pictures, was comforting the Russian girl who had buried her head in his chest.

Already the German television correspondent was doing a terrified piece to camera in flak jacket and helmet, a member of his crew dutifully holding the rejuvenating pink reflector up against the hail of sand. He must have been set up for something else to get it together this fast. I tried to shake the stuff out of my hair and noticed that along with a substantial amount of desert were some pieces of plaster and chips of paint. The hotel had been hit.

'Oh shit. Joshua!' I shouted, turning my head around desperately to find him, though I knew he'd gone upstairs.

An American woman was screaming. 'Where's Ed? I can't find Ed! Ed's gone. He was right in the room!' She ran past me, her face contorted with terror. I felt like the lead character in a film, standing still, a spotlight on me, completely motionless with chaos all around me. Nobody was looking for me. I put my hand over my eyes and tried to see through the darkness. The hotel had a big hole in it. Looked like a shell wound, which meant a tank, which meant the Americans. Why the fuck were the Americans attacking us? I mean, Jesus, I had broken a story that very day justifying their whole sodding war.

I needed Josh. McCaughrean was whispering to this girl. 'It's all right, baby. It's going to be all right.' I had never heard his voice sound like that before. I had never thought about how his size (enormous) could be comforting, his talent (undeniable) could be impressive, his essential kindness (considerable) could be, well . . . appreciated. Why shouldn't she fall for Don McCaughrean? No reason at all.

I put my head in my hands and I didn't go anywhere. The wire services were setting up little working tents on the front lawn of the hotel, flashing their enormous industrial torches all over the place, showing flickers of people's crumpled faces. There had to be casualties. An ambulance pulled up and the crew ran into the hotel, emerging a minute or so later with a dust-covered lifeless person on a stretcher. The American woman recognised him immediately.

'Ed!' she screamed, running along beside the paramedics, her face pressed down to his. It didn't look very hopeful. He'd gone a funny shape, like dead people do. It's hard to say exactly how you can see they are dead, but the way their bodies lie isn't right. Living ones don't do that.

Pip was in his element. His revoltingly dyed hair seemed to glow in the unnatural light and he was bullying his crew. This was exactly his kind of piece – personal adversity, grave danger, first-person heroics. If he pulled it off tonight, the Americans might come begging. 'We're not in Kansas any more, Toto,' he shouted to his sound man who I'm pretty sure muttered 'Cunt' under his breath as he approached to adjust Pip's mike. I wished Eden was here. More than that, I wanted Joshua. I didn't feel like taking down quotes, inspecting the damage, talking to the Americans. I wanted someone to . . . to take me home. Ha. Haven't even got one. If I'd had a phone I'd have called Evie.

And then it happened. At first I felt a sharp pain in my shoulder, like when I was shot or like the memory of it. My face and hands were unbearably hot and tingling and my breath was short. I felt my heart thudding in my chest as though it might burst and my vision blurred. I staggered slightly, letting the frenzy of news production, grief and confusion swirl round me. And I knew I was dying. An allergic reaction? Some sort of anaphylactic shock brought on by the oil fumes or the sand or something? A heart attack. That's what it felt like. A heart attack. Or a stroke. I threw myself towards the open doors of the ambulance where what was left of Ed had been taken. A young nurse, horror and fear in his face, stopped pumping Ed's chest when he saw me and the American woman fell on top of her friend, shaking with sobs.

'Help me,' I said to the nurse, falling heavily into his arms, unbalancing him.

'You were upstairs?' he asked, immediately looking into my eyes to keep me alert, pulling my jacket off.

'No,' I muttered, about to faint. 'My heart.'

'Heart,' he said to himself in English, glancing out at the disaster scene, afraid the attack might continue, clearly wishing he was at home with his family.

He put his stethoscope to my chest and I wished he would hurry. I needed something intravenous, I wanted him to knock me out, take me to a white bed under a white ceiling with fluttering white curtains at the windows and sweet tea on a tray. He smelt of sweat and cloying aftershave. His moustache glistened.

'Please help me,' I said again. 'Do something.'

He sighed. 'Heart fine. Pulse quick, but strong. Good.'

He shouted something to his colleague in Arabic, put a pill into my mouth, handed me a small paper cup of water and pushed me out down the metal slope, back into the insanity. He was trying to get the American woman out as well so that he could bring some more injured people on board. I looked back at him.

'Why won't you take me with you?' I asked, my hands hanging by my side.

'Panic attack. Healthy,' he said, barely meeting my eyes, throwing his arms out at the scene as though to suggest that anybody in their right mind would have a panic attack in the middle of this. Anybody except me.

'*What?*' I wailed, knowing already that it was true. Feeling ridiculous. What was wrong with me? What was happening? First the brain tumour, now this.

I knew, though. This is what life is like if there is some kind of point to it. This is what life is like if you really care whether somebody else lives or dies. This is what life is like if you really care whether you live or die. Suddenly life is fragile, precious, precarious. For the first time since I could remember, I didn't want to die. Because of Joshua Klein. I mean, of course, I have never actually wanted to die. But I don't usually care much. You've got to go sometime, and all that. And I'd rather be shot in the back of the head than lie on a morphine drip for two years after eight courses of chemotherapy. But now . . . If I could be with that man every second of the rest of my life I would feel short-changed. Shit.

'Some tosser looking for you, Eff Zed,' McCaughrean shouted across to me now, fag between his lips, camera hanging by his side.

'Where's Irochka?' I asked him, genuinely concerned.

'Sent her up to my room. Managed to persuade her they won't do it again. Fucking morons. How hard is it to see the fucking Corona?'

'Quite hard in this, I'd have thought,' I said, knowing that there would be enough conspiracy theories about why the Americans had hit the press to keep everyone going for a long time. Knowing also that it was probably just some boy in a tank who fucked up. The ordinariness of this exchange with Don was making my heart slow to normal. Or was that the Valium the nurse had given me? I had seen where the hole in the hotel was. I knew it was floors away from Joshua. He was fine. I felt it in my bones.

'Who's looking for me?' I asked.

'Fuck do I know?' Don shrugged, putting his camera on his face and walking away.

Breathing half normally now I started to wander around and take things in. I was deeply ashamed of my pathetic episode and hoped nobody had seen me begging and pleading and gasping. Someone was pointing at me and a young man walked towards me through the smoke, the hotel debris littering the floor, never mind the sand, which seemed to be letting up a bit.

'Faith Zanetti?' he asked.

'Mmm hmmm.' I nodded, reaching for a cigarette and offering him one. I inhaled deeply and now really did start to feel better. 'What can I do for you?'

He sounded English and had floppy brown hair and big melty eyes. Jeans, trainers, T-shirt, bit of acne. That's right, I thought. He's a teenager.

'I'm Fernando. Carly's stepson. Well, sort of. You know. I came to bring her home, but the hospital won't release her and I don't know . . . She mentioned you. Said you were here and were her friend. You know . . .' He was glaring straight at me, shuffling his feet, trying to pretend not to be shy, not to be completely terrified. 'I was in the lobby when . . .' he said, pointing his cigarette at the hole in the building up on what must have been about the tenth floor.

'Fuck. Poor you. I'm so sorry about Carly. She's going to be fine though. She's holding up great,' I told him. Hopeless. Come on, help him out. I was not coping well with this. I remembered it well from people not coping with my bereavement when I was little. English people are terrible at grief, even consolation at grave injury, as in this case. None of us was mentioning the possibility of her not walking again. These things embarrass the English. Everything embarrasses them – social faux pas, death, joy, social interaction. In my case people preferred just not to mention my bereavement at all and later, when I was a teenager and wanted to drone on about it a bit, everyone changed the subject or tried not to meet my eyes. And now here I was doing the same.

'Who cares? She's a bitch,' Fernando said. 'If she'd looked after him, Dad might not have topped himself.'

OK, I really didn't feel like talking about this just this second, standing outside in a fucking war zone. He was doing well at diminishing my sympathy. Anyway, what the hell was he doing here?

'Well, I don't think you can ever really save anyone from themselves, Freddie,' I said, wishing I wasn't smoking so that I could light a cigarette and pause this nightmare exchange.

'Fernando,' he sneered.

'Can you hear the drums, Fernando?' I sang under my breath.

'What?'

'Oh nothing.'

'Hey, have they started looting the Iraq Museum yet? Might go and get my girlfriend some Sumerian gold shit,' he said. Ah, a joke. What on earth was I going to do with this boy? Help!

'Hmm. Good plan,' I told him, watching Karim from reception taking the duct tape away so that we could all go back inside. Apparently only one room had been obliterated. One room and three journalists – nobody I knew well, thank God.

I put my arm round Fernando's shoulders and he didn't shake me off. It's such a terrible age, this. Whatever it was.

'How old are you, Fernando?' I asked him, walking him across the marble floor, my boots clopping, his trainers squeaking.

'Seventeen,' he said.

So, seventeen. Terrible age. You want to give them a hug but they're at the kind of stage where everything is sexual. He might wonder why this crone friend of his stepmother's is making a pass at him. On the other hand, he might need a hug and a cup of tea and his teddy bear. Poor boy. And expelled from school. Was that what Carly had said?

Inside, Klein strode up to us as I'd known he would, unsullied by sand or rubble or any aspect of war. 'Oh God, Joshua,' I said, relieved, falling into his arms. He pushed me away and stood me up, brushing my stomach with his hands to show me we were still us. Would always be us.

'Faith. And who are you, young man?' he asked, gripping Fernando's hand in his, staring, rapt, into his face. Amazing.

Fernando smiled, visibly relaxing. Here was somebody, he realised, who could help.

'My dad's girlfriend was hurt the other night. I came for her, but . . .' He smiled at Joshua who was taking it all in and coming up with plans to help.

'Hell did you get here, son?' Klein beamed. It was a very good point and one I had been wanting to make.

'Friend's dad's in the army,' Fernando mumbled, acting his age, and Joshua and I both nodded in realisation.

Klein was taking control. Oh, thank you thank you thank you.

'Well, I think we are going to have to get Carly back home to you when this is all over, Fernando. I'll take care of it. In the meantime let's concentrate on getting you back to England. For tonight, come with me,' he said quickly, excitable but firm.

He led Fernando out of the hotel, news production still in full swing on the front lawn, stench of heat and smoke and oil still obliterating normality.

'Hey!' I shouted after them. 'Where the fuck are you going?'

Joshua smiled at my hysteria. 'I thought Fernando here might like to stay with . . . um . . . Ziggy and Anita tonight. At the Sheraton. It's in a safe zone now. They must be about your age,' he said to Fernando. The Sheraton is cool. It's got external glass lifts and these balconies with latticed wooden shutters that are supposed to look like the hanging balconies of old Baghdad, however they might have worked. There aren't any left now except on the Sheraton. Safe zone, my arse. The Corona was supposed to be in a safe zone.

He kept walking and I kept running after them, shrieking.

'Ziggy is staying at the Sheraton? How is that possible? And how do you know?' I squealed at him. I wanted to go to the Sheraton actually. It's got a huge anti-George Bush mural or mosaic in it. And a big pool.

Joshua and Fernando stopped walking for a little while. Klein turned to explain.

'I didn't like the other place they found. Too dangerous. They seemed only too pleased to move to the Sheraton,' he said, and disappeared with Fernando into the frenzied throng.

I suppose I knew the first time I saw him with the dreadlocked boy. But I didn't fully register until much later. I didn't fully register even now. Though he had tried to tell me.

I wanted to lie down. I mean, normally when I'm in a state I want to pace around, talk to people, phone the desk in London, file a piece. Right now, I just wanted to be asleep. What I did, of course, was phone the desk, file an immediate piece to copy, find McCaughrean and make sure he would provide the pictures.

'I'm on it, Zanetti,' he said. 'Hey, could you check on Irochka?' He looked up so meek, so loving. He was doing some shots of the smoke-filled corridors on the tenth floor, sheets of paper blowing about, bits of computer exploded on to the carpet. Eerie carnage shots that there was no way they'd use. Leave the arty stuff alone, Don. Take the fucking picture. What they wanted was either a body (too late – they'd been carted off already while he was cuddling Ira) or the hole in the hotel. That wouldn't be bad because of the weird balconies. Half a spider's web moulded in white cement.

In room 1409 Irochka was, get this, painting her toenails. She was lovely in that amazing Russian way. High Slavic cheekbones and pale green eyes, glowing skin, the whole business. You knew immediately that she wore very expensive lacy underwear and spent a lot of time rubbing cream into her already creamy skin. She was white blonde. I glanced out of her window. The skyline was pretty much obscured by smoke. Minarets, domes and Saddam's samovar-shaped trophy buildings were barely visible in the haze. The bridges that span the Tigris downtown were vanishing in the fog and the river looked almost gold.

'Hi. I'm Faith,' I said. 'Don wanted me to make sure you're OK.'

She looked bemused. Oh my goodness. She doesn't speak English. I said it again in Russian and she smiled.

'He's such a sweetheart,' she said. She wasn't being patronising. She wasn't a tart on the make. She really was a student at the university in Baghdad, transferred for a year from Moscow to practise her Arabic. She really had fallen for Don McCaughrean. I sat on the edge of the bed and stared at her as she concentrated on her task.

'I know it seems crazy,' she said, understanding my bafflement without my needing to voice it. 'But it doesn't matter what is going on around you. You are either a queen or a chicken. I don't want to be a chicken.'

So this is how you become a queen. Paint your nails. Interesting.

This is what I have always loved about Russians, my ex-husband included. No, I did love him. I used him to escape going to university and to escape London and all the other things that needed escaping from. But he was funny and he was kind and he loved me. He bought me bootleg pears and roses from the old women who stood all night in the snow outside Belorusskiy Voksal.

'Are you a queen or a chicken?' Irochka asked me, earnestly. She had the eyes of someone who has lived through tragedy.

I lit a cigarette. I looked at my dusty boots and my raggedy jeans.

'Um. A chicken,' I decided. 'Definitely a chicken.'

Irochka shook her head in deep disapproval.

'That's bad,' she said. 'Bad.'

I laughed and left her. She was definitely, and would always be, all right.

CHAPTER TWELVE

I, on the other hand, would not always be all right. I waited in my room, cowering there, hoping my phone might ring. I felt like the kind of teenaged girl that I never was. He didn't make me wait to despairing, though. He was kind enough to recognise need when he saw it. At the time I even thought he somehow 'knew' I was waiting in my room for him to get back from the Sheraton. When he was around I trusted him with my life. Reliability itself. When he wasn't, a swirling fog of fear and insecurity engulfed me. It rang.

'You want to get something to eat?' Klein's voice asked my ear, without saying who it was or anything.

'Sure,' I said. Cool, huh? Retaining some dignity. Mmm hmmm.

I think this really is the best thing about my job. Going out for dinner while the world ends. The smallest things feel so momentous, take so much courage, involve so much risk.

'I know somewhere that's open,' he said when I found him on the front steps, the whole city rumbling with noise. Boom. Boom. Crack. Boom. Though you do almost get used to it, you sleep like a dead person for a week after you get home.

We walked out into the burning parking lot where an old man in white robes and bare feet was perfectly happily guarding the few cars that dared to stay there. He smiled pleasantly as though there wasn't a war going on and showed his two teeth. One on the top. One on the bottom. When I was little, Americans used to be appalled at the state of British dental work. They would wince at all the crooked, haphazard yellowing or brown teeth we seemed to feel perfectly at liberty to display. Now, though, most people in England have more or less straight white-ish teeth and it is endlessly surprising to see the state of people's mouths in places where dental care is an enormous luxury – more an exercise in pain management than hygiene or, more ludicrous, aesthetics. Men especially have teeth stained so dark brown that it almost looks as if they've done it on purpose. The things stick out at all kinds of angles and bad breath is more or less obligatory.

The same is true for facial disfigurement. People born with hideous deformities mostly can't afford to be operated on and there is a boy who I think works in the kitchens at the Corona, I've seen him twice scuttling through the lobby, with a vast goitre on the side of his head. The infant mortality rate is, no surprises here, very high in Iraq and a lot of weak babies are left to die. The cancer ward at the main paediatric hospital in Baghdad has, apparently, a hundred per cent fatality rate. Well done, guys. Or maybe it is our fault. Sanctions and invasions.

'Let's sing a song,' Klein said, turning the key in the ignition.

'Let's not.' I laughed, sitting back, waiting for the chill of the air conditioning to wake me up properly. Shouldn't have taken so many pills. 'What happened with those kids and the Sheraton? What the hell were they doing in your room anyway?'

148

'I'm crazy,' he began, ignoring my efforts at being serious and pulling out on to the almost deserted main road along the river lined with stringy palms. A felucca actually bobbed about there. Someone, a bedraggled boy, was pulling a car engine along the middle of the four-lane road on a kind of go-cart made of the base of a pram and some planks. 'Crazy for feeling so lonely.'

Patsy Cline. He paused.

'Come on!' he commanded.

I can't disobey this man.

'I'm crazy!' I sang, as quietly as I thought I could get away with.

'Louder!' Joshua shouted.

'Crazy for feeling so blue!' we went on together, getting into the swing.

We were still singing when Klein pulled over outside Baghdad's flashiest restaurant, the Khan Murjan. 'I wanted to take you to the revolving place at the top of the Saddam International Tower, but I guess this might not be the safest moment for it.'

'No thanks,' I said. 'Those things make me feel sick anyway.'

The cobbled alley, so often full of people parading themselves about, quite apart from the mosque-goers from across the way, was completely empty. Just the odd pile of fly-infested garbage. Nobody was clearing it at the moment. All very Day of the Triffids. What would cities look like with no traffic and no people, everything eerie, silent and dead? Well, like this. Although in Iraq one has to factor in the almost tangible presence of the appalling heat. We walked past a beauty salon with its shutters closed and a wedding dress shop, the mannequins surreal in their vast clouds of netting and satin and sequins. 'Your wife wear something like that?' I wondered, pointing at a particularly lurid bejewelled thing.

'Don't remember.' He smiled, lying brazenly.

He knocked on the ornate restaurant door. I didn't think we should get our hopes up. However, Klein gets what he wants, and an emaciated old man, his tux hanging loose round his shoulders, let us in with delighted greetings, Allah this, that and the other.

'Hello hello, welcome welcome.' Hello hello is a standard greeting here.

I had heard about this place but had never been here. It was not open, of course, but had been opened for our benefit. The maître d' switched the lights on to show us an enormous brick-vaulted room that looked as though it had been built as a mosque. In fact it's a caravanserai, built to house students from the mosque opposite and their camels and what have you. Now little white-clothed tables sit hundreds of feet below the echoing ceiling, their lamps bright as lilies on a black pond. Klein was pleased with his gift to me and pulled a chair out for me to sit down on the edge of what might, in pleasanter times, be a dance floor.

'What do you think?' he asked.

'Fantastic,' I said. 'On the imposing side, though.'

Should have put my skirt on. I do own one. I just don't like it, but sometimes, depending on the sleazeball in question, it is necessary to bow to convention.

The thin man, on duty alone apparently, brought us a bottle of Lebanese rosé and poured us a glass each. Beautiful color. Like a sunset.

'Happy?' Klein wanted to know.

I thought about it for a second. Part of me didn't want to give him the satisfaction. It was difficult to beat this guy, though. Difficult not to plunge willingly into whatever trap he was setting. And I was sure it was a trap of some kind.

'Very,' I said, aware of the inappropriateness of the location, timing and company. 'What happened to conflicted?'

He sparkled at me and stroked the back of my hand. 'You are hard to resist, Faith Cleopatra Zanetti. Very, very difficult.'

'You do a fucking good job, then,' I said. Seriously. I don't remember ever being resisted to this extent.

We were brought some steaming flatbread and I looked at Klein, confused.

'I really hate you,' I said.

'Thanks.'

'No. I do. What the fuck are you so perky about the whole time? The world is ending out there and you are always in this bloody fantastic mood. What is with you?' I rapped my fork on the tablecloth in irritation. Irritated not that he was so constantly happy, but that it was so infectious.

'My mother always said everything would turn out for the best,' he said, already finishing his glass of wine. Presumably he'd got up before me and for him this wasn't breakfast.

'A Jewish woman?'

'Mmm hmm.'

'Who was an adult during the Second World War?'

He laughed. 'Yes, well. She may have been slightly over-optimistic, but you can't ruin your whole life wallowing in misery just because the world isn't perfect,' he said, lifting up my shirt with his eyes.

'Funny,' I said, lighting a cigarette. 'That has always been exactly my policy. I mean, how can you not sink into an abyss of misery when you see everything that goes on?'

'How?' he wondered, chewing enthusiastically. 'I don't know. There's no point, is there?'

I laughed, choking on my smoke. 'Point? Of course there's no point. There's no fucking point in anything. But how do you help it?'

He shrugged, pouring us more wine. He was wearing red braces today. For reasons as inexplicable to me as the theory of relativity, the very sight of them made my eyes half close in swimming lust. Especially odd since red braces are what makes a newspaper editor out of a mere man. Seriously. All you have to do is be chauffeured into work and read the papers on the way (therefore living in the suburbs is helpful – gives you more time).

Then, once you are in the office, you hold the morning conference. Here you need to remove your jacket, thereby appearing more human and exposing your red braces. You must lean far back in your chair and cross one leg over your knee in manly but authoritative fashion. Then you just ask all the representatives of the different sections what they've got planned for the paper that day and if one of them is talking about something you don't understand you say, 'Well, Joanna, what exactly is that all about?' giving the impression, always, that it's Joanna who hasn't explained it properly or has taken the wrong line on it. She will then tell you what it's about and you will be enlightened and you will nod. Always be sure to do away with a couple of proposed items and ask somebody else for their ideas on what should be there instead. It is also helpful to have a few personal obsessions with which to cram the paper (Catholicism, fox hunting, anient China – anything really). Then it's off to lunch (in chauffeured Jag) with luminary before evening conference (see notes on morning conference) and various glittering functions where everyone is nice to you because they want your paper to be on their side. Back to bed with doting though neglected second wife, first edition of your paper to be biked over to you in the night hot off presses.

And then it dawned on me.

'Oh no!' I shouted, my voice bouncing around this empty cave, an enormous cavern of a place that could easily seat a thousand people. Couldn't even hear the bombs down here.

He stopped eating to look up at me. Some of that mazgouf fish had arrived. I already couldn't stand the sight of it and I'd only been there a week.

'You believe in God, don't you?' I accused, nodding to myself in utter certainty. It was the only explanation for his constant state of teeth-grating serenity.

'Sure. Why not?' He shrugged, batting the gravity of the accusation away.

'Why not? Why not! Well, because He doesn't exist, because children get raped and tortured – I mean, have you READ *The Brothers Karamazov?*' I whined. Very much hoped he wouldn't call me on this since it had been some time since I last read it and I now can't quite remember why it compounded my atheism but I felt sure that it was significant in my own lack of spirituality in some schoolgirlish way. And this man always made me feel like a schoolgirl in a pink and white candy-striped dress with railway tracks on my teeth instead of the tough and occasionally intrepid reporter that I am. Aren't I?

'Sure. My favourite book. I thought it was about how God does exist.' He smiled, wiping his mouth with a starched napkin. He was bloody charmed again. Charmed by my excitable atheism, my silly ideas and my unnecessary railing.

'No! It's not! Well, OK, maybe it is, but in any case He doesn't. Look at the world – look at this place. Nobody in their right mind would believe anything except that God is a product of human intelligence. Not the other bloody way round!' I was embarrassed at how worked up I was getting. I felt as though I was president of the debating society and my team was losing. My hair was flying everywhere and I could feel the beads of sweat on my forehead. And Joshua Klein was laughing at me.

'Art is a product of human intelligence. Or abstract things – truth, beauty. Do they not exist just because we invented them? You want some fish?' He had already swilled down another glass of wine and was looking at me expectantly.

'What? Oh, um, no thanks.'

Baghdad. A war. Work to do. And I'm shaking my belief system because of some old man? My belief system working as follows: everything's shit but if you're not going to kill yourself you might as well plough on through it. Complicated, I know, but you get into the swing of it after a while. Joshua Klein, however, had noticed a tiny little chink of hope and had stuck a chisel into it. It appeared to be turning into a gushing wound.

'So you think there's a point to everything, do you? Right and wrong?'

He thought about it for a second, just to humour me. 'I suppose I do. I think what my country is doing here is right. I think Saddam's regime is wrong. Don't you?'

Hmm. America right. Saddam wrong. Tricky one.

'Um. No. I wouldn't say that at all. What about us? Are we right or wrong?' I smirked. I felt suddenly that I might win the argument after all.

Klein's gorgeous face was grave. He looked his age when he wasn't smiling. He twisted his signet ring round his little finger.

'That, Faith Zanetti, I don't know. That I don't know.'

I sat back and laughed, pleased that at last it was him, not me, who was shaken.

'Feels so right it can't be wrong,' I sang. The theme tune from *Happy Days*.

He smiled too at that. The waiter brought half-melted pistachio ice cream in metal bowls on stalks, a Walls triangular wafer stuck in the side.

'Yes, it does,' he said. 'It's . . . irresistible. But I'm married, Faith.'

I leant forwards on my elbows, almost kissing him. 'So what? I'm not proposing.'

Should it matter that he's married? Should again. I am able to get feminist about this. Why is the perception always of a little wife at home feeling betrayed? Maybe she has been fucking around her whole life. Maybe she is a miserable bully. Maybe she has spent years longing for a guilt-freee way out of a dreadful marriage. I don't want to feel sorry for a woman I don't even know. After all, she doesn't need my pity.

Oh, I don't know. Maybe I was wrong. It turned out that I was. But anyone who's ever had these feelings knows you can't walk away from them. They are what life is all about.

It was when we were standing by the till and his credit card was running through a machine. I let him pay. Standards slipping. When the man (who turned out to be called Mohammed – what a shocker) went to phone the card details through (fat chance – phone lines down), Joshua took my face in both his hands and pulled my head towards him.

You know when you watch films – American, English, French, whatever – and there is always a love interest, a big passionate love scene? Characters whose lives are overturned by desire, who can't help themselves. Humphrey Bogart kisses Ingrid Bergman and his life, his lost hope, his soul, something bigger than both of them depends on it. Anyway, it always makes me flinch. Nobody kisses anyone like that. Nobody gazes wetly into somebody else's face with all that love and trust and honesty and kisses them like that. It's bullshit. It's Hollywood. It's what we wish would happen but know never will. It's for people who are one hundred per cent . . . what? Yes. One hundred per cent fictional. All the best people are.

But I was wrong. I do. I kiss people like that. It's real, it happens, it happened to me. It was magic and music and poetry and stuff, something ineffable that we touched with the swirling power of it all. The choking physical desire, as pure and as perfect as angels' wings. Seriously. I thought my heart might give out. More to the point, I thought his might.

'Stop. Stop! I'm going to fall,' I said. I was going to. Perhaps. Feeling faint. I backed away from him and looked into his face.

He said, 'Wow.'

I swear only Scarlett O'Hara has ever been kissed like that. Perhaps I am becoming fictional myself, what with all this passion and joy.

When we came out of the restaurant, back into the blazing alleyway by the mosque, I felt unsteady on my feet. Not because of the wine, but because I wasn't myself. The sandstorm had blown away, leaving streets that looked as though someone was trying to make a beach out of them. If there is a point to things, then how is one to live? I think that's why I had a panic attack back there at the hotel. What are you supposed to do now?

'It's not easy,' Klein said when I asked him.

(Incidentally, it is not that difficult to become fictional. You just need to cook dinner very thoughtfully, occasionally tasting the sauce and adding a missing ingredient. You must shave your legs in the bath, poking one leg gracefully right up in the air at right angles to your body. Sometimes, if things are getting on top of you, you might surround your bath with candles and fill it with foam, plunging right under the water to purge your demons.)

CHAPTER THIRTEEN

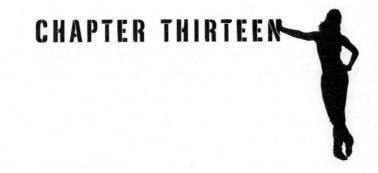

What you actually do when your whole world changes is, of course, carry on exactly as you did before. I was being slack not filing at greater length on the hotel attack. When colleagues are dead it looks a bit ropy not to get on to it in a big way. Look, I know I sound shitty not being more concerned, but Carly is a close friend and that was bad enough. I don't have room to come apart when people I barely know bite the dust. And I don't think they are the heroes they want to be either. Any more than I am. Or my father was. We are the few people at war who choose to be here. We know the risks.

When we got back Klein seemed reluctant to leave me to write.

'Will you still feel the same later?' he asked me. 'I know I will.'

I laughed and pushed him away from my door. Number 621.

'Get out! You know perfectly well it's always you who's walking away from me, not the other way round.'

'Never again,' he said. 'Never again.' He kissed me.

'Off!' I said.

'One more!' he said and I was in no mood for resistance. He had been afraid of losing control. Well, he'd lost it.

'I'll give you forty-five minutes,' he said.

My room felt dark and empty. Only the emergency generator lights were on, so there was a kind of blue glow and nothing else. I wondered why I had so few belongings. I imagine that to be a queen rather than a chicken you need things like jewellery, make-up, things made out of silk and cashmere. I had with me a short-wave radio, a toothbrush, toothpaste, bottle of Valium, one black skirt and a pair of high heels for emergencies only, a man's white shirt, two T-shirts, two pairs of jeans, two pairs of socks, two pairs of pants and a bra. Oh, and my passport, lighter, air tickets, computer, notebook and Pearlcorder. No photos of loved ones in my purse or the kinds of lucky charms some of the others carry. Eden has a postcard, a black and white photograph of a very young Elvis walking alone down a street in the rain, his shoulders hunched. Don has his cameras (and now Irochka!) and someone once told me that Grant Bradford carries his girlfriend's knickers around in his pocket. Worn.

I talked my longer piece over distractedly, opening and shutting the mini bar in the hope that a miracle would this time provide some alcohol, lighting cigarettes and putting them out again in disgust, chewing at the skin around my fingers like I used to do when I was little and still living with Mum. When I'd finished I sat down on the bed and sighed. The dreadful fear of earlier had evaporated with the elation of dinner and I knew the hotel wouldn't be, couldn't be hit again. I would live to spend more time with Joshua Klein if he would have me. Not a feeling I was used to. I smiled and lay back on the bed, rolling my head over towards the door as it began to open on cue to the second, the little green light that showed it was unlocked glowing at me.

Klein walked in holding a bottle of champagne and two glasses. He looked unreal in the blue light and I smiled at him.

'Hey,' I said, leaning up on one elbow.

'Hey.' He nodded. 'Pilfered from the Sheraton.'

'Nice one.' I beamed.

He eased the cork out, without a bang, and poured me a glass, bringing it over to the bed as though we did this every night. That was the thing. It was all exciting and passionate, that's true. But I felt more relaxed than I ever had before when I was with Klein. As though we'd had our little jokes and glances and routines for forty years already. (I love the New York use of 'already'. I was on a plane once and the couple next to me were arguing about something when the bloke shouted, 'The future is now already!' Grammatically odd.)

I took a sip of deliciousness and he said, 'I think we should give our relationship more depth.'

Oh no. Oh, don't do this. I tried to think what Carly would say. He's scared of what happened earlier. He's going to try and pull back. But WHEN are we going to get laid?

'Hello?' I said. I mean MORE depth? Listen, honey, I am having a lot of trouble with the depth we've already got ourselves. I don't do depth. There is so much depth going down here that I am drowning. 'More depth?'

'Uh-huh. Why not? If this is going to be an ongoing thing I think we should chat,' he said, apparently serious.

'Chat,' I said, contemplating this. Or rather, not so much as giving it the time of day. 'And what shall we chat about?' I asked. 'You know that bit in *The Graduate* when Dustin Hoffman wants to talk about art? Would you like to talk about art?'

'Art,' Klein pondered. 'Sure. Art. Why not?' He laughed.

Then he stood up.

'I always chat better with my trousers off,' he said, and he removed

159

his trousers, hopping about on one leg for the notoriously difficult bit, and then he lay down on the bed next to me, socks on. Thank God. At last there was going to be some concrete evidence of his much vaunted lack of ability to resist me. Look, I'm not going to revolt anyone with graphic descriptions which leave me with a serious vocabulary problem. But, well, I've never done it before. I swear, I never knew what all the fuss was about. I mean, no wonder people get in such a flap when their lover is unfaithful if THAT is what they're doing. To describe it as sex would be belittling it pathetically and ignoring the endless well of pent-up . . . love, I suppose, pouring out of both of us into each other. But to describe it as making love would be to omit the desperation, dirtiness and almost violence of it. Anyway, when I had recovered, after more than half an hour of lying still in each other's arms, I thought, and I said, 'Oh, I see.'

And he just laughed. Nothing to say now. Nothing to say from someone who had talked almost nonstop throughout the . . . what? Sex? Love? The Experience. He told me how beautiful all the parts of me that he was kissing were. He told me what he was about to do and what he wanted me to do. He told me how he felt and I told him. Now I know it doesn't sound very believable but I've never said it before. Or if I have (and who can remember through the haze of alcohol?) I've never meant it before. And even tonight it didn't carry all the meaning I wanted for it.

'I love you,' I whispered. I wanted to add, 'More than words can wield the matter,' but didn't have time. And I needed to hear it back.

'Say it,' I told him.

And he did. 'Faith,' he repeated over and over again. 'Faith. I love you.'

And later I made him promise. I made him promise me that when we had to give each other up it should be me who is allowed to do it.

'Please,' I said. 'Don't do that thing with the note again. Let me do it.'

'I promise,' he said.

'You know you asked me if I'd still feel the same later? I will. I will always feel the same,' I said.

When I sighed despairingly in the dark he seemed to know what I was thinking and he squeezed my hand.

'The future. This has no future. I don't want to look for your wallet for the rest of my life. You don't want to nag me about my drinking until I punch you in the head.' I said it quietly, smiling, but I knew it was true.

'That's not the future,' he said, holding on to me tightly. 'The future is days on the beach, going to the opera, deciding where to go for supper. Waking up with each other every morning and laughing.'

I thought about this for a while and my tear ducts were simply unable to cope with that much hope and optimism, thank you very much. I don't *do* hope. I am hard-wired to snipe and quip. Defensive banter – that's me.

He kissed the tears from my eyes and I said, 'If that's true then we're in a lot of trouble, Josh Klein. A lot of trouble.'

'I want to sleep with you,' he said, and I put my head on his shoulder. He had sucked me in and I didn't want to get out any more. I wanted to hold my hands up in surrender, so I did. I can't remember the last time I approached someone with my fists unclenched.

I thought at the time and perhaps I think now that he meant it all as much as I did. That it was as difficult for him to admit and to say, to wrench out of a lifetime of thinking he would never feel and say it, as it was for me. But I don't know.

Perhaps he just knew it had to be said. It's the fuck protocol. Maybe. And now I'll never know. You see, a cynic like I used to be would just laugh over his pint. 'If a girl wants to hear it, you say it.' But that cynic hasn't done what Joshua Klein and I did. So how would he know?

I fell asleep that night after the Corona Hotel got shelled and I felt safe for the first and last time in my life. I had my recurring dream about Dad coming home, alive after two decades hiding from the Inland Revenue in Panama and wondering who'd got his jacket.

CHAPTER FOURTEEN

'Where are my socks?' Klein asked me, rummaging about under the bed, already alert and on the go like a five-year-old boy. The tanks which had been a 'show of force' were doing more than showing now and the appalling booming of the bombardments was accompanied by the distant crack of street fighting. Not that I gave a toss.

I sat up, dishevelled and happy, my hair in a wild halo around my head, our champagne bottle half full on the floor. I think that may be the first time that I have abandoned a bottle of anything without finishing it. In Russia it shows disrespect for the host – that's my excuse.

I laughed at Klein on his hands and knees, scrabbling around in a panic as though he was going to be late for school or his mum might catch us or something.

'Men,' I said, reaching for my cigarettes. 'Beforehand you're all like,

ANNA BLUNDY

"Oh God, I can't live without you." Then you have one orgasm and it's "Where are my socks?"' '

'That's good,' he acknowledged, smiling. 'That's good.'

He found his socks and sat on the floor putting them on. He moves like a child.

He knelt by the bed and held my hand, about to say something, but instead he kissed my hand and looked at me.

'I have to live without you,' he whispered, and walked out of the door.

Have to. Have to. Should. Ought. Silly man. A shower might be a good idea.

It was odd to see the same old face in the hotel mirror. A steel-framed thing with a medicine cabinet behind it – plastic cups with flannels in plastic bags, shower cap, shampoo in a sachet, little black ones with English and Arabic on them. Black is still classy in Iraq. I expected to have changed somehow now that I had found him. And it felt like that. Found him. As though that's what everyone is trying to do. I never had been. I really wasn't looking. I have always known that it's not a man who is going to solve my problems and make my life complete. I was wrong though. It is, and he's here and he loves me too. Memo to self – must read more poetry. Everything was more clearly defined and perfect than I have ever noticed before. The chrome showerhead, the wisps of paper round the hotel soaps, the fragment of kilim rug in a gilt frame above the bed, my old leather doctor's bag suitcase with the brass clasp. The heat beating through the sliding balcony doors was caressing rather than brutal.

I washed a lifetime of cynicism and despondency out of my hair and wound a towel on top of my head like a turban. I found Klein's signet ring on the floor and in a gesture of total lunacy I put it on. This turned out to be a fatal mistake. You know, actually fatal. I didn't just slip it on for safekeeping. I thought about the symbolism and I knew what it meant

164

and I loved it. I've never worn a ring before and I loved that it was his. My trophy. It had JFK engraved on it. I wondered what the F stood for.

Down in the lobby everyone was understandably grim. There were a few faces missing and no secret as to what that meant. There were some other people missing too – all the Ministry of Information stooges and the secret policemen. I think they must have acknowledged that they were fighting a losing battle and buggered off home to change their allegiances and decide whether or not to get out of the country to avoid a lynching. The Republican Guard's feared retaliation was now fairly obviously not going to happen. Allied occupation was the only realistic outcome to this. The driver, Samy, was still ploughing through his copy of *Marie Claire* and Grant Bradford seemed to have been sent back to Baghdad to do the shelled hotel story. He was sitting stony-faced in front of the lobby television, smoking intensely. Must ask him about those knickers.

'Hey, Bradford,' I shouted, trying to liven things up a bit. 'Is it true about your girlfriend's pants?' She is a go-go dancer from Louisiana.

Grant didn't turn to look at me. He kept his cigarette in his mouth and screwed up his face to stop the smoke going in his eyes. He pulled a ball of red lace out of his multi-pocketed khaki jacket and held them up to me, not once taking his eyes off the screen.

'Yuk,' I said. I leant over the back of his chair.

Don was next to him, with Irochka, bizarrely, on his knee. Fat tears were rolling down his substantial cheeks. Weird. He hadn't been this upset yesterday. I kissed the top of his head and Karim brought a bottle of vodka and some teacups over to their little brass table and plonked it down without a word. Irochka met my gaze first and she nudged her armchair with her elbows so that it too looked up to face me. He pushed Irochka off and fell into my arms with a loud sob.

'I'm so sorry, Faithy. I'm so sorry,' he cried.

Oh God, what?

'Don. What is it?' I asked him, pushing him back and holding him

165

by the shoulders. It seemed that everyone in the hotel lobby had turned round to look at me, to watch my reaction to the news. I was determined to take it well, whatever it was. I had been falling apart too much since my conversion to optimism, not that I had had much of a chance to practise it yet.

'It's Eden,' Don said and I immediately felt sick. Oh, please let him be all right, oh please don't let him be dead. I wanted to start saying sorry now for having dismissed him this past week since I met Joshua. 'The division he was with got ambushed. They were lost or something. All dead.'

OK, I thought. It could be worse. He hadn't been killed individually in a shooting or a car crash. His whole division was taken out. That meant he might have been the only one to have crawled away or maybe he hadn't actually gone with them from the base that morning or, well, any number of things. I was going to practise my optimism right now and refuse to believe that he was dead.

'Eden's going to be fine, Don,' I told him, trying to cheer him up too. I raised my hand to his clammy shoulder; the cotton of his shirt sticking to his flesh.

The Corona hotel seemed to let out a collective wince.

'No, Faith,' Don told me, wiping both his eyes with the backs of his hands. 'He's dead.'

'You don't know that,' I insisted, brightly.

Don was completely confused and he brought out a crumpled cigarette packet from his pocket and lit a fag, wheezing as he did so. He offered me one.

'No thanks, I'm cutting down,' I said and he looked even more baffled.

'Faithy, why don't you sit down. Listen, I've seen the pictures of their vehicles. The Iraqis are behaving like they've won the fucking war. Even if he survived the attack, they'll have killed him by now.'

I laughed. I knew that Eden Jones couldn't die. He couldn't die. The world is not that awful a place. He isn't dead.

'McCaughrean, you pessimistic bastard. I'm going to make you buy me a drink when I walk back in here with Eden Jones. I don't want to hear anyone saying that that man is dead. He is not dead. OK?' I was shouting now and beginning to be aware that I appeared very mad. I leant down and poured myself a vodka, drinking it quickly in one out of a thick-rimmed hotel cup.

'OK?' I asked, a bit more quietly.

'OK, Zanetti,' Don mumbled, reaching out for Irochka's comforting fingers. He shuffled around on the marble floor, a fan whirring over his head.

You see, I just wasn't going to let this happen to me again. Not again. No thank you. When Evie told me that Dad had been shot, he still wasn't dead yet. 'He's going to be fine, sugar baby,' she said. 'Sure as eggs is eggs.' A surgeon called us at home from some hospital in Belfast. I'd been with them for more than two years and Mum still wasn't even allowed to contact me or come within a certain distance of the house. I told my friends at school she was dead. So that day I got home and put my black canvas bag down on the table and reached for the cupboard where the crisps were.

'Faith honey,' Evie said in that awful tone that people would use with me for years to come. A tone of sympathy and condolence. You know the one that some women use pretty much all the time? 'Oh hello, how *are* you?' they say, and you wonder who died.

Well, in this case, my dad.

'Faith honey,' she said, and took my hands in hers. She was wearing a soft brown halter-neck dress and coquettish heels. 'Your daddy's been hurt.'

Hurt, my arse. Well, yes, it must have hurt. He certainly looked hurt when we saw him on the news that night being rushed into the emergency room on a stretcher.

They operated, but the bullet was deep inside him somewhere and he died from multiple heart attacks during the operation. Ironic in a very, very bleak way, because he'd always been terrified of dying of a heart attack. He imagined, and often talked about, the pain that would sear up and down his left arm, the breathless agony. Well, I guess he never actually had to experience it.

My point being that I will not be going through all that again. I will not lie on my bed screaming for someone who is never coming back.

I was wrong, of course. I would soon be doing exactly that. But I didn't know it at the time and, as my first lover told me (I was fifteen, he was twenty-six and had been married three months), 'What you don't know can't hurt ya.'

I stomped towards the lobby doors, determined, fag in mouth, to find a driver who would take me out to where the ambush had been. I wasn't even going to bother to ask Samy, who was clearly filling in a questionnaire that would tell him whether or not he was a sensitive lover (not, would have been my guess). I didn't quite get outside though, because I walked straight into Ziggy, Anita and Fernando who were coming in, sweating from the churning street. This lot again. The very presence of western teenagers was surreal in the circumstances. The only teenagers around here were soldiers. This bunch looked like something out of a film about teen angst set in Beverly Hills.

'Seen JK?' Ziggy asked me, an aggressive sneer all over his face.

'Not for an hour,' I told him honestly.

'Dude.' He nodded. Anita glowered at me as though I was personally responsible for whatever civilian casualties had so far taken place. Actually, she is a very capable glowerer and I did start feeling a bit guilty.

'Fernando, how are you? Did you manage to get any sleep?' I asked him, ignoring the two teenagers from hell who, in my opinion, should have been at home in America doing whatever coursework they had to do, or serving people cobb salads and pitchers of beer. It was dangerous here and they were angry and stupid.

'Not really.' He grinned, giving the impression that he had been up all night getting stoned or drunk or having an orgy. 'Joshua's got me out of here today. The airport's open and there's a Hercules going back to England in a couple of hours.'

'Cool,' Ziggy commented.

We were conspicuous and in everybody's way.

'So . . .' I said, hoping to wind this up.

'Dunno where to go when I get back though,' said Fernando, glumly, looking around the lobby at all the hacks and trying to pretend not to be interested.

Oh, here we go. Great. A stroppy teenager to deal with.

I made them sit down and order coffee on my room while I went to stand in the corner and phone Evie. I surrounded myself with a cloud of cigarette smoke and dialled her number.

'Hey, pumpkin,' she crowed, hoping I wasn't going to mention the war, babbling immediately. 'Oh, baby. I have a bee in here. Just fogged it's bumbly ass.' She was breathless as though she had just chased this insect round the house with her spray can.

I interrupted her. I explained Fernando's situation and begged and pleaded.

'I'll make it up to you, Eves,' I whined. 'Honest. Come on, he can have Mo's room until he gets back from school. Pleeeeeeease. I owe it to a friend. You know? The woman who got shot? When she's better he'll leave. We're trying to get her medivaced to London now.'

I knew she was going to say yes. I only had to sound desperate enough. I thought I would omit to mention that he had just been expelled from his sixth form college for dealing dope. She'd be trying to score off him if she knew.

I was writing down the address when Ziggy noticed the ring. He pointed a dirty finger at it and snorted, plonking his coffee cup back down on its saucer with a splosh.

'So he's doing you too, is he?' he leered. Anita twisted her nose stud around, embarrassed. She leant down to pick at the nail on her big toe.

I smiled, feeling the weight of the ring and all the candyfloss things it symbolised.

'Don't know what you mean, sweetheart,' I said. None of this kid's business. Go and protest against the war and stop hassling me. I dare say the Iraqi people is seriously appreciative of your contribution to the anti-war effort – sullenness. I'm sure there are plenty of Iraqis who don't want to be bombed, but I can't imagine any of them pinning much hope on this specimen.

'Joshua Klein. He's doing you,' he went on. Drop it, kid. 'You're wearing his ring.'

I laughed. 'That's a beautiful way of putting it, Ziggy,' I said. 'You are a very eloquent young man and will clearly go on to great things.'

I was unruffled by the whole exchange so far. But then he said, 'OK, dude. This time I'm telling Mom.'

The penny, which had been teetering at the top of the metaphorical slot machine for some time now, dropped. Well he's hardly going to put any old kid and his girlfriend up at the Sheraton, is he? Ugh.

I didn't dignify this with an answer, or, at least, I didn't have time to dignify it with an answer because I could see, above the glow of Grant Bradford's head, pictures of the ambush in which Eden had been. I put my hand over my mouth in acknowledgement that it looked very, very bad.

The whole lobby stared at the screen in silence and when I turned away, the minions of Satan had disappeared over towards the ground floor pizza place. The ambush had happened near Tikrit and Iraqi television showed burnt-out armoured personnel carriers and overturned jeeps, on fire, spewing black smoke into the air, a few locals jumping for joy and some Republican Guard soldiers looking pleased with themselves and firing into the air. Oh, Eden, don't be dead.

CHAPTER FIFTEEN

I must have left a thousand messages for Joshua, begging him to help me. I was hitting redial on my mobile over and over again. 'I'm downstairs. Please come urgently.' I paced up and down, ignoring the glowers of Ziggy and Anita and the pitying stares of everybody else. It already felt like a funeral.

When Klein did eventually emerge from the lift he looked like a character in a play coming through the curtains to solemn applause. Nothing seemed completely real any more. Joshua was not, however, in a playful mood. 'Faith,' he said, not even looking at me like that or trying to touch me or anything. 'I need to talk to you.'

It was all I could do not to simper or plead for some reassurance but fortunately I had not sunk that low. Yet.

He pulled me without affection, as though last night hadn't happened, as though he hadn't said those things, out into the searing parking lot and clunked the alarm off his car, tossing some coins to the car park boab.

'Get in,' he said, so I did. No opera this time, no singing, not even any talking. He turned away from the river and down some back streets. We drove past a square where people were kneeling over little wooden box coffins and screaming. Ought to tell Don. The left-wing papers love those shots. Desperate bereaved people wailing as though representing for all of us the agony of war. I can't look at those pictures. Klein pulled up, in no time at all, in a quiet, shady alley, near one of the old colonial buildings not far from the Iraq Museum.

Near the museum I could see that the looting had begun. I'd spoken to someone who works there before I came out to Iraq (she'd done some exchange thing with the British Museum) and she said she'd already started sandbagging everything and hiding the most valuable relics at her mum's house in the mountains where they normally went out for picnics at weekends. My favourite joke when Evie tried to take me to see ancient relics for my general edification was always, 'Why do we have to go out to look at old stuff? Can't you just look in the mirror.' Actually, of course, Evie was and is incredibly beautiful. The age gap of ten years, which seemed so huge when Dad met her, has now narrowed and you couldn't see that there is a day between us any more. Especially as she has youngish children now and I should have. Should. Should.

Klein and I stepped out of the car and a child poked her head out of a window hung with washing to have a look at us. He opened an old green door with a big brass knocker by punching a code into a panel on the outside wall. It was cool and very dark inside and we walked up some stone steps to the first apartment. A smell of spices and putrefaction. The lift, a clunking thing with iron gates and ceramic buttons, was defunct halfway between the ground and the first floor. The flat had a name in Arabic under the bell. The second we were inside I could see it was owned by rich people. There were lavish rugs on the walls, heavy drapes on the window to keep in the cool, and lots of gilt chairs scattered around in front of an enormous central television. The sofa, a red velvet thing with gold feet, was purely ornamental and there were lovely old china things in glass cabinets around the room. Blue and gold bowls, a Russian samovar and some miniature teacups. The light shone from a low green glass globe in the middle of the ceiling. I had the feeling that we had not come here to get laid. I was afriad even to try to touch Klein in this mood. I was terrified of the brush-off that I could see I would get if I approached him. Normally I would go straight for a confrontation or make a joke. What had happened? What did I do wrong? And, much more to the point, why was I of all people – impenetrable Faith Zanetti, someone once called me – wondering any of this shit?

'It's OK. It's a friend's place. We're safe here,' he said. I didn't like this tone. If we were safe here, that strongly suggested we were not safe elsewhere. And safe from what? He wasn't talking about the war. I looked at the pictures in the frames. A couple getting married, a couple on horses, a couple in Venice. Not just any couple, I realised, sidling up closer, but Nur and Hugo. In fact, they even had ornamental carpets depicting them both, hanging on the walls. So this was their place in the centre. Well, they'd wanted us to meet, thought he'd be useful to me. And was I to be useful to him too in their plan? I wondered if they'd gone yet. Certainly no sign of anyone having been here recently. It was sepulchral.

'Great, Joshua. Why am I here?' I asked, lighting a cigarette with a vast onyx lighter that I lifted with great difficulty off a smoked-glass coffee table. 'Are you going to get your kit off or shall we go back to the hotel?' I was sniping at him and I knew it. But I was gearing up for the scene I felt was coming. And it should come as no surprise. He'd done it before, after all. He gets close and then he backs off – fight or flight. He probably can't help it. Probably barely knows he's doing it. My inclination would be the same, if only I'd had any kind of a grip on my inclinations.

'I saw the news about Eden Jones,' he told me, standing, feet slightly apart, arms crossed, a shard of light glancing across him from a gap in the curtains. He might have been interviewing me for a job. As an assassin. I stayed as still as possible. Perhaps if I could just stay forever in this moment then we wouldn't have to face whatever was coming next. I didn't dare breathe.

'I do have . . . sources have provided me with a bit of information about what happened out there,' he began.

'Uh-huh,' I said. Don't hope. Do not hope. 'Like?'

'Well, we believe that not everyone in the unit was killed,' he said and he looked at me significantly. We? Okey dokey. 'It is not clear who did and who did not make it, but at least two injured people en route for the Engineer Battalion HQ were taken into custody somewhere just outside of Tikrit. I am not saying that Eden Jones is one of them. But he could be.'

My reaction was not particularly measured.

'Eden's alive! He's alive and I'm going to find him!'

'Faith. Please be calm. Nobody is at all clear about whether or not he is alive. But I should tell you that we are going in to rescue our men. We hope to reach them before they are executed by their interrogators. It is a very dangerous operation and there may well be further casualties. But we never abandon a man down. Never.'

This speech could have been made from a rostrum spiked with a million media microphones. Where did he get this tone from? Who the fuck did he think he was talking to? Since when was he 'we'?

'Uh-huh.' I nodded, whispering in fear. I couldn't pin down what it was I was scared of, but I think it was Josh Klein. JFK. One of my inner voices was beginning to hate him. For his wanky initials, for what he was doing to me, for not loving me properly, goddammit. For seeming

174

as though he would take me under his wing but actually just fucking me. Not that it wasn't . . . oh, I don't know. I tell you one thing. I was missing the simplicity of Eden Jones. We take the piss out of each other, we occasionally have sex, we know we ought to be capable of more and we know that we aren't. You know where you are with someone as fucked-up as you are. With a bouncy optimist who knows right from wrong, on the other hand . . . Well, you're screwed, aren't you?

'Ah,' he said, looking at my left hand. 'You found my ring.' He held out his hand, palm up, and there was nothing I could do but slip his ring off my finger and give it back to him. Now didn't seem like the moment to bring up Ziggy. What was his real name? Daniel. That's right. Daniel.

'Yes,' I said. 'I did.'

He put it back on as though I were a lost property agent and carried on talking.

'Faith. I can arrange for you to go with the rescue party,' he said, looking expectantly into my face. 'But I want you to make me a promise first.'

'Anything!' I said, flicking my ash into an ashtray the size of a planet. If I could go with the rescue party then it must be true. Eden must be alive. I knew it. I didn't give a shit if nobody else believed it. I wasn't letting this ever happen to me again. It would make amazing copy and be a fantastic scoop and I love travelling with the military. Almost as much as Eden does, if I'm admitting it. Everybody likes you on these stories. They want you there to make them look good and they can keep you safe and minimise the hassle. The 'independents' wandering around where they shouldn't be and dying all the time are, one general told me, 'a huge pain in the butt'.

'If the mission isn't successful, I don't want you to write about it,' he said, totally straight-faced as though that was the kind of thing you could ask of someone.

'What? I can't do that, Joshua. You know I can't do that.' I shook my head and sat down on a flimsy little Louis XVI fake, with my elbows on my splayed knees.

'Then you can't go,' Klein said, not moving a muscle. He was so uncharacteristically still, it was sort of unnatural.

'Joshua. Why is this in your power? What are you talking about? Who are you?'

He smiled indulgently at me and came over to where I sat, squatting next to me and holding my hands now. What the fuck are you playing at, mate?

I heard a car drive by outside. No fighting though.

'You know where my loyalties lie, Faith. I don't want my people to look bad right now. Now would not be a good time to fail. Do you want to go or not?'

'I want to go,' I whispered.

'And you promise?' he asked, his face close to mine in the green gloom of the flat.

'Yes. I promise,' I said, and I wanted to be promising something else. This was the most compromised I'd ever been. This isn't telling Colonel Gaddafi you're going to be nice about him (which I did). This isn't offering editorial control to the most minor contacts (do it all the time). This was a promise to report only one version of the truth. I was on side and I didn't like it.

I really felt the atmosphere needed breaking, so I stood up and started pacing about. Could I flirt him back? There must be a way of snapping him. There must be a way of getting him to look at me like that again. How could it all be over so fast? How could he give so little a shit about me when he had seemed . . .

'So,' I grinned. 'Are we going to live together in a nice house in Primrose Hill? Or do you prefer Richmond? Evie, my dad's last girl-friend, lives in Richmond. It might be nice to be near her. I think she would appreciate it if after the wedding you would call her Mom.'

Klein is fifteen years older than Evie. That was the joke I was making.

'I believe that you know I live in Washington DC,' he said, and he might as well have punched me in the head, or disembowelled me right there. He paused and drew in breath. 'Are we done?' he asked.

It was happening again. My heart, my brain, my lungs, my vision. I wasn't sure if I was going to be able to stand up but there was no fucking way I was going to die in front of this bastard.

'Oh, I see,' I said. 'You're an arsehole. Great. Well done.' And I walked over towards the door, watching it melt in front of me like a Dali painting (I hate Dali. Stupid moustache, stupid pictures.).

'Faith,' he said, when my back was turned.

Yes? What? He's going to call me back and kiss me and hold me and make the world all right again. He's going to hold my hand forever and never let go. We can just laugh at everything together until we die.

'You will be picked up at the hotel tomorrow at five,' he said.

'Sure.' I nodded, and started down the stairs to the street.

He followed me out and drove me back to the hotel in silence.

'What about the beach?' I asked him as we pulled up.

'What about it?' he asked.

'Fuck it, Joshua. Are you "conflicted" or what? This is bullshit,' I shouted at him, but all my self-assurance was long gone. Apart from the hole in its side, the hotel was almost back to normal, and cars were pulling up outside, delivering high-heeled ladies and sharp-suited men as though Baghdad was a normal city governed by a normal regime. Well, apart from the all too public looting. Shopfronts smashed, fridges and air conditioners, filing cabinets and computers dragged along the street by the desperate and barefoot. Perhaps I was going mad. Perhaps everything that had happened between us hadn't really happened. Perhaps I had fucked it up in some way I didn't understand. Perhaps I had invented the intensity of it. Perhaps . . .

'Something like that,' he said, and he clearly wanted me to just fuck off and die. OK then, I thought. I will.

I fucked off, in fact, in a taxi out to Nur and Hugo's. The phone lines were down and there was no other way of finding them. I wasn't going to be having any of their evasive shit this time. I was being manipulated by Joshua Klein and they, I was pretty sure, had suggested me for this manipulation. They'd tried to make it sound like he'd be a good source for me, but I was beginning to suspect it might be the other way round.

There were people out in the streets near their house, pottering about their business. An old man with a plate of couscous on his head, a woman with some children out on the scavenge. The sentryman at the bottom of their pretentious drive was not there and the gates were fastened with a big rusty chain. I could see from here, though, that the front door was open. The taxi driver waited incredulous in his Tacchini tracksuit while I climbed the gate. Their poor lawn had been replaced by dust and sand, their potted palms were dead. I pushed the enormous door open, knowing what I would find. The pathetic sight of a looted house. Picture shadows on the walls where even the abysmal artwork had been removed. The cushions gone from the sofas and chairs, all the glass stuff gone, some broken on the floor. I imagine Nur probably took everything she wanted with her to London or Paris. Nobody planned to come back here. It was depressing. I found a bottle of whisky that had been left on top of a glass table held up by a brass eagle and took a swig. I went back to the hotel, bleak and empty.

I spent all night in my room kicking pieces of furniture and saying 'Fuck' with varying degrees of intensity. Also 'Bastard'. I hurt my toe on the chair. Bastard though, really. Why doesn't he love me?

I tried Carly's mobile, expecting to fail. But she picked it up.

'Why doesn't he love me?' I asked her.

'Zanetti? What is wrong with you? He does,' she crackled.

'Then why does he go so cold and professional? He's offering me this story. I'll tell you about it when it's over, but he'll hardly even look at me.'

'You've had sex then?' She laughed, inhaling on a cigarette.

'I prefer to call it making passionate love. Who got you the fags?'

'Do you indeed. The nurse. Well, you're in for some agony then.'

'Why?'

'You just said love. Love equals agony. Didn't anybody ever teach you anything?'

'Apparently not,' I admitted and hung up, defeated.

I filed two totally shit three-hundred-word pieces that were both humiliating collections of the wires and television reports about Eden's ambush and the house-to-house fighting in Baghdad. The paper didn't need much, though, because they had good pictures of some American soldiers kicking back in one of Saddam's deserted palaces. They would take up most of the front page. And, let's face it, public interest was beginning to wane.

Somebody did a survey once and I think it was a week – readers can sustain interest in a particular crisis for a week. Even the twin towers didn't manage longer than that at the top of the news. Let alone wars 'abroad'. Hussein's palaces are fantastic photo spreads. I mean, if you're going to be vulgar you might as well really go for it. That was clearly his view. Great big gold taps and huge paintings of nude blondes with snakes writhing round their legs, like the kind of thing you can win at the fair, except framed in solid gold. There was a brilliant mural about four hundred feet high of a bunch (English not American usage – it really looked like a bunch of, say, asparagus or something) of missiles piercing the sky. It doesn't do them justice to call them phallic. They weren't phallic. They were penises. Then, just for good measure, a few slightly more tasteful paintings of Baghdad's big beautiful gold mosque, all hanging lanterns, carpets and dim holy light; next to some

Glastonbury-ish things of white blonde warriors with swords and loin-cloths, rippling muscles and glinting daggers. Honestly, the taste of the man. This is not to mention the artwork involving himself. Please. Seriously, he deserves taking out for this alone. The Blogger, who until recently was holed up in his cellar, just delivered twenty-four pizzas to some American soldiers, my computer told me. This guy really cannot decide whose side he is on. And nobody much cares any more.

CHAPTER SIXTEEN

Having not had so much as a wink of sleep, such was my hatred for Joshua F. Klein, I plodded downstairs at five to find Hunter (no, honestly) waiting for me in the lobby: helmet, flak jacket, dog tag, slightly nervous blue eyes. The Americans were in control now but anyone could still meander up and chuck a grenade at them and they knew it. Most, but not all, people were glad to see the back of Saddam. I'm not going to bother cataloguing the guy and his sons' repulsive crimes. They deserved it, by any standards.

Hunter had blond bristle all over his big fat head and I could see the bags under my eyes in the glimmer of his reflector shades. A Green Beret. That's what he was, though not what he was wearing on his head today. He called me ma'am. Relentlessly. What am I? The Queen?

'Ma'am?' he said, which I translated as meaning, 'Are you Faith Zanetti?'

'Yes,' I told him, nodding. He looked me up and down with faint disgust as though we were going out on a date and I hadn't really put the effort in. It was true. I stank, I was filthy. Hey, what's new?

He walked away from me, his shoulders as broad as the doorway, out into the seriously beautiful dawn. You know, palms swaying on the river, light tingeing the edges of the velvet blue sky, bright stars a-twinkling in the heavens, birdies a-tweeting. All right, all right, I'll stop. It was, though.

'Where are we going?' I asked my escort.

'That's classified, ma'am,' he said, putting his shades on and climbing up into his Humvee. He said I could sit up front with him. 'Indigenous intelligence assets have supplied us with the location.' (That's a grass to you and me.)

'Where're you from, Hunter?' I asked, getting all chatty now. Oooh yes. On the ball, me.

'North Carolina, ma'am. Been in the US Army seven years now.'

His 'daddy' works in a branch of the Wiz out at the local mall and his 'mommy' teaches first grade. I can wheedle that top secret information out of anyone with my journalistic prowess.

Oh yes, and he is in Iraq in the hope of 'kicking some Iraqi ass'. There was some ass I quite wanted to see kicked and was thinking of enlisting Hunter's help, though I could see he might have a bit of a conflict of interest problem there since JFK had set this whole thing up for me in the first place and Hunter here appeared to be, at least at some level, under the bastard's command.

Wasn't it fun? Didn't he want to do it again? What happened to the beach and the opera and where we're going for dinner? What happened to the whispers in my ear and the touch of his hand? I put my own shades on and glowered out of the window. The fear had entirely left me now. I was fucking angry. Fine, fuck me and chuck me, but don't do all this lovey dovey shit first. Bastard!

The few people about at this time stared at us in our Humvee as we passed, too fast – I suppose so that there was no time for an ambush. A small group of old men with their robes hoisted up out of the sand, some children out looking for water – the supply was off and the big lorries of the stuff had not yet arrived. Enterprising tossers were apparently making holes in the pipes out of town and charging locals for fill-ups. We hurtled quickly down the deserted six-lane highway out of the city, out past Karrada where all the usually busy shops and beauty salons were boarded up. We took a road lined with squat white buildings and strewn with electricity wires. There were a few abandoned cars, some burnt out, some not, and the odd big hole in the road from the bombardments. Mostly, though, it looked relatively peaceful. Satellite dishes and aerials dominated most of the buildings and low creamy mosques with delicate minarets occasionally glided past. The pavements were sandy and the palms were tall and spindly.

Before Hunter had even called me ma'am a dozen times we were out in the countryside, if that's what it was, following enormous swirling signs in two languages, which looked as though they should lead you on to a toll-paying motorway but in fact sent you on to narrow desert roads with red sand flying up on both sides. We passed two Iraqis with machine guns, young men with headscarves and ammunition strapped to them, their allegiances unclear. Neither of them raised their RPKs at us, but Hunter's grip on the black steering wheel tightened, his freckled knuckles whitening. He flicked the display screen on and checked our direction on a digital colour map. Then he flicked it off again, satisfied.

'Who are they?' I asked.

'Saddam fedayeen, displaced Baathists, Islamic extremists, Army of Muhammad, Wahabis, Al Qaida terrorists, Iranian-backed Shia – could be any one of 'em,' he said, glumly.

We drove alongside a shallow river, shaded by thick date palms, and we saw some young men and boys washing their horses. Fifteen glossy animals stood up to their haunches in the water and twenty or so boys splashed around with them, some sitting on their backs tipping plastic buckets of water over the horses' heads, and some of them swimming round the animals' legs, squealing, shouting and fighting playfully. A few of the gleaming, toasted, almond-coloured men wore white rags round their groins, but most of them were blissfully naked. When they saw the American Humvee they all froze like a scene in a painting. Hunter slowed down to show his lack of menace and, in an instant, they took a silent and collective decision to like us and they started to wave. I leant all the way out of the window to wave back and the boys cheered.

'Watch yourself, ma'am,' Hunter said, and I came back inside and lit a cigarette.

'Hmm. Not such a shit world after all,' I said.

'Ma'am?' Hunter asked.

'Nothing.' I smiled, and smoked peacefully, Joshua Klein banished briefly.

I had actually fallen asleep and was lurched awake by the Humvee shuddering to a halt by a small white breeze-block hut in the middle of the desert. Groggy and puffy-eyed (about four hours' sleep in twenty-four), I schlomped down into the sand and looked around. There was an armoured personnel carrier, a military ambulance, a huge hemmit, and two more Humvees. Also, what looked like an awful lot of burly young men in khakis.

'Hey,' I said, holding up a hand.

'Hey,' they all shouted in unison, turning round from their games of chess, weapon-cleaning activities and general lounging around in the sun to look at me. The equipment was astonishing. Hunter gave me a tour of all the things we would be taking with us. There were night vision goggles and heat-seeking this, that and the other – you know, those things that zoom along the streets like horizontal fireworks looking for a warm thing to pierce and destroy (i.e. a person). We were taking semi-automatic and automatic weapons, handguns, assault rifles with lights mounted on them, grenades, a rocket launcher and some things that make obscuring smoke. As well as radios and walkie-talkies and even some sushi knives. Well, that's what they looked like.

'You gotta get them in the stomach, right here,' Hunter told me, patting what were surely some very well-toned abs under all that protective business. 'Any higher and you can't retrieve your weapon.'

'Because it's stuck in someone's rib cage,' I said.

'Right,' he concurred.

I looked around at the dreamy swoop of the desert and wondered if we would all come back alive.

'Should I be nervous?' I asked Hunter, and one of his colleagues, lying in the sand with a Discman on, raised his leg to kick Hunter in the shin.

'Ma'am?' he wondered.

'Nervous. Are you nervous? How dangerous is the mission?' I asked again.

'Pretty dangerous,' he said. 'I believe it will be pretty dangerous.'

I didn't get where the signal came from or why everyone obeyed it, but moments later the whole division was praying. And me? I closed my eyes and joined in. It seemed like the moment to participate.

'Our father, who art in heaven, hallowed be thy name . . .'

It was very, very hot. If Don had been here he'd be wanting to do his egg frying caper. He likes to prove, whenever the opportunity arises, that you can fry an egg on a hot car bonnet. So far, the evidence I have witnessed suggests to me that you can't. Sometimes it goes a bit white round the edges. He'd say it was hot as an A-rab's armpit or a camel's arsehole or something. I missed him.

When we'd stopped praying and were hauling our behinds into the vehicles, I thought I'd try it myself.

'Hot as a camel's arsehole out here, isn't it?' I said to a man with acne and a Boston accent.

'I'm sorry?' he said.

'Oh, nothing,' I mumbled and took my seat on a bench in the back of the jeep. Now, I've been on these types of expeditions before and normally there's a real atmosphere of fear and excitement, but this lot, eight of them sitting in my section at the back, were pretty solemn. I think it was because it was a rescue mission and they really didn't want to fail. Usually you are out to get someone dead or alive. Banging on the corrugated iron doors of stinking slums in the middle of the night, knee high in raw sewage. This time the people needed to be alive and that is always an extremely difficult requirement. Also, there was no question of managing it without, presumably, killing a fair number of other people. A grim prospect. We rolled on to Highway One.

'How you doing, dude?' one boy asked his neighbour very quietly.

'Dude,' the other one answered, apparently a positive response.

Hunter had given me an army issue bulletproof vest and helmet and I was beginning to feel seriously faint in the heat. I don't know how they do it with all their gear on their backs and guns on their chests. You have to be very, very fit (and young) to be a soldier. Basically.

We must have driven for five hours. One man, a soldier-medic whom the others called LB, leant out the back at one point to throw up. My spine was rattled by the lurching journey and nobody really said much, the exchange of cigarettes and fat Zippo lighters aside. Hunter, who I'd considered my guide, was obviously a driver and navigation man and was upfront in one of the other vehicles with the young Iraqi translator who was risking his life for a pittance that might get him to America one day.

'Do you know who actually survived the ambush?' I asked them.

'One Bonnita Hernandez,' LB told me. 'Don't know her. Possibly one or two others though they may have died already.' That was not what I wanted to hear. So far I had done a pretty good job of pretending Eden was alive. It was getting harder every minute.

I tried to do a bit of interviewing. Find out what they thought about everything. Salt of the earth vox pops again. 'I wanna get in there and I wanna get dirty. Take revenge for nine eleven,' a bloke I couldn't see

186

shouted. No matter that there was no discernible connection. But he soon got a chance to get in there.

We got underway so fast that I ended up worrying more about keeping myself alive than wondering whether or not Eden had managed the same thing. LB was put in charge of looking after me, which seemed to mean either dragging me around by the wrist or sort of pushing me forward with his chest. The communication was excellent and despite the pitch dark everyone seemed to know which way to run, who to shout at and what to fire at whom. It's easy to describe the technicalities of this kind of mission, but the unbelievable terror of death when the guns start firing and things start burning is impossible to make real. Because it doesn't feel real even when you're there. I think my brain just sort of deletes it.

We stopped outside a group of low buildings where a few fluorescent strips gave out a dull light. All the soldiers jumped out of the vehicles and started moving towards the buildings, crouched low, scanning the air with their weapons. We had created a blaze of light that was directed at what looked to me to be some kind of official complex. There was no resistance. Not yet.

'Third door on the right, ground floor,' LB said to me, from behind his goggles, just before he was shot in the shoulder. I know it sounds ridiculous and sudden but that's what happens. Somebody says something to you and then they just drop to the ground, screaming. One of the thousands of ear-bursting bangs had made contact with LB. Happens all the time. Someone had fired from the first and highest floor. I actually saw his shadow come to the window but it was all too fast for anyone to get him properly in their sights before he fired himself. But once he had, he was dead. Even before LB hit the ground. In less than five seconds the whole building was under obliterating attack. And I had seen Eden. I may be mad, I may have been hallucinating, but I could have sworn I saw his shape move behind the glare of one of the downstairs explosions.

Someone yelled, 'Come on!' to the paramedics who rushed behind the rest of them carrying two stretchers. I heard the chok-chok-chok of a helicopter and saw that we were being protected from above. Or was this thing landing?

All the downstairs windows had been smashed by automatic fire and the sky was alight with flares and flames from inside. It is amazing how fast you can breathe and how hard your heart can pound without you dying.

'We're going in,' I heard Hunter's voice say through the chaos.

I knelt on the floor with LB, shouting for help.

'Man down!' I yelled and LB groaned.

'I'm fine,' he said. 'Really. Fine.'

He wasn't though. His body had started to spasm and he was foaming at the mouth. A young woman in fatigues, a combat lifesaver, leapt out of the ambulance and injected LB with something. You have to be quick. If you don't save them in the first hour, the golden hour, you don't save them at all.

'You take his shoulders, OK?' she instructed me, grabbing his feet. This seemed somewhat unfair to me but this perhaps wasn't the place for getting shitty. We dragged him over to the ambulance thing in what felt like a hail of bullets but actually we were set back a bit from the firefight and it was almost quiet over here near what smelt like a ditch.

'Is he going to make it?' I asked her.

Inside, it looked like America. Clean, white and sterile with masses of very hi-tech life-saving equipment already being brought into play by an expert team.

'Sure, it went straight through him. ABC! CCT! DCAP – BTLS!' she shouted incomprehensibly.

Was that a good thing? I knew though, if honest, that it must be better than it getting stuck inside.

I staggered out to watch the amazing display that seemed to be concluding before my eyes. The medics had two people on stretchers and were surrounded by four soldiers each, all of whom turned occasionally to open fire back towards the buildings. The noise was incredible, every crackle of gunfire almost deafening. The helicopter landed in what might have been a parking lot and the rescued parties were rushed towards it.

'Hey! Hey! Eden! Wait!' I screamed, running towards the Black Hawk whose enormous blades were blowing us all backwards. Was he there? Had they got him? I wished somebody would tell me something. I was forgetting to doubt anything in the certainty of crisis.

'Please! Let me go with them,' I was shouting, to anyone who would or could listen. Maybe the guns were quiet now, but with the helicopter and all the Humvees starting up again it was hard to tell.

'Climb on, lady,' a butch bloke leaning out of the helicopter said to me, and he grabbed my forearms and dragged me, legs flailing, on board just as the thing actually left the ground. Inside, Eden and Bonnita lay unconscious on stretchers, attended to by four men in white coats and flak jackets. He was there. He was going to be OK. I had seen his hand hanging over the side of the green khaki bed.

The noise of take-off was just astonishing, as was the size of the thing. We could have rescued all kinds of people in this monster. It was space age. Nothing like the rickety old open-sided machines you get in African wars, people hopping on and off, firing handguns out of the doors. This probably had a cruise missile capacity.

I elbowed someone out of the way, hurting my elbow, and I went to kneel by the man who must be Eden. 'Is he alive? Is he OK? Oh God. Oh God,' I muttered madly. You sort of forget about dignity when the chips are down. I held his hand and kissed it. I pressed it to my cheek and realised that it was not his hand. Too bony. Fingers too long. I screamed.

'It's not him!'

'Ma'am. We have not yet made a full assessment of their injuries. It

189

looks like they have been severely mistreated but they are both going to make it,' said a serious-faced bloke called Hirsch. Must have been twenty-two if he was a day.

'I said it's not fucking him. It's not him! We've got to go back!' I had to shout so loud to be heard in this thing that my lungs hurt.

'We brought out the only people we found, ma'am. I'm sorry,' Hirsch told me.

OK, this was urgent.

'I saw him. He's in there. We have to go back.'

Hirsch lurched towards the cockpit and came back shaking his head. 'I'm sorry.'

I shoved Hirsch aside and went to the cockpit myself. Falling twice on the way, ripping the headphones off a teenaged girl who was flying the helicopter and screaming in her ear, 'Go back. There is a British journalist in there. We have to go back. If we leave him and he survives there will be no good stories to come out of this. I know he is in there.'

'If you would step back and calm down!' the girl shouted. I threw my hands up and carried on staring at her expectantly.

'Take your seat, Miss Zanetti,' she said again, but the look in her eyes told me she would try something.

And thirty seconds later I felt the machine turn round. God, I'd better be right. If it wasn't him I was toast. Two men lying on the floor sent out covering fire while we landed. This time they knew we were coming and they weren't having any of it. Two boys in heavy camouflage jumped out of the copter and started crawling through the dirt towards the building, most of which was now on fire.

I jumped down after them, falling and getting a face full of dust. Hirsch jumped on top of me. He lay there pinning my arms to the ground, the filth swirling around us under the deafening whir of the blades.

'Don't even think about it,' he yelled into my ear. He was hurting my arms. With an enormous effort I rolled over and shoved him off, crouching down to follow the two soldiers who had taken the lead.

In the obscurity of the smoke and flames we had let loose twenty minutes earlier we managed to creep round to the back of the building. Every now and then one of them would wave a big gun at me to fuck off and go back. I didn't. The first boy, unnecessarily in my view, used the butt of his semi-automatic to smash a window and he dived through. The second one followed him and I realised I was going to have to do the same. Gracelessly, and cutting my wrist on my way, I hauled my arse up through the broken glass and ran after my leaders across some kind of waiting area. Saddam Hussein smiled down at me. Well, he could fuck off. We ran down a corridor kicking doors open on both sides and spanning the area with weapons as we went (well, not me actually). I was covered in soot and dirt from head to toe, my wrist was bleeding badly now and I was gasping so much I thought I might inhale too much smoke and pass out. I had twisted my ankle in the jump, I now realised. Fuck it. He's not here.

We went into a storage room of some kind. There were some chemicals in glass bottles beginning to burn in the corner. The bottles exploded and flames shot around the room as the fire spread. The boys, weighed down by helmets and smoke gear and guns, started kicking the cupboards open. One of them had people in it.

'Eden Jones?' shouted the first boy like Darth Vader through his mask.

Oh, for Christ's sake, he's not in a sodding cupboard, I thought. Somebody was, though. A man wandered out, dazed and mad, accepting his imminent fate. It didn't come. The soldiers shoved him out of the way and carried on shouting for Eden.

'He's not here, lady,' one of them turned to yell at me.

'He fucking is,' I screamed. I was coughing badly now. There was something chemical burning. I threw my head back. 'Eeeeeeeden!'

191

It felt like it might end up being my last breath. But I heard an answer. I was sure I heard someone say, 'Faith.'

'Did you hear that?' I asked the soldiers.

'What? Didn't hear a thing.'

'Kick those cupboards down,' I said, hunched over with coughing. I pointed at the cupboards not yet kicked in. To my amazement they obeyed me. Well, not so amazing maybe. Kicking things down is, after all, their forte.

Out of the smoke and the stench and the dust and the pandemonium, Eden Jones emerged with wild eyes, filthy and determined. I grinned.

'I'm not leaving without these people,' he screamed, holding the wrists of two Iraqi doctors or nurses and raising his arms as though they had all won a prize. The Iraqis looked terrified. There were another five of them in there. The boys looked at each other and took a call. One of them hit Eden over the head with his gun, the other one caught him as he fell and, requisitioning me to grab the unconscious Eden under the other shoulder, we hauled him away into the night. Me breaking my fucking back and bleeding from the wrist, and one guy covering us as we hobbled to the helicopter.

'That was a motherfucking stupid thing you did,' Hirsch told me when I had clambered back in. I can't deny that the two soldiers (Jonas and Dean, it turned out) slapped hands in a high five.

'Shut up and bandage my wrist,' I hissed and slumped quietly down into my seat. I even put my seat belt on. I was too shattered to speak or move. I couldn't believe we'd done it. But, I thought as we rose up into the air again, I'm alive. And so is Eden. We'd got them. Mission success-fully accomplished. Beautiful Bonnita rescued from the horrors of capture by Iraqi forces. I could write my piece now. Joshua Klein wouldn't try to stop me, because of course I had decided to file even if the mission had been a failure. There we are. I hadn't thought about the man for hours and hours and that, let's face it, is why we all do the job we do. If you need to escape from yourself, go on a very dangerous army mission and you will forget, for a time, whatever it is you might have thought you needed to worry about. Survival instinct is a very good emotion block. I find.

'Anyone have any idea of the body count?' I asked, wondering if Joshua had known perfectly well that Eden was alive, but nervous in case we killed him in the rescue. Then he could tell me the Iraqis had killed him or something.

A burly man sitting at the side of the helicopter against the dark green camouflage paint of the door shrugged. I recognised him from the Humvee. The killed and wounded eventually go up on the Defense Department website.

'Not more'n twenty,' he said. 'I reckon.' He told me the Israeli army were all for bulldozing after a raid, but that they, the Americans, didn't have anything to hide. Oh good.

Eden twitched and mumbled something. He, Bonnita and whoever the hell the other bloke was were now safely strapped to their stretchers. I could have sworn he said, 'Faith.'

I unhooked myself from my station ('Ma'am. Ma'am? Could you take your seat please, ma'am.') and staggered over to him in the dark.

'I'm here,' I shouted at full pitch, unromantically but necessarily. 'Eden! I'm here.'

'He's out cold,' Hirsch shouted, and I had the distinct feeling that they had now been heavily doped, never mind the smack in the skull. I imagined they would probably be grateful.

I felt the machine falling out of the air after about an hour of flying. By now I had been handed a printout done on board that gave the details of the location of the rescue (a disused school on the outskirts of Tikrit), the number of Iraqi casualties (eleven), and all the other things that would be condensed into a first paragraph. There was also a disturbing list of

Bonnita's injuries (including the traces of torture) and those of a man who turned out to be Iraqi but in some way on the Allies' side. Nothing about Eden. This was an army rescue and the television news pieces tomorrow would probably end with the line, 'Also rescued was British journalist Eden Jones.' This after a good twenty minutes of maundering on about Bonnita. I already knew that this was going to be the feelgood story that would change public opinion and get the world on side. You had to be thankful that Bonnita was a girl. And from what I could see she looked stunning. Get her army graduation photo (must call pictures in London and have them get on it) and we were made. All a very, very slick operation.

It always amazes me that survival stories amid appalling carnage are effective and are so unashamedly upbeat. Child rescued from rubble in earthquake that killed five thousand. People love it. It is treated like a glimmer of hope in the despair, but really you might reasonably expect the despair to be the main thing. In this case one measly survivor in a division of twenty. Plus Eden. How had he made it when they didn't? Why was Bonnita seized instead of shot? I was desperate to know.

We landed in the gardens of an astonishingly ornate Mesopotamian-style palace.

'Uday's,' Hirsch told me, as the blades finally stopped whirring and the world pulled into some kind of focus.

'Wow,' I said. There were some big tents on the lawn and Eden, Bonnita and their friend were taken off towards them in the dark, a huge team of medical staff having met the stretchers off the helicopter with drip stands and blankets. I wanted to follow but a petite blonde woman who introduced herself as Sergeant Skvorecky had already pounced on me.

'Hi. Good to meet you. Come this way,' she said.

'Sure. Thanks.' I nodded, now in what seemed like supreme safety, at last taking my flak jacket and helmet off.

'Heavy going in this heat.' She laughed. 'Let me take that.' She carried the jacket for me; she herself in a white shirt and khaki trousers. We walked into the palace through impossibly ornate fifty-foot-high copper doors, arched to an Islamic point. Enormous free-standing air conditioners were dotted about inside a mosaic ballroom with green onyx floors where army functionaries sat at foldaway desks, working on their laptops. Sergeant Skvorecky showed me to an empty desk with a carafe of iced water and a satellite phone perched eagerly next to the computer.

'There you go,' she said. 'Yell if you need anything.' And she stepped energetically away to leave me to break my story. First I drank all the water straight from the carafe, half of it pouring down my chin and neck. The man at the desk nearest to me laughed.

'You were on the rescue, right?' he asked. He was called Carl and would have had ginger hair if it hadn't all been shaved off.

'Right,' I said.

I phoned Tamsin in London.

'Fuck me. That's amazing,' she said and I promised to file within an hour. She said she'd get the pictures sorted out.

I waved to Sergeant Skvorecky and she skipped towards me, absolutely dying to provide me with information. Facts, figures, statistics. She had 'em all. She had the atmosphere of a human clipboard.

'A shower,' I smiled, lighting a cigarette. 'I'd love a shower.'

She laughed. 'I'm afraid we only have running water during the day. Would you settle for a swim?' she suggested and I jumped out of my seat with bounding glee. Which was good, because I almost had to run to keep up with her as she led me down a labyrinth of corridors, heavily graffitied by the occupying soldiers. Under a family mosaic of Saddam and sons someone had painted 'Cocksuckers' in red paint. Fair point.

At last we were outside. The whole palace was ablaze with army floodlights. Half of it had kind of disintegrated under the weight of a cruise missile, but the other half was all complicated brickwork and gold-topped towers. The naffness was confined to the interior decoration of the private quarters, apparently.

Anyway, most importantly, here was the glorious, turquoise, empty, submerged-lighting, Olympic-size pool. Swimming on a story is the best thing in the world. All the death and despair can be completely alleviated for as long as you are in the water. Something biblical about it. Purification and all that. I always do it. I especially remember a time I made Don McCaughrean strip and swim with me in Israel. I tore all my clothes off and jumped in off the tiled side. Some blokes perched high on the perimeter walls cheered and waved at me. Honestly, soldiers a long way from home and naked women . . .

I swam under water as far as I could and splashed about like a happy seal. I tell you what. Uday Hussein had a really nice palace. I found out later that there was a special little bunker in the grounds where he did all his seduction (this involved pointing a gun at teenage virgins and then beating them unconscious with a truncheon). If he had been a nice man, perhaps he would have found candidates queuing up to share his home with him. The riding stables and boathouse were, I heard, just down the road. This was all before he was killed, of course.

When I got out of the icy water I found a rough towel neatly folded, a pair of khaki trousers and a pressed white T-shirt. My leather jacket and boots lay next to them. Everything else appeared to have gone to the laundry tent. Not too shabby for Faith C. Zanetti.

I wrote my rescue story with the help of the espresso machine and ten cigarettes and then lay down on the canvas camp bed I had been allocated all by myself in an upstairs suite. I splashed my face in a sink that was shaped like a large scallop and went straight to sleep. Eden Jones could wait until morning. I dreamt I was chasing Joshua through London rain. In an underpass near Piccadilly I gave up and kicked the yellow tiled wall in frustration. At that he ran back towards me and kissed my face. 'Baby, don't cry,' he said. 'I just wanted to get there faster because it's raining. You know I'd never leave you.'

CHAPTER SEVENTEEN

'Ma'am?' Hirsch was saying, standing over me, his stethoscope swinging. They really expect you just to leap into life, these army types.

'Mmm hmmm,' I answered, rubbing my eyes. I sat up, bleary, a pale dawn light coming through the slits of windows, dark engraved wooden shutters closed over them.

'Mr Jones is conscious,' he said and I jumped up, suddenly as alert as required.

Sergeant Skvorecky was behind Hirsch with a printout of the *Chronicle*'s front page and my enormous Bonnita Hernandez rescue story. Not just one picture of Bonnita (in her uniform) but two. She'd been prom queen at high school last year! What more could anyone want? There she was, ludicrous hair, frosted lipstick and fright of a dress for all the world to sympathise with. At CentCom in Qatar they had already been briefed about the rescue and the whole world was buzzing with the stories. Completely without my noticing it, some footage had apparently been shot last night, possibly from the helicopter while it was on the ground, and a tiny snippet had been released for the delectation of the television people. Whichever way you looked at it, this was huge, and I had been the only journalist there. Well, properly conscious at any rate. LB, who had been shot right in front of me, for fuck's sake, was fine, nobody else had even sustained an injury and the snail was basically in his shell. Not only this but I had had a whole night's sleep, more or less, a refreshing swim and Eden Jones was awake. I could almost have been described as being in a good mood, despite having had my heart trampled all over by some poncy bloody Savile Row shoes. (Bastard!)

The combat support hospital was a very long way away and Uday's palace was even cooler than it had looked last night. Absolutely no expense whatsoever spared. A whole room dedicated solely to the storage of McCulloch chain saws, a stone reproduction of the Venus de Milo, and corridors guarded by life-size porcelain leopards. Skvorecky pointed out the vast peach-coloured sunken jacuzzi baths (three in a row, free-standing in a sixty-foot-square bathroom), and the fully equipped bowling alley parallel to the ballroom. Outside and before the hospital was 'the pen'. People were held there before being interrogated by the counter-intelligence men, 'the CI guys'. It's hot in the pen. They usually talk.

Eden was sitting up in bed drinking milky tea, a fan aimed at his bed, a drip in his arm and a preposterous white nightie on that looked worryingly as though it might be backless, you know how they are. I mean, admittedly the equipment had come on a bit since MASH, but that was the basic scene. He was not expecting me. In fact he looked appalled to see me.

'What the hell are you doing here, Faith? You join the US Army or what?' he pretty much snapped.

'Listen, sweetheart,' I said, walking towards his bed across a canvas floor, 'I single-handedly rescued you from the clutches of evil.' I sat down next to him on a folding chair. There was no sign of Hernandez. 'Where's Hernandez?' I asked, looking around.

'That's what I'd like to know,' he said. There were about ten beds in here, Eden and then a few boys suffering from heat exhaustion or something uncombat-related like that. No bandages or drips and all of them sitting up reasonably happy, reading *People* magazine and old copies of *Time*. Eden was the only patient without a tattoo.

Klein had kissed my tattoo. He laughed and traced it with his finger. I have Elvis's signature tattooed on my right-hand pelvic bone. I once had to write a piece about Graceland and got a bit overcome. There is a salon in Memphis which specialises in Elvis tattoos. I like mine, though it's going a bit green. 'He'd have been about your age,' I said.

'Thanks.' Klein laughed.

'When did you wake up?' I asked Eden, reading what was in his drip bag. Sugar and salt.

He put his tea down on his steel table. 'When did I go to fucking sleep more like? I'm lying in bed and suddenly world war three breaks out. Then someone hits me on the head with an assault rifle and gives me a general anaesthetic. I had a sprained ankle, for fuck's sake. A general anaesthetic!' he shouted, for Hirsch's benefit apparently. 'Bonnie's screaming because she doesn't want to be moved – she got some internal bruising – and they jab a needle into her arm and haul her outside. Nobody knows what's going on. I dragged some people into the cupboard with me. They shot Dr Harmal in the fucking head, Faith. He was just standing there,' Eden wailed. Bonnie, huh.

'Well, you're OK now.' I sighed. I couldn't believe he was complaining about being safe and well in the lovely Palace of Eternal Vulgarity. 'Here. Look at my piece.' I handed him the printout and he scowled down at it, reading every word with increasing rage. He looked like a cartoon character whose face swells up all red and steam puffs out of his ears.

Hirsch came over. 'How are we doing here, Mr Jones?' he asked, flipping through his notepad.

'I'M FINE!' Eden shouted, and Hirsch, who was clean-shaven and fragrant as though he hadn't been up all night, smiled and patted Eden's shoulder before meandering away to polish his instruments or whatever.

'Jesus, what is with you?' I asked Eden, beginning to feel a bit exasperated by his total lack of gratitude at being rescued, presumably at amazing expense to the American taxpayer, and, of course, his lack of pleasure at seeing me.

He stared at me and ripped my article in two, throwing the pieces to the floor.

'This is a total fucking pile of shit, Faith,' he said. 'Did you actually come on the rescue?'

OK, now I was seriously pissed off. The heat was seeping into the hospital tent from outside and I could feel a sweat breaking. Didn't he see me there! I saved his life.

'Yes, I bloody did. It was fucking dangerous. Everyone's been so worried about you. We thought you were dead. Then . . . well, I got the chance to come, and it was incredibly slick. Had you both out in no time. WHAT are you complaining about?' I had stood up now to make my point, and the other patients were staring at me.

'Well, it amazes me that if you were inside the hospital while all those idiots were shooting everyone, you didn't notice that nobody was armed or that Bonnie and I had been very well looked after,' he hissed, as slowly, loudly and clearly as he could. I had never seen Eden in a righteous rage before. It was quite a spectacle.

'What hospital?' I asked, feeling more than a little nervous now.

'The hospital in which Bonnie and I were being treated,' he said, looking at me with total hatred. 'Faith. Were you inside the hospital?'

He had me there. Shit. I had known it was something official. Some kind of complex. It hadn't occurred to me for a moment that it was a hospital. Disused school, didn't they say? I had stayed outside with LB for the first bit. Well, I'd had to, hadn't I?

'Not at first, I wasn't. A kid got shot by a sniper and I stayed outside with him. By the time we came back for you it wasn't all that recognisable,' I said quietly.

'A sniper, you reckon? Hardly likely.' Eden groaned.

He could see the uncertainty in my face and calmed down, aware that he could get me on side, I suppose.

'I came round and I was here, Bonnie gone fuck knows where. Did they bring us both in on the same helicopter?' he asked, getting excited. I felt shattered. If there was something wrong with this story I was going to look a complete idiot. Taken in by the American army and fed a line. Bollocks. I could already smell the mendacity. Eden didn't make stuff up.

'Yes,' I told him. 'They brought her in here with you. Must have moved her in the night. She's probably in some clearing centre in Virginia by now.' Then something awful occurred to me. There's a film with Tom Cruise in it where he joins a law firm and they turn out to be part of the Mafia and he begins to realise that everyone he trusts is in on it and there's no escape. My blood seemed to chill at the possibility that I might be Tom, being fed lies by smiling people like Sergeant Skvorecky and the frankly quite handsome Dr Hirsch.

'Listen. They examined you both on the helicopter and gave me a report on Hernandez's injuries. They said she'd been tortured. Is that possible?' I asked him.

His entirely mirthless laughter did not bode well. 'Fuck me,' he said, shaking his head. 'THE LENGTHS THESE PEOPLE WILL GO TO.' He threw his arms up in amazement.

'Eden, stop it. Listen. I filed that piece. It's in today. It's big news. Her high school fucking prom picture is being beamed all over the world. Talk to me,' I whispered, already feeling we had something to hide, wanting to get Eden out of here before they gave him another general anaesthetic or some arsenic.

'OK, here's the deal,' Eden said, leaning towards me in his ridiculous nightie, his breath smelling of minty toothpaste and tea. 'Basically we got lost. Seriously. Lost. You know the sandstorm that night? Well, all the equipment got fucked somehow and we were driving through an untaken bit of Tikrit in this whole fucking convoy. Nobody was telling me anything but I could feel they were all really nervous. Anyway, I'd kind of got to know Bonnita . . .' He coughed.

'Oh, you have to be joking!' I said, smiling at him almost in admiration. 'You were only with them about twenty-five seconds.'

'Do you want to hear this story or not?'

'I don't know now.'

'OK, listen. She was, is, pretty junior. She was just working the phones and the navigation stuff basically. Anyway, it had all got fairly intense and we were lost in this shithole. So I said to her, "Are we lost?" and she nods at me. She looked really scared and she told me we might get ambushed.' He went completely silent and even smiled when Hirsch came and put a paper cup in front of him, little red pills rattling in the bottom. 'Thanks, doc,' he said.

'Jesus. Go on,' I told him when Hirsch had gone.

'Well, it was hot in this thing,' he said.

'What thing?'

'We were in an armoured personnel carrier and I hate being trapped like that in the heat and I just had this vision of us burning alive in there. I kind of felt . . . Well, I don't know, but something made me jump,' he said, nodding to himself in amazement at his own prescience.

'You jumped out of an armoured personnel carrier?'

'We jumped out.' He smiled.

'You jumped out of an armoured personnel carrier in the middle of Tikrit with Bonnita Hernandez?' I shook my head, laughing. Stunned.

'Uh-huh,' Eden confirmed.

'And the other people in the vehicle?'

'Well, they were fairly surprised. Shouted at us a lot. What were they going to do?'

I couldn't stop laughing. It was so perfect. 'And then?'

'We dived into the nearest doorway and this bloke opened the door and took us in. Bonnie's having a total hysterical fit because she thinks she's going to get court martialled for deserting. This guy, Rashid, spoke English, was an orderly at the hospital just out of town. "Was" being the operative fucking word. He dragged us inside and I thought we were toast, but then he's like giving us iced water and looking at our injuries. Bonnie really hurt herself jumping down and I fucked up my foot. So, he says we should wait until night and he'll take us to hospital in his uncle's car. That's when we heard the attack on the convoy happening. Everyone died.'

'Oh Christ,' I breathed. And what I wondered was this: how much did Joshua Klein know about this? I begged myself to believe that as far as he was concerned Eden and Hernandez had been captured and needed rescuing. I begged myself to believe it. 'But do you think she might have had marks on her that *looked* like torture?' I tried.

'Faith, don't bother. If you've been whipped with electric cables, it shows. She was hurt, but any army doctor is trained to know what torture looks like. Fuck. *We* know what torture looks like.' He went all loud again now. 'THEY JUST NEEDED A FACE-SAVING OPER-ATION TO TAKE THE WORLD'S MIND OFF THEM LOSING A WHOLE FUCKING UNIT THROUGH INCOMPETENCE,' he shouted.

A bloke playing patience on his bedspread looked up.

'Any chance of shutting the fuck up, friend?' he asked, eyebrows knitted. He was naked to the waist, a vast dragon tattoo occupying most of his back.

203

'Slim,' Eden sneered and picked up his teacup in impotent rage. His foot was plastered and hanging in traction. It occurred to me now that perhaps this wasn't necessary. Perhaps they'd done it to stop him moving.

'Where's Bonnita?' I yelled over to Hirsch.

He smiled indulgently (cute). 'She was flown home last night. Despite your friend here's beliefs, she was not very well. Shouldn't think she'll be up and about for a while now,' he said.

'Not if you lot can help it,' Eden muttered.

It was already fairly worrying but then it went and got worse.

'And the Iraqi bloke?' I asked Eden.

'Dunno. Stuffed him in some Iraqi hospital by now I should think. He was just an orderly at the hospital. Must have given them the tip-off. Anyway, how did you get in on the rescue party?' he asked. 'Your friend Klein?'

'No,' I lied. 'Why?'

'Because he's a creep. Because he fed you the Jamal thing and the chemical weapons and you believe everything he says because you've fallen "in love",' he mocked. It was Eden, not me, who put 'in love' in nasty sneery inverted commas.

I stood up. 'Fuck you,' I said. 'It's you who fucked up with the gas explosion. Not me. I happened to have the contact who knew the truth. And if you're jealous about the weapons lab, well, tough shit.'

Eden rolled his eyes. 'There was zero evidence in the weapons lab and you know it. It was a one-man deliberate feed and you just swallowed every fucking line. You didn't even try and put any independent corroboration in your piece, Faith. Not even a pretence at it.'

I leant forward to punch him in the head, but it didn't seem like the location for it. 'Don't let the jealousy consume you, Jones,' I said, and walked out of the tent into the blinding heat of Uday Hussein's front lawn. Ungrateful arsehole.

*　　*　　*

204

I badgered Skvorecky for half an hour before she called through to get someone to take me back to Baghdad. In the end it was Hunter again and I was pleased to see him. I was standing out by these insane electric security gates when he pulled up in his nice reassuring Humvee.

'Hunter! Hey!' I said, smiling.

'Ma'am.' He nodded.

'Oooh, tell us another.' I grinned at him, and climbed in.

Things had obviously gone the Allies' way, because now little groups of children were waving wildly at us, all white robes and knotty hair. An old man in a crocheted cap held up a two hundred and fifty dinar note and tore it in half, ripping Saddam Hussein's face in two. I saw a billboard of Saddam with an American flag draped over it. Makeshift street markets had started up again – old women laying out all their cutlery on a blanket by the side of the road, old men with a collection of plugs, wires and adaptors, and younger people with bunches of flowers (hmm, handy) and a few vegetables. We drove through the Al Mansour district and nobody was bothering to crouch behind the sandbags. There had been a big leaflet drop here and the streets were littered with the 'This time we won't abandon you' fliers, the friendly Allied message in swirling Arabic. I wondered if that would prove to be true. Even the double-decker buses had started running again. Hunter was not devastatingly forthcoming on the subject of the Bonnie rescue.

'We're feeling pretty upbeat about it,' was all I could get out of him. I bet they were.

At the Corona I kissed him on the cheek and hopped out.

'Thanks for the ride!' I waved, and felt almost as if I was coming home.

Apparently overnight the hotel lobby had become a normal place. Hardly a sign of the carnage of the other day or all the ministry stooges who had hung around so menacingly at the beginning. Don was sitting in front of the television, watching the rescue footage on CNN and drinking a beer. Both these things – foreign news channel in public place plus alcoholic beverage – were signs that Saddam was on his way out.

'Eff Zed!' he said, getting to his feet, delighted. 'Fuck me. You must have been hot as a—'

I stopped him.

'I was,' I said. 'I really was.'

He slapped me hard between my shoulder blades, a sign of admission that I'd been right about Eden and that he should have known, should have had faith in me. 'Hey. Me and Grant did a brilliant piece yesterday. All these families have just, like, moved into the Defence Ministry. Brilliant. They've got these signs up – "House. No guns. Mother, Father, Baby, Wife." Khalid and Nawal this couple were called. Brilliant.'

'Cool,' I said.

'Carly made it back to London. She's in St Thomas's. They think she'll walk.'

So Klein had somehow fulfilled his promise to Fernando and got her on a medical plane home.

'God, that's great.'

'So, when's Jonesey coming back?' he said, offering me a cigarette.

'Ta,' I said. 'Dunno. Don't care. See you later.'

I was about to go over to the lift, with the intention of beating Joshua Klein's door down and kicking the shit out of him, for all kinds of reasons, when Don called me back. He looked at me a bit shyly and drew his breath in.

'Faithy, I wanted to tell you something,' he said.

I grinned, knowing what it was.

'Yes, Don?' I said.

'Faithy. Me and Irochka are getting married. Back home in a couple of months. When all this is over. I hope you're not too . . . you know, upset.'

I laughed. 'No, Don, darling. I'll get over it. Hey, congratulations.' I put my arms round his big neck and kissed him on the cheek. He smelt of sweat and fags and beer.

'Incidentally, Eff Zed. What the fuck are you wearing?'

I walked away again. 'I'm on side now, Don,' I said, and felt ashamed of my khakis.

I had pressed the big green up button when he beckoned me back a second time.

'Forgot to mention it, what with all the excitement. That nice weapons inspector bloke, Klein, is it? Went back to Washington. Asked me to give you this.' He said, fumbling about in his trouser pocket and brought out a crumpled note.

'I didn't read it or anything,' he said, hanging his head. 'Sorry. It's got a bit . . .' He tried to straighten it but I snatched it away.

'Thanks,' I said, and slumped down into a chair behind McCaughrean's coffee table. Karim ran over with a big smile and a shot of vodka for me in a proper glass. Times were changing.

'Thanks, habibi,' I said and he grinned. Even his white jacket looked cleaner, somehow. And there was a woman on reception. A busty, red-lipsticked type with a hairdo.

I unfolded the slip of paper. Typed again.

Dear Faith,

I was glad to hear that your mission was successful and that your friend is in excellent health. I am sorry if I have failed you in other ways and I am sure that my returning to the States will seem like a bit of a cop-out to you, but I feel it is the best thing to do at this time. I hope you understand.

This time he couldn't even bring himself to the emotional intensity of signing his fucking name. And no, I did not understand. And why did he keep dumping me when I wasn't even asking for anything? It was as though he just wanted to humiliate me. I already knew I was dumped, he didn't have to take it any further, trample me into the ground any harder.

I called the Sheraton and asked for Daniel Klein. He had, what a shocker, checked out that morning.

'You all right, Faithy?' Don asked.

'Yeah.' I nodded. 'Ever seen *La Traviata*?'

'My favourite Verdi opera,' he said. 'Why?'

'No reason,' I said. 'It's really nothing.'

Nothing at all.

CHAPTER EIGHTEEN

So basically I was relieved when Tamsin phoned to transfer me to CentCom in Qatar. Everyone else was dying to get out of there – trapped in the middle of the desert at an eternal press conference like some kind of Sartrian vision of hell. It was some prefab huts outside a Dohar industrial estate where people were just being drip fed every word of the US and UK military perspective. Not much to laugh at but personally I'd have gone anywhere to get out of Baghdad. Even the Blogger, whose entries on his website had been fairly perky while I'd been busy rescuing people, was now getting a bit downhearted about the nutters showing up in Baghdad. All sorts of wannabes returning from abroad in the hope of running the country. And the suicide bombing maniacs trying to kill Americans. He said he was scared of being murdered himself since it is 'halal' to kill anyone who associates with the infidel. Poor fucker.

This had not been a good trip. I had no particular desire to think about it, but Eden had been right about that mobile weapons lab. It hadn't even occurred to me to question Klein and not only because I had assumed this was his job and why would he lie about it. But also because we were dancing around our sexual attraction even while a tank was trying to blast us to smithereens.

And never mind Bonnita Hernandez, Eden's version (they had gone in to get their woman back, knowing she was alive, knowing she was a deserter who needed keeping under wraps, knowing also that it could be pulled off as a big positive publicity coup) was quite obviously true, though it was still possible (oh, please, please) that at least the Americans hadn't known the place was a hospital and had genuinely believed that Eden and Bonnie had been captured and taken there. But even in my own mind, pacing up and down my room, throwing stuff into my suit-case (where the fuck was my washbag?), this didn't ring very true. Their maps of Iraq looked pretty good to me on the Humvee screen and things like hospitals and government buildings must have been clearly marked. And then there was the claim that she'd been tortured which had now been elaborated on in the US.

The last news I'd seen had her in Virginia (no surprises there – she'd be debriefed to death) with all kinds of injuries and – weh hey – amnesia. So, with any luck she'd have forgotten Eden Jones and the fact that she basically deserted at the first sign of danger. Obviously, I was going to have to do this story, but I wanted to talk to Klein first. As long as Eden was completely sure of his version I could just run it as a first-person account from him. His paper was so fucking pleased about the rescue that they splashed Bonnita Hernandez-style mawkishness all over their front page for two days. I wasn't at all sure they'd want his refutation. If we ever made up, perhaps we'd do the story together. I ought to have phoned to find out where he'd be going and when. Sod him though. Let him rot.

In the meantime, I was on my way to Qatar.

It was strange to be back at Saddam International, now Baghdad International Airport, with my bag on my shoulder. Having been such a quagmire of officialdom, it was now a runway with a huge heap of rubble at one end where all the buildings had been. No passports or check-in or baggage carousels (not that I ever have anything but hand luggage – who needs the hassle?). No cups of Turkish coffee or crowds of heavily scented taxi drivers. Grant Bradford, who appeared to be covering the whole of the war on Iraq single-handedly, was coming with me on some sort of semi-military flight into Qatar. Then we'd be bussed to CentCom. I was going to replace Mary Polanski who'd lost her mind with boredom and begged to be brought home. 'I'll do home news. Features. Anything,' she'd screamed and Tamsin promised she'd ask me if I'd stand in for a week. She was expecting me to resign or something rather than go, but I was desperate.

All the way to Qatar I listened to Grant going on about his time with the Brits up near Basra.

'Great blokes,' he kept saying, sort of to himself. 'Great blokes.' I got the feeling he'd liked to have been a soldier.

'Were they, Grant?' I'd occasionally say.

'Yup. Really great. Fusiliers built a bloody water pipeline in four days.'

They had had a helmets-off, berets-on policy going, trying to get on with the locals. This had meant a lot of schtick from the Yanks who basically thought they were poofs nancing about with feather boas and socialising while they tried to win the war with actual weapons rather than a handshake. 'Haven't got a fucking clue,' was Grant's verdict on the Americans.

No peanuts on this flight, that's for sure, so I tried to read a report I'd been sent about this dossier Blair had gone to war on. Big news in England where for some reason the whole war had been pinned on the genuineness or otherwise of a document cataloguing Saddam's biological weapons capabilities. Bloody hell, everyone knows he's been gassing Kurds left right and centre. Who cares if a student wrote the dossier? I was about to fall asleep with the mind-numbing tedium of the thing (isn't this bloody home news anyway?) when Joshua Klein's card slid out from between the pages.

I stared at it, feeling that some sense could be made of it if I could only decipher it. Just his name, swirling and embossed, made my insides lurch in lust and anger and despair. And just possibly love if he'd only offer some back (bastard!). Joshua F. Klein, US Government Research. Research into what? How to screw people over as effectively as possible? Research into how to be a total arsehole? If it was either of these he was extremely good at his job. There was a phone number and an email address.

CHAPTER NINETEEN

Bumpy landing in Qatar and I could feel the heat through the plane even with air conditioning on. We were still rattling along the runway when I made the first of a million calls to Josh Klein's mobile phone.

'You have reached the phone of Joshua Klein. Please leave a message.' So I did. After all, I had obeyed the man in every particular so far.

'Josh, hi, it's Faith. I'd like to talk to you. Please call me back on this number.'

Grant chortled.

'Phoning your boyfriend, Zanetti?'

'Fuck off, Bradford,' I told him and dialled the number again in case Klein had heard it ringing but not got to it in time. This time I said, 'Me again. Call me. I need to hear your voice.'

I hung up and clamped my hand to my mouth. Was that true? Shit. Shit. Shit.

Grant was shaking with laughter. 'Faith Zanetti in love,' he spluttered. 'Bradford,' I said. 'Mention this to anyone and I'll chop your plums off.' He wiped the tears from his eyes. 'I bet you will.' He beamed.

We juddered to a halt and the pilot said, 'OK, people. This is Qatar. Get off my plane.'

Hmm. Not exactly BA. I was dying for a drink.

A little white bus was waiting for us at the bottom of the steps under the aircraft's roaring, stinking engines. The heat was appalling and around the edges of the airport I could see men in white robes and headdresses, neat palm trees and banks of gleaming Mercedes. Qatar, it was clear, is on the affluent side.

'Hello, darling,' Grant said to the pretty black soldier in a soft khaki cap who was driving us to CentCom. To the Coalition Media Centre.

'Sir.' She nodded, without a smile. I doubted Bradford was her type. Ginger-haired, freckled, 45-year-old alcoholic with a preference for strippers. I think he was rebelling against his ex-wife who was a venture capitalist with a flat chest and short back and sides. Like she cares who he's sleeping with now. She can't possibly need the alimony she makes him pay and was probably only too glad to be shot of him. A photographer he was having a thing with in Rwanda accidentally called him at home. He'd told her he lived with his sister and a tricky misunderstanding ensued. It concluded, according to Grant, with his wife saying, 'Oh, the cunt.' She then sent him a text message asking for a divorce. He was remorseful and devastated. She was steadfast. He is now on his tenth table dancer. He writes mournful letters to his kids on paper napkins from the bar when he's pissed.

We drove along pristine tarmacked and almost entirely deserted motorways, through sparkling toll booths and past low creamy palaces with guards outside. The odd brand new, air-conditioned (usually metallic pea-green) Mercedes swooshed past us, driven, invariably, by a man in a white headdress with a black rope round it.

'How're you finding Qatar?' Grant asked Private Wendell. I kicked him.

'A little on the warm side, thank you, sir,' she said, as though he had asked her name, age and rank, almost shouting the 'sir'.

'Mmmm. Most illuminating,' he muttered and I kicked him again.

We hadn't seen a building for twenty minutes by the time we pulled up in the sweltering sand at Central Command. It had been slapped up especially for the purpose of briefing the press during the war and was basically an enormous warehouse in the desert with something passing for a hotel Sellotaped to the side of it.

'Welcome,' said Private Wendell, turning off her engine. We jumped down into the sand and squinted around. She handed us both some ID to hang round our necks.

'What's your first name, Wendell?' Grant begged as she walked away, leaving us to fend for ourselves.

'Ashanti,' she called back over her shoulder.

'Lovely!' Grant shouted, but she didn't give a shit.

Nor, to be fair, did Grant once we were inside.

'Oh, fantastic!' he said with genuine enthusiasm as we walked into the absolutely freezing chill of the colossally air-conditioned interior.

'Cold as a . . . what would Don say?' I smiled.

'Dunno.' Grant laughed. 'Cold as a polar bear's cunt?'

We giggled and walked down a brightly-lit disinfected corridor in high spirits. There was a fizzy drinks dispenser and a cigarette machine and one of those things that sends bars of chocolates and bags of crisps swirling down the end of a metal spring and out through a big hole in the bottom. There were televisions blaring all over the place and, in the main area, all the television companies in the whole world had set up little desks for their anchors, with Baghdad or war graphic backdrops slung behind them on a curtain. A Chinese American woman I vaguely recognised was having her lipstick touched up while her producer, a fat

215

girl with railway track braces and headphones clamped to her ears, shouted at her.

'Ten seconds, Lily,' she screamed, terrified of missing the link. The autocue was already rolling on the desk. 'Five seconds, Lily!'

Lily, a pro, turned to face the camera with half a second to go, beautifully made up and coifed. She smiled.

'Good afternoon, from Central Command in Qatar. I'm Lily Fang.'

The producer breathed a sigh of relief and rolled her eyes at me. Lily's backdrop was flames and an F-15. Excellent choice.

Grant found his desk, the lurid font of his tabloid glaring out at him from a little flag attached to the back of the chair. Someone was shouting down the phone, 'Look. Is Chemical Ali dead or not? It's a simple question.' Special office chairs and curved screens, headpieces for the telephone – everything to ensure that nobody filed a lawsuit when it was all over. 'Did my back in on those chairs', 'Went blind staring at that screen', 'Got whiplash using the phones all week'. No sirree. The friendliest people in the army had been billeted here and were going around chatting to the journalists, smiling whitely and generally giving all the carnage an upbeat feel. Hey, it was working on me. Love my job. Always someone trying to make you feel at home, always someone to call in the middle of the night (even if it is just the desk) and always someone worrying about you. That's quite apart from the pleasure of seeing familiar faces wherever you are all over the world. Grant was slapping hands with everyone around him. They'd put all the tabs together. There was hardly anyone western here I hadn't met before and I grinned and waved at a few. Maybe this was going to be fun.

Ooooh, and check it out. They really know how to keep us happy. Over in the far corner was, yes, you guessed it – the bar! I sidled over across the gleaming white lino and sat up on a high stool. A boy in a white apron with 'Faulks' on his name tag came up to me and smiled.

I dug the heels of my cowboy boots over the low rungs on my stool like I was in stirrups and winked at Faulks.

'Hello, darling,' I said. 'Double espresso and a vodka.'

'You want ice and lemon in that?' he asked me, already drying a glass and flicking the coffee machine on.

'What? In my espresso?' I quipped (ha ha) and he smiled dutifully.

Well, I was relatively happy. I can do these exchanges. Sometimes the peaks and fucking troughs of passion and despair can be bit wearing. How the hell do people do it? Fall in love and hope for things? I mean, you are just setting yourself right on up for disaster. And here I was. In the disaster. A textbook life error. Rule One: Do not enter into any kind of sincere or emotional engagement with anyone. Rule Two: Keep all goals and desires to a realistic minimum (i.e. 'quite fancy a coffee') in order to avoid disappointment/devastation/possible suicide. Rule Three: Be sure never to give the slightest toss about anyone ever.

Oooh. I had really fucked up. The trouble was, and I hate to admit it, I missed him. I had tasted something amazing and I wanted more. You see, usually I get what I want and I couldn't understand how this wasn't happening now. Only child syndrome, I guess. I was determined but entirely without a plan. He had taken me to the top of a mountain and shown me paradise on the other side and now I wanted to go and live there, thank you very much. Didn't he?

I turned round to see a hundred people shuffling towards some institutional swing doors with a groaning lack of enthusiasm. I raised my eyebrows at Faulks in a question.

'Two o'clock briefing,' he said. 'They do it now to time it right for breakfast news in the US.'

'Right.' I sighed. Now, there's nothing wrong with that, of course. They've got to have the briefing some time and, considering that it is sort of home news for them, you can only expect them to do it at a convenient US time. But I felt the nasty chill of cynicism sweep over me and hated the slickness of the whole thing. One of the left-wing papers ran a mad rant from a novelist the other day, which Tamsin emailed me, but one of the things she said rang true. It was about the American warplanes that the pilots had painted with teeth to look like sharks and how Disney this all was, as though nobody was really aware any more that real people were dying. No way of saying that without sounding pious, but the impressive level of organisation does make one's blood run a bit cold.

And then I saw someone I'd rather not have seen. LB, looking as lively as an otter. He was walking past the bar carrying armfuls of documents.

'LB? Hi,' I said, smiling. 'How are you?'

'I'm good, ma'am,' he answered, but he recognised me in the middle of answering and blushed deeply. 'M-much better. It really wasn't as bad as ...' He couldn't finish the sentence and he rushed off, absolutely desperate to get away from me. So when he threw up out the back of the Humvee, was he perhaps nervous about his forthcoming perform-ance as an actor not as a soldier. And had I fallen for it? Could I really have fallen for it? Wasn't there blood everywhere? God, I couldn't remember. But I had seen the sniper. Hadn't I?

I'd go to the conference, but I wanted a cigarette first, and I moved to slope back outside, dragging my crumpled packet out of my jacket pocket. Faulks the barman swept past me, an armful of paper piled up to his chin. 'I would not advise you to go out there. Some kind of demon-stration.' Hmmm. Everything, but everything was giving me a bad feeling. I didn't like this at all. I almost knew who I was going to find here.

There was no fresh air and it was so bright that it took me a couple of seconds of focusing before I properly honed in on Daniel 'Ziggy' Klein and Anita standing outside the electric gates near a kind of sentry box with a few other straggly types, holding up placards. God, but what the hell were they up to now? How had they got here? They were like a Greek chorus or something. Popping up to remind you of things you were trying not to think about. Unreal.

Daniel's sign said, 'Don't believe the spin' and Anita's said, 'US troops out of Iraq'. Their crappy looking jeep was parked next to them.

Daniel had seen me first. He looked surprised but completely elated. I was glad there was a gate keeping him out.

'Hey! Slut!' he shouted. 'You didn't think he was going to marry you, did you?'

'Fuck you, Ziggy. Go home and get a job,' I yelled back.

I went back inside and put my unlit cigarette behind my ear. The exchange had really rattled me. I didn't like that kid, and there was no point in pretending that it was his hairstyle that bothered me. The unenthusiastic cogs in my brain processed all the things I had against Ziggy Klein, whirring and creaking as they did so. Well, first there was his presence at all. There's something wrong with someone like that getting access to all this. Even given his father's grace. Then there's the politics. At first I had him down as an idiot student who didn't understand the issues. Now, though, I felt that it was perhaps I who had got the wrong end of the political stick.

Plus there was the fact that he was really just rebelling against his very establishment father and probably had no idea what the actual issues were, just that his dad was in the wrong because he's . . . well, I don't know, got a serious job or something. And that bothered me because Klein obviously had complicated family 'issues' that I didn't like knowing about. And why does Klein indulge his son's wankiness so much? And lastly there was that thing Ziggy had said, so gleefully. 'You didn't think he was going to marry you, did you?'

This got me twice. Once with the realisation that Klein had told his son he'd dumped me. And then again with the stomach-twisting admission to myself that yes, I would like to be Mrs Faith C. Klein. I NEVER thought this would happen to me.

'Ah, Mrs Klein, your usual table?'
'Why, thank you, Alfonse.'
Ugh.

CHAPTER TWENTY

I sat down at the back of the whirring auditorium we were crammed into (the American networks got the best seats up front) and I actually opened the notebook I'd been handed. Little blue biro too. All the equipment. I drew a camel and then wrote 'bastard'. It was going to be an edifying afternoon. The British Army press officer bloke came and said hello to me, a round-faced cheery type, professionally genial, who had obviously got his job because of his general air of total openness. He was a Yorkshireman, smiling and joshing.

'Zanetti,' he said. 'Got some Italian in you?'

'A great-great-grandfather, I think,' I whispered. Things seemed to be starting at the front.

'Bet you like ice cream!' he said and I laughed as required. He patted me on the shoulder, anything I can do and all that.

The serious black soldier, thin and depressed-looking, was standing at the rostrum, the stars and stripes deliberately in shot behind him and the presidential logo thing on the stand in front of him.

'Good afternoon, ladies and gentlemen,' he said.

A very ugly bald man in a velvet suit (*Rolling Stone* magazine, surely?) groaned so loudly that everyone laughed.

'Glad to hear that I'm amusing everyone already,' said Vince, and everyone stopped laughing as though to embarrass him on purpose. The atmosphere wasn't great. Agitated, tense.

He launched into an unbearably boring account of which divisions were where and who had achieved what. He made sure never to say that whole towns had been taken, but always that 'large areas have been secured'. He gave no casualty figures for either side and really not enough detail to write even the driest, most unreadable piece. After what felt like about two years and lots of yawning and sighing and rustling on our part, he said, 'Any questions?' and over a hundred people put their hands up. He peered around for a long time as though his criteria for choosing someone were extremely complex and nobody was quite fulfilling all of them. The air conditioners buzzed loudly and the camera crews shuffled about on their stepladders at the back.

'Yes,' he said, pointing at the bald bloke who had groaned.

'Spencer Ellroy, *Rolling Stone*,' he said (yes!). 'Why are we here?'

Vince sighed. 'So that we can provide you with information to the best of our ability,' he said softly, not smiling. Far from amused.

'But you won't tell us anything!' Ellroy suggested.

Vince ignored him, but one of the shifty-looking types standing in the wings took a long route round the back of the hall to get to Ellroy and whispered in his ear while Vince took another question ('Are you pleased with the progress of the war so far?' A pretty obvious American television question. Music to Vince's ears. His answer could be succinctly summed up as 'Yes'.) Ellroy left the hall accompanied by an armyish looking type in plain clothes. I didn't see him again.

I was seriously beginning to feel the CentCom torpor everyone talked about (the only danger around here was obesity) when Vince picked me. I'd forgotten I still had my hand up, I was so bored. I stood up and people had a good look at me because I was new and entertainment was thin on the ground. I waved.

'Faith Zanetti, the London *Chronicle*,' I said. 'I wanted to ask you about Bonnita Hernandez.'

At this Vince smiled. His very favourite subject.

'Is it true that Hernandez in fact deserted with her lover and was being treated for minor injuries in a Tikrit hospital when American troops went in to supposedly rescue her?' I asked.

There was an enormous silence and the sinister sideline blokes shuffled their papers, talked quietly into their mouthpieces and flicked their eyes around the room. I was relieved to see that they looked confused rather than frightened. Most of them, at least, had very clearly not known. After a long pause all the journalists burst out laughing, some of them staring at me incredulous, some of them, mostly the Arabs, actually clapping.

'To my knowledge, that was not the case, no. Private Hernandez was captured by Iraqi forces loyal to Saddam, along with British journalist Eden Jones,' he said, looking at me questioningly.

I remained standing. 'Eden Jones says he was in hospital with Hernandez and that they were being well treated when troops burst in and gave them both a general anaesthetic before removing them from the scene. He says the firefight was entirely unnecessary.'

Vince looked off to the side and one of the White House press guys came over to him with a note. Vince read it out.

'It is our understanding that the enemy fired first. We don't yet have all the information but I believe a sniper was stationed on the upper floor of the prison where the victims were being held. An American soldier was injured in an attack and a firefight then ensued,' he said. Prison. Victims. Attack. Jesus.

'Well, I just saw that soldier out here at CentCom and he looked absolutely fine to me,' I said and the hall roared with laughter. I don't think anybody was taking me very seriously, but at least everyone was enjoying themselves.

'We don't have any information to corroborate what you are saying, Miss Zanetti. Next.'

And I was dismissed. I sat down on my plastic school chair to some mild applause and I noticed that the men and women in the sidelines looked rattled. They were passing notes to each other and some of them were on the phone. I wondered where Eden was. I was aware that I really ought to have cleared it with him before breaking his story. I mean, the CIA might bump him off or something . . .

It was then that a door opened at the side of the stage where these types were hanging nervously around. A man walked out briskly. He stood there in the wings and chatted in an ordinary way to the other White House stooges. He was expected. He worked here. He was an American government spin doctor. He was Joshua Klein.

The woman next to him, in a pinstriped skirt suit and black high heels out here in the desert, leant in to say something to Klein and he immediately looked over at me. I could see that he hadn't known I'd been stationed here. He was shocked and even, just possibly, embarrassed. He almost ran back where he'd come from. Vince called it a day.

The Americans were going live on air any second and they all rushed over to their funny booths to put bizarrely inappropriate clothes and make-up on. I was reeling from having seen Klein and I couldn't believe I hadn't guessed straight away. Was that why he'd slept with me? So that I would run his spun stories for him? What do they call those spies who seduce people – honey traps? I shoved my way through the crowds trying to get out and up towards the rostrum.

'Hey, Faith,' someone from Reuters said, looking bemused as I hurtled past him. 'Good questions.'

I tried the door but it was locked. It was like *The Lion, the Witch and the Wardrobe* or something. A magic door that sometimes leads to other worlds and sometimes just leads to a cupboard full of clothes. Actually, that's exactly what Klein was like himself.

I stood there, in the emptying hall, and dialled Klein's number. I had long since given up hope of his answering, but I did think he might not delete my messages without listening.

'Hi. It's me. I just saw you at CentCom. You absolute shit.'

The thing is, I now felt like a stalker. He had, in a certain way, behaved impeccably. He had offered me stories and he had offered me sex and I was all grown up and completely at liberty to accept or refuse. I had accepted. In the case of the sex, he then backed away and isn't it everyone's right to change their mind? Hey, it's not as though I haven't slept with people and said nice things to them and regretted it in my time. So now I'm calling and most certainly planning a barrage of emails and I am . . . yes, I suppose I am defiant. Powerless, crushed and pissed off. And I want to tell him. But you know what else? I want to tell him about Uday's palace and Sergeant Skvorecky and being in the helicopter. I want to tell him about Eden in the hospital tent and how cross he was and how MASH it looked. I want to tell him about Don and Irochka's wedding and the knickers in Grant's pocket. I don't want to be on my own any more.

I crept back outside, checking for Ziggy and Anita and their friends with just the top of my head before I put my whole body into their line of abuse. They had gone. Back, presumably, to the very nice hotel that Klein had checked them into. Plenty of them to be had in Dohar. I chatted to the Reuters bloke while I smoked. He had about ten different press passes round his neck and he said he was here 'for the duration' and had never been so bored. 'I can't believe they expect us to swallow it,' he said. 'They're so fucking intent on not lying that they just don't say anything. Seriously, we get more off the telly.'

'It was a bit like that in Baghdad,' I said, stamping my fag out under my foot.

He laughed, but I wasn't completely joking. Alex, I think he's called. I didn't dare ask because he knew my name and I must have met him a hundred times. I think my friend Shiv had a thing with him but I didn't dare ask him that either. She is dead now and he might cry or something awful.

I wandered back in, leaving Alex to finish his cigarette. Everyone was beavering away over their copy or their pieces to camera now and the air of antagonism from the briefing had lifted. I was looking for someone official and it didn't take me long to find her. She was moving from table to table, giving out fact sheets. I tapped her on the shoulder.

'Ma'am?' she said. I was getting sick of this. For one thing, shouldn't I be 'miss'?

'Hi. I'm Faith Zanetti from the London *Chronicle* and I was wondering where I might find Joshua Klein. I had arranged to see him, but nobody seems to know where his office is,' I said innocently.

'Oh, right. Sure thing. Just one moment,' she chirped and picked up her walkie-talkie. 'Got a lady here to see Josh? Shall I send her over?' she asked someone, urgent, earnest. The answer was affirmative and she directed me outside the main building and back in again round the corner. 'You will need your ID to re-enter,' she told me, and checked the piece of plastic round my neck. 'You're all set,' she confirmed.

He was in a special plush bit with carpet (that Brillo Pad stuff) and slightly more expensive lighting. The guard on the outside door scowled at me but hit all the right buttons and gestured me through to the opulent cool with his gun. I was on a long corridor with a series of doors off to the left. There were spotlights on the ceiling and everything was quiet. The fifth door had a plaque by its side reading, Joshua F. Klein. I opened it and took a deep breath.

He was sitting behind his desk in a white shirt with his sleeves rolled up. He was tapping at a computer and he wore glasses that had slipped down his nose. He was listening to *La Traviata* on a tiny portable CD player with cigarette packet-sized speakers. He didn't *look* like Satan. My rage evaporated now that I was actually in front of him and I smiled.

'Hi,' I said.

He stopped working and put his glasses down on his desk. Then he put them back on again. He leant on his elbows and looked at me a bit sadly. He sighed.

'Faith Cleopatra Zanetti,' he said. 'What have we done?'

I sat down in the foldaway chair in front of the desk and lit a cigarette. Blowing smoke over towards him. I rested my boots up in front of him and laughed.

'I don't know, JFK. You tell me,' I said. 'Why didn't you answer my calls?'

'I didn't know what to say. I don't know what to say to you,' he said, picking up a paper clip.

'You could just say, "Hi, how are you. Nice to hear from you."' I suggested, walking over to his water cooler to get a paper cup to use as an ashtray. 'Like a normal person.'

'I can't though, can I? How can I just say that? We can't get any further into this, or we will never be able to get back to our old lives. I will never be able to get back to my old life,' he corrected himself.

'What's so great about our old lives?' I asked him, sitting back down. 'Mine's no great shakes.'

He laughed. He always makes me feel as though I've said something incredibly witty. It's what charisma is all about, isn't it? Not being fascinating yourself, but making whoever you're talking to feel fascinating. Bill Clinton is the world expert in this, but even your more minor figures like Colonel Gaddafi and Michael Portillo do a pretty good job.

Klein sighed again. 'I can't, Faith. I can't do this,' he said.

I was beginning to feel tearful and I hated myself. What am I? Ingrid Bergman getting on the plane? Vivien Leigh chasing Clark Gable out into the fog? It was absurd. I needed to think about the matters at hand. Klein had a window behind him that looked out over some sand and a razor-wire fence.

'Nice view,' I said. It's a trick I have. Whenever you feel awkward, concentrate really hard on some aspect of your physical surroundings and talk about that instead. Never fails. Except this time.

'Faith,' he said and started to get up. No! Do NOT suck me into this. No!

'Sit down!' I shouted.

He looked around as though unsure how to respond to a command. But then he sat down.

'Look, never mind all this crap. I get it. You're conflicted. Life's complicated. OK. Fuck off. I'll deal with it or I won't. Either way. But why didn't you tell me you're a spin doctor? Why did you feed me the shit about Jamal and the smallpox lab and Bonnita ratfucking Hernandez? Is that why you slept with me? So that I would write your crap for you?'

Klein is not used to anyone talking to him like this. Directly, emotionally, challenging. He is, as far as I can see, someone who deflects conflict. Keep your head down, smile and it will pass. Well, not this time, baby. The first time he called me baby I thought I would die with pleasure and lust and trust. Now the word sounds like an insult.

'Can we, uh, can we get a few things straight?' he asked, exhausted. And, oh God, I wanted to hug him and apologise. What was wrong with me? I had come in here expecting a confrontation with the antichrist and I had found a slightly sad man, full of self-doubt and abandoned hopes, unwillingly compromised and foundering in the vastness of, well, life. Goddammit.

I nodded, pretty fucking defeated myself. This time I used the water cooler as nature intended and took him over a cup as well – a peace offering.

'When I told you about Jamal it was because I knew the truth of the thing and you had been a victim of Saddam's spin. I am, I was, a weapons inspector and I did not lie to you about that. Jamal was injured in a gas explosion. As for the smallpox lab, I did deceive you, but not like you think. That was a chemical weapons lab, and it did come from a complex producing, almost certainly, weapons of mass destruction. I believe I was right that it was used to produce the smallpox virus. However, as you suggest, I did not have absolute proof of that, and I hoped you would run your story anyway. And you did. I was at college with Iraqis who went on to work on the biological weapons programme. I know they are doing it. Public opinion needs proof. I don't. I already have it. But if public opinion needs it then I am going to supply it because what we are doing here is right.' He had fixed me with his gaze and I looked at him quizzically. He wasn't lying. That is, he believed himself. And I believed him too. What I create in his absence isn't Joshua Klein. This is.

'And Hernandez?' I asked, lighting another cigarette, wishing this was all over.

Klein sighed deeply and stood up. He put his head outside his office and glanced both ways down the corridor. Then he walked over to a small basin near a filing cabinet and turned both taps on.

'You never know,' he said. It's an old trick I know from Russia. Running water interferes with the way some bugs work.

'We knew Hernandez had deserted with her friend. Your friend. Faith, we need to win this war quickly. I care about Iraq. I spent time here when I was a student, before Saddam, before this mess, when it felt like what it is, the birthplace of civilisation. I wrote a paper on Iraqi poetry. I want to get rid of these people and I want to start helping to rebuild this place. That's why they put me on this job.'

'Oh Jesus, Josh,' I said quietly. I was laughing quietly, hysterically. 'Jesus, I can't believe you did this to me.' My voice was getting louder. 'Fuck you, Klein! I am going to lose my job, my whole fucking reputation. Fuck you!' I had stood up and was pacing about, getting breathless.

Klein stood up too, grabbing my wrists and staring at me. I thought he might kiss me. Or I might kiss him. I had no idea what was going on.

'Faith. Faith, baby. Please calm down. Sit down,' he said.

'Fuck you,' I whispered and sat down. 'So you sent me in to maybe get killed?'

Klein banged his fist on the desk and his glasses fell off. 'You KNOW that's not true! I made every effort to try and make sure you didn't even go inside the building. We did know it was a hospital. We did know they weren't captured. We did not know whether or not the place was guarded. There was a real danger of a serious battle over this and we could not afford to lose. Christ, Faith. You know how powerful the media is. You know what effect an example of cowardice and desertion in the US Army would have done to us. Do you want Saddam Hussein to stay in power? Well, do you?'

Oh, God, but it all sounded just about reasonable.

'Faith? She knew her colleagues were about to die and she ran away because she didn't want to die with them. Is that the kind of picture we want to be presenting here? Faith?'

I felt like a schoolgirl again and I looked at my boots. I knew he was wrong but I couldn't pin it down.

'Joshua. It's not about what kind of picture we want to present. It's about the truth,' I mumbled.

And now he, quite rightly, roared with laughter. 'Faith Cleopatra Zanetti. Faith Without Doubt. The sword of truth. You don't give two shits about the truth. You want a story. You want a good story and I gave you – yes, I gave you – three of them. You'll probably win an award for this war. You think your newspaper cares about truth? You think a right-wing British rag that passes for a broadsheet only because of its size cares about the truth? Hell, the *New York Times* doesn't even take leads on *British* stories from the British press because you are all so slapdash with the truth. Don't talk to me about truth. You don't care about Iraq or the Iraqi people. You are just doing your job.' He crossed his arms and sat back.

I smiled.

'Touché,' I said and put my face in my hands. It was only when he knelt down next to me and took me in his arms that I realised I was sobbing.

He brushed my tears away with his fingers.

'Is it why you seduced me? So I'd do all this? This was fucking set up by Nur and Hugo!'

He held my head to his chest and kissed the top of it. 'Is that what you really think, Faith? Is that what you think, you silly girl?'

CHAPTER TWENTY-ONE

Things felt different next morning at CentCom. Faulks the barman made me a coffee and LB high-fived me when I walked past him. I had spent the night with Joshua Klein. The sky outside was blue enough to give you a headache and the desert had a kind of pale butteriness about it that made it look like a film set rather than a life-threatening element with a twisted mind of its own.

'There's so much I want to say to you,' Klein had said to me as we lay on the floor, curled into each other. 'But can I show you instead?' First he showed me a by-line picture of myself that he had in his breast pocket. 'You know, I kiss this good night. That is where I'm coming from.'

Then he stood me up and he pushed me down again, a big hand in the small of my back and his mouth on mine. And it felt like the truth. It felt like everything that is good and right and real, under a starchy sheet on a sofa bed, me biting his hand to try and keep quiet.

'So passionate, baby,' he said and I kissed his eyes. Every now and then I had to take stock to make sure that I hadn't died in ecstasy. There just isn't a tack-free way of saying this kind of thing, without Shakespeare's help, but it was true anyway. And I would have been happy to die there. What more can you possibly expect out of life, Faith C. Zanetti? Not more than this. Definitely not more than this.

Lying there in the glow of so many machines, little red and green blips flickering in the darkness, I smoked and asked him about Daniel. I suppose my thought train was – sex, love, oh God, he's done it all before and she even conceived and everything. I wanted him all to myself but I knew I was sharing him.

'What's the deal with your son?'

'Daniel? Hmm. Well, his mother was . . . his mother is very difficult. He has a lot of problems. He's been in hospital, for . . . various things.' He stroked the scar on my shoulder. It's messy – gunshot wound from El Salvador.

'Right. Still, that's no reason to put him up at five-star hotels in war zones,' I said, hoping he was going to say something not weird. Suddenly, though, everything was falling into place. All the duplicity I had seen and felt to be so sinister now had a logic to it that I understood. It wasn't murky and evil. It was straightforward and necessary. Klein laughed. I was jealous of all the Joshua Klein laughs I hadn't heard. Decades of them before I was even born.

'No, that's true. But this way I can keep an eye on him and he thinks he is working. His protest against me, against what I do, against American imperialism, gives him a purpose and keeps him out of hospital. He needs to fight me. Anita is a friend from hospital and she has no family so I . . . so I suppose I help her too. She's a nice girl really.'

He was talking but he was staring at my face and smiling.

'What?' I asked.

'You,' he said.

'Yeah. What?' I asked.

'You're . . . pretty.'

Yup. I could see what he'd meant about wanting to show rather than tell. Yeats, he ain't, as a friend of mine once said of a boyfriend who wrote very disappointing emails.

'You too,' I said, and there was a part of me that I would like to have trodden on that couldn't believe that somebody as beautiful and wonderful and right as him could have noticed a worm like me. A queen or a chicken? Well, I'd admitted to Irochka that I was a chicken so it should be no surprise.

So I sat down at my desk that morning, showered and adored, and I wrote a piece about the progress of the war, copied pretty much word for word from the photocopies I'd found waiting for me. Once, when I was filling in for the Moscow correspondent, the desk had wanted some kind of economics story that had just broken over their wires in London. 'We haven't got anything on that here yet,' I said. I had no time to make calls because the paper would be 'put to bed' in under an hour's time. If I'd called Reuters and got them to fax me over the wires from their Moscow bureau in a big hotel just down the road, the whole calling and faxing process across the Moscow lines would have taken well over an hour. So the desk in London faxed me the wire copy back to Moscow and I wrote the piece. 'Faith Zanetti in Moscow.' Rewriting the wires from London. It's often the way.

Television news tries to fudge it by not showing the correspondent. So they have all these great pictures that they've bought from the pool but their correspondent is in Azerbaijan that day, not Chechnya. So they get someone in London to do a voiceover to the pictures and then they just miss the country off the sign-off. So, instead of ending 'This is Pip Deakin in Chechnya', it just ends, 'This is Pip Deakin'. Whenever I'm watching these pieces I can't help shouting at the television, 'Nowhere fucking near Chechnya,' just to complete the sign-off for them.

Anyway, the coffee was good and hot this morning, the phones and computers worked, and someone had turned one of the televisions to MTV. There was a boy band singing a song on a boat. They were all under twenty and were gazing meltily into the camera in a grotesque parody of loving honesty. 'You make me wanna call you in the middle of the night. You make me wanna hold you till the morning light. You make me wanna look. You make me wanna fall. You make me wanna – surrender my soul,' they crooned. And I knew just what they meant.

Today I had gone into God bless America mode. I was once on a plane to the States, a bit hungover, tired, not looking forward to the long flight and the boring job at the other end (a piece about pollution in Texas and the North American Free Trade Agreement – bored yet?). Then this mobile phone advert came blaring on to the screen at the front of my section (that's right – I was flying working class) and it showed London in the rain, red phone boxes, black taxis, grey pavements. Someone then picks up the phone and there is this blare of music and suddenly you see people waving the Stars and Stripes at an American football match, cheerleaders with white teeth and brown legs leaping into the air, waving red and white pompoms, and the spectators eating hot dogs, laughing and cheering. Suddenly, weh hey, I was on my way to America.

They, or rather we, were winning. That was good. That was the message. So I wrote it and dutifully filed to Tamsin who said, 'Bit short on scoops out in Qatar, Zanetti?' Still, she never was one for gushing. Today I was glad to be here, safe and slick and cared for – on the winning side. I decided that John Lennon was right, America was the Roman Empire and obviously anybody not a part of it feels a bit angry and bitter and wants to bring it down and prove it's corrupt. On the other hand people flock there from all over the world if they can, hoping for a better life. Even the most rampant anti-Americans want a cut of the profits – to study at their universities, to take advantage of their research, to lie on their beaches and ski in their mountains. Go anywhere and you'll find people who are clamouring to throw off the oppression of their way of life (from wearing a burka and being kept at home twenty-four hours a day to just feeling that the British class system is obstructive) and to start again in America opening a nail salon, walking people's dogs or driving a taxi. And who wouldn't prefer air-conditioned splendour and a bottle of Bud to a rat-infested, stinking, sweltering hellhole and a glass of amoeba-filled water?

CHAPTER TWENTY-TWO

'What happened, Zanetti?' Eden Jones asked me, standing by my desk and leaning on his crutch. 'Where's the piece?'

He was still angry but I was pleased to see him. Hell, I was just plain pleased anyway.

'Hi.' I smiled up to him. 'How's the foot? How come you're here?'

'Better. That bastard Hirsch released me. Can you believe they tried to make me sign something? Actually said I'd regret it if I didn't. Now the paper wants a big feature about CentCom. Where's the piece? I didn't write it. I was waiting for you.'

'What piece?'

'The piece about what really happened to me and Bonnie. Are you still researching or what? I would have expected you to have done it by now. A big Faith Zanetti investigation.'

I smiled again. 'I don't think it's what anyone needs right now. The war's nearly won,' I said, admittedly with a tiny weeny little edge of condescension in my voice.

'Fuck me.' Eden groaned, rolling his eyes towards the chipboard ceiling which was coming away at the edges with the weight of all the wires it had to support. 'What's with the Stepford Wives thing, Faithy? Come on!'

Alex walked past and commented, 'Eden Jones.'

Eden Jones was holding both my shoulders and leaning too hard because of the cast on his leg. I didn't want to give him the pleasure of telling him about the questions I'd asked at the briefing yesterday. Anyway, that had been yesterday.

'Get off, Jones. Listen, it's your story anyway. If you want to write it, be my guest. There's a computer over there.' Grant Bradford waved back as I gestured in his direction.

'Hey! Jonesey! Is it true?' he shouted, his hair glowing enthusiastically.

'Yes,' Eden yelled back. I imagine my performance had kicked off rumours. Most people, though, just thought I was trying to wind Vince up.

Eden dragged a chair over to me and sat in it.

'Boyfriend got to you again, I see.' He sighed, staring into my face. He'd got really intense lately. Can't believe I never noticed it before. This clear-sighted dynamism.

'I don't get it, Eden.' I laughed at him. 'Why are you so suspicious of everything? Why do you want to bring everyone and everything down? Has it never occurred to you that the way you and Bonnie were dealt with was for a . . . well, a greater good? Do you want the Allies to lose this war? Let Saddam Hussein keep on torturing and gassing people? Can't you see that the media is just desperate for a story, anything to pull governments down and overcomplicate things that can be simple? It's not all vicious lies, you know. It's a war effort. Historically speaking, war efforts have always involved propaganda. You can't win without it.'

It was a long speech. I watched Eden Jones' face while I made it. He hadn't shaved lately and he kept taking a cigarette out of his packet, putting it in his mouth and then putting it back in the packet again. He rapped his fingers on my desk.

'Jesus,' he said. 'Jesus Christ.'

With enormous effort he hauled himself up to standing. He had one of those blue foam things on his foot with his toes poking out of the end. Lily Fang was doing her thing again over in her booth. She was beginning to give me the creeps. LB walked past and touched my shoulder.

'Ma'am,' he said, but he was winking. I felt like a member of the team and it was good.

'You know what, Zanetti,' Eden said, getting ready to walk away. 'Firstly, a lot of doctors and nurses standing around doing their job got killed in that propaganda exercise. Secondly, Stalin was very keen on a few sacrifices for the greater good, a bit of caressing the truth to suit his goals. How far do you go with it, Faith? We're not just parasites out to ruin people's careers and make everything shit with our tawdry exposures. We're part of the democratic process. We're here to keep them honest. If we become part of the lie then the whole thing falls apart. Can't you see that, Zanetti, you stupid bitch?'

He had raised his voice a bit too much and people were staring. Particularly an attractive private with a long auburn plait down her back. He couldn't stop himself smiling at her.

'What I can see, Eden, is that you are a very angry and cynical person. When the war is over and a new regime is taking shape, the recriminations and the endless sniping can start. Meantime we just need to get this over with,' I told him, smiling again. I had my hair pulled back in a neat ponytail and was still wearing the khakis Skvorecky had given me over at the palace. I felt it possible that I even looked like one of them.

'We?' he sneered.

'Sometimes, Eden, there is nothing wrong with taking sides,' I said.

He hit the base of his hand against his forehead and limped away from me. His jeans looked as though he had been sleeping in them for weeks on end. And those teeth could do with bleaching.

At the two o'clock briefing Klein was openly in the wings, wearing a fabulous three-piece suit, under which I could see his red braces. His gold cufflinks flashed in the spotlights when he moved his arms, nodding and shaking his head at Vince when he looked his way, indicating which questions could and couldn't be answered. Joshua F. Klein caught my eye and smiled. I could have flown with happiness. 'I want you,' he mouthed and I thought I might actually melt or die or something. Eden sat at the front and kept his hand up throughout the briefing but Vince didn't pick him. Everyone but me was bored and angry. I could no longer understand what they were all so pissed off about.

Afterwards I went round to Klein's office. Now I could try to pretend that this was a journalism-related trip (indeed, that is exactly what I did pretend when talking to the burly security man) but it wasn't. I wanted to throw my arms round Joshua's neck and tell him how much I love him. A woman in a trouser suit chased me up his corridor, squealing, her heels clacking, a pair of glasses swinging on a black ribbon.

'Now is not a good time,' she whined, but I ignored her and pushed the door open, breathing in blissfully as I turned the light steel handle. After all, it was almost my room too. The most wonderful night of my life had been spent in it. And if I'd known how it would all end, would I still have done it? Almost certainly.

But now was not a good time. Daniel and Anita were there, slumped in the cheapest office chairs on the US market and picking their spots. It was even colder in here than it was in the rest of the compound. Something very depressing by Mendelssohn was droning out of the little speakers. Klein faced the couple, concerned and weary. He didn't smile when he saw me. In fact, he dismissed me as though he was talking to his least favourite secretary. A slight wave of the hand. No, not that part of my life at the moment, thanks – fuck off.

'Not now, Faith,' he said. Another command I was expected to obey.

At the sound of my name Daniel stood up and spun to face me, his dreadlocks following him. Today he was wearing a marijuana leaf T-shirt above his combat trousers. I mean, don't people ever understand that they are a caricature of themselves? He was like a cartoon of a troubled teenager. I hadn't removed my head from round the door and Daniel spat at it. My head, that is. A huge glob of green phlegm landed almost in my mouth and I retched. The thought of his pierced tongue and the fags and joints and lack of toothpaste left me gagging. I was expecting to be somehow rescued, or at least apologised to but Joshua, in a gesture that would perhaps be comprehensible to a parent, but not to me, put his arm round Daniel's shoulders and sat him back down, ignoring me for while.

'Danny,' he said, kindly.

'Ziggy,' Daniel corrected him.

'Ziggy.' He smiled.

Oooh. I was getting pissed off. Angry now, I walked into the room.

'Hey!' I said, my arms thrown wide in amazement. I had wiped my face with the bottom of my T-shirt.

'Please, Faith. This is not a good time,' Klein told me again, more firmly, nothing but indifference in his beautiful face. I could have died. That first time he looked at me 'like that' back in the hospital in Baghdad might have been two hundred years ago.

I once had a boyfriend who was handsome but, after two days with him, I realised he was a real pain in the arse. I dumped him but he wouldn't leave me alone. He called endlessly and would have emailed if they'd been invented then. He stood outside restaurants where I was having dinner with another man. I began to loathe him and all he could say was, 'How can you treat me like this after you did and said all those things?'

How? Dunno. Changed my mind. Quite fancied you, now I think you're a tosser.

And now I was getting my comeuppance. Perhaps it is a moral universe after all. Klein's belief in God was becoming more and more convincing.

'Dad, can you get rid of this whore?' Daniel moaned. Anita appeared to be shivering.

'Faith?' Klein said, really beginning to get angry with me. 'Please leave. This is a family issue.'

OK, now he'd really got me. I've always hated people with proper families. Families who take a picnic to the lake and laugh about the last time they were here when so-and-so got stung by a bee or some totally fucking banal event. They roar with laughter. 'Oh, it was so funny. You should have seen your face!' they say. I mean, big shit. You see, there are certain things I just can't bear. One is waiting for people who don't turn up. When Evie said Dad was coming home, I used to look out of our suburban window in the orange mediocrity of the street lamps and count the cars till he came. Often he changed his mind and went to a bar instead. Or on another story. I would be mad with joy because he was coming. Crazed with worry because something had happened. Speechless with rage that he had rejected me. Violent with self-hatred because I deserved it. And the other one is people putting their families before me. Even in the most minor way. So a good friend says, 'My mum's coming over later so let's have lunch tomorrow instead.' And my spiral starts. I hate them for wanting someone else more than me. And I hate myself because, hey, who'd want me? Then I hate myself a bit extra for the self-pity and childish bollockyness of it all. I want a family who puts me first. And yet, of course, I don't. I would hate to have had someone telling me what time to be home, making me share the biscuits, forcing compromise on what I wanted to watch on television, talking about me to my teachers with a disapproving shake of the head and a joint agreement to cajole me into submission. Mostly I just think, thank fucking God it's all over.

But it wasn't though, was it? Because here I was, begging for attention and getting kicked out for 'family reasons'. What's so fucking great about families? Don't seem to have made Klein very bloody happy. I had come to see him as a lover and, yet again, he'd turned me into a stalker.

'Josh? How can you . . .' I began and Klein actually got up to manhandle me out of his office. Now that I didn't think I could bear.

'I'm going,' I said. 'I'm going.'

My eyes burned in the heat on the way back to the main compound. I could actually feel my skin cooking, just on a fifty-second walk. The razor wire glinted hideously and the sun was making the sand and the sky shimmer into each other. The ground seemed to shift under my feet and I put my hand out to the wall to steady myself.

A black soldier I hadn't seen before was on the door and he straightened himself up from his happy slouch to offer his help.

'You OK, ma'am?' he asked, his helmet tilted coquettishly forwards.

'Me? I'm fine. Why?' I snapped at him and then tried to turn it into a smile.

'Just asking,' he mumbled and went back to his sun-drenched slump. Sun-drenched. Sun-drenched. There's that song, I thought, trying to stay focused on the swing doors that would take me back through to the cool clarity of the story. 'I want my sun-drenched, windswept, Ingrid Bergman kiss. Not in the next life. I want it in this. I want it in this.' 'Beautiful South', I think.

And I had had mine. But now what? I want it again. And again. And again. You see, the song does not offer any advice on what to do once you've had it. Because once you've had it and you know what it's like, you can't live without it any longer. It's impossible. Like some sort of

Greek myth. You know, the half lion, half unicorn knows that if it kisses the swan the ecstasy will be unbearable and it will then die of loss when the swan turns into a serpent. Well, that kind of thing.

I got to the doors and pushed them open, gasping for breath as I leant back against the magnesium white wall, trying to get some sort of grip. I had longed for the cool, but now I found I was covered with goose pimples and my lips felt blue. The buzz of the drinks machine seemed terribly loud.

'Faith? Faithy?' Eden said, and his face looked too big leaning into mine.

'I'm fine,' I said, or at least I was sure I had said it.

'What, darling? What are you trying to tell me?' he asked, putting his arms round me. Why was he calling me darling? All his anger had evaporated in his concern. I must look terrible.

'Leave me alone. I'm fine,' I shouted, but he couldn't hear me.

He wiped my mouth with his sleeve and I think I must have been foaming or something. He put one arm all the way round me under my shoulders and with his other he leant on his crutch, hopping us both through into the main lounge and sitting me down on the edge of all the news production stuff on a little hard blue sofa with a red plastic rim round the brittle nylon upholstery.

'Faith? Faith? Do you know who I am?' he asked me, standing up.

I nodded, no longer certain enough to try speaking.

'OK. Stay there,' he said.

He seemed to be gone for hours and I couldn't stop shaking. I was just glad that everybody else was too busy to notice. The fat producer woman with the braces gave me a quick but dismissive glance, her headphones round her neck like something orthopaedic.

'You're my girl,' Eden said when he got back, and he knelt in front of me, rubbing my arms. He had put a cup of Styrofoam tea and a cheese sandwich on a white paper plate down beside me and he lifted the tea to my mouth. He squatted there until I had eaten every bit of the sandwich and finished every sip of the tea. It wasn't easy. The food tasted like gravel and I had to force it down my throat, but he'd made the right call. Things were pulling into focus and when I said, 'Thanks,' Eden said, 'My pleasure.' Clearly, then, motor functions were looking up.

'Jesus, Zanetti. You had me worried. Had a row with Klein or something?'

I scoffed. 'Maybe heatstroke,' I said.

'Hmmm. Well, your mind certainly seems addled. That's for fucking sure,' he said. He was holding my hand and it was comforting.

'Friends?' I asked, thinking he'd be justified in telling me to get lost.

'Always,' he said, and he clambered up to standing at last, swaying a bit on one leg. 'Listen. Will you be OK? I want to try and have a private word with Vince,' he said.

'Fat chance.' I smiled, feeling a trickle of cynicism run back into my blood.

As soon as he was out of sight I took my phone out of my pocket.

'You have reached the phone of Joshua Klein. Please leave a message.'

'Josh,' I said. 'What's happening? Why do I feel nervous to phone you? Why don't I have the right to talk to you?'

Then I called a couple more times in case he suddenly felt the urge to pick up. Then I left another message.

'Do you hate me so much that you can't even pick up the fucking phone to me?'

I sat there on the sofa thinking a horrible thought: That Josh Klein is not my friend. Eden brings me tea and a sandwich. Eden would call me before I ever had a chance to call him. Eden would reassure me constantly, not that I would ever even need it. Josh Klein does not give a fuck about me. And as I thought this, the whole clean, whirring, buzzing, brightly-lit thing of it lost its allure. Faulks developed the

247

puffy-eyed look of an alcoholic, the guns got a menacing glint about them, the beaming fresh-faced innocence of the American staff was facile and empty rather than helpful and earnest. Was the whole thing a lie? The whole world?

I can't have been staring into space at my desk for more than a couple of minutes when the girl who'd told me I was 'all set' to go and see Joshua the day before slapped an A4 envelope on my desk. It was addressed to Faith C. Zanetti and it boded ill. There was one sheet of paper in it with a tiny typed note in the middle. Oh, here we go. Again.

Faith –
    I will be leaving for DC this afternoon with Daniel and Anita. Please do not try to contact me again. I trust you will understand.
    JFK

I put my head in my hands and pulled at the spirals of my hair. This whole thing was very ill-fated. Not that I have any time at all for fate or destiny or anything. But I should have known before we started. Spotted him for a fuck-up. Known myself well enough to understand that I am too weak to handle anything real. It's like asking a heavyweight boxer to sit a history of art exam. I just can't do it. My toughness crumbles and I'm sitting there in my silk shorts with a mouthpiece in and a towel round my neck, staring at a question about the Russian Realists. (Actually, I love the Russian Realists.) I was feeling so fucking sorry for myself that I could hardly breathe and would probably have started drawing broken hearts with Joshua 4 Faith written on them if the whole of CentCom hadn't suddenly fallen completely silent.

Phone conversations were halted mid-sentence, Dictaphones switched off, autocues left whirring by themselves. Open-mouthed and clutching pens, cups, sheets of paper, computer mouses and bars of chocolate, everyone was staring at their nearest television screen.

Bonnita Hernandez had gone missing. Gone missing? From some military hospital while suffering from amnesia? Didn't they have cameras? Guards?

My heart was pounding. Words like democracy, facilitate, manipulate spun round my head. Eden. Eden. Eden might be in danger. Might he? I wanted to take some Valium, drink a couple of shots of vodka and lie down. I realised, looking down at the bag by my feet, that I didn't even know where my room was. Didn't have anywhere to go. I looked at my bag again and realised it wasn't my bag. I crawled under the table and examined the brass clasp. It was just like the clasp on my battered leather bag but it had been painted that colour. Recently. The marks in the leather were nearly the same, but it had just been dragged along the floor to look worn. There was a tiny wire, almost imperceptible, snaking out of the corner and it dawned on me as my heart lurched – a bomb!

'Help! Help! Bomb! Bomb! Everybody out!' I screamed. And I screamed and screamed and carried on screaming until my knees buckled under me and somebody jabbed a needle into my arm.

CHAPTER TWENTY-THREE

'Need anything babe?' Evie asked me, leaning her head round the door to my room. The spare room. I shook my head.

She and Fernando were getting stoned downstairs. He seemed to have moved in on some kind of a permanent basis. At least until Carly got out of hospital.

'Sure?' she asked.

'Sure,' I said.

They sedated me at CentCom and flew me back to London off my face on morphine to be treated at some private psychiatric hospital on Harley Street. The consultant wasn't that worried about me though – he was as silver-haired and reliable looking as Blake Carrington and he had madder patients. He said I was suffering from chronic exhaustion and would be all right after a couple of weeks' sleep and a bit of Prozac.

I preferred not to open my eyes, ideally. If I opened them at night the glow from the street lamps and the lines of cars outside frightened me. I didn't understand why I could never see the sky. Only orange clouds that seemed to come in lower and lower, making it difficult to breathe. Things in the house buzzed. The fridge, a computer, a clock radio. The radiators gurgled and whenever the washing machine was on I worried the house might fall down. Well, it might. There were planes overheard all day and all night, flying very low, perhaps about to plunge straight into us.

During the day the sunlight coming through the rose velvet curtains hurt my eyes. So I liked to keep them shut. Evie has Radio Four on all the time and when I hear the chimes of the news I freeze in terror. I am worried that a nuclear war will be announced, that chemical weapons might have been found seeping into all our houses through air vents. The whole world is at war. Children abducted and raped, politicians found hanged, earthquakes and floods kill thousands, gentle gorillas are poached for their body parts and the seas are all full of oil.

Evie tried to take me to the cinema to see a film about an old man who is reassessing his life after his wife dies. I couldn't stop crying. At least until I turned round to see a sniper in the back row, about to pull out a gun and take aim at us.

'Nothing's gonna happen, sugar,' Evie said. But it already has. It already has. And I found out where Nur and Hugo got to in the end. London. Not Paris. They put their fucking Save-Iraq-Using-Faith-Zanetti's-Idiocy-And-Joshua-Klein's-Looks plan into action and got the fuck out. Typical of an old hack to become a zealot in his old age. Typical of Dad to have gone for a young zealot when he did. It turns out the Americans did have Nur's brother lined up to run the sodding place once it's all over. Unbelievable. Or rather, so bloody believable.

One morning I heard my dad come home. He rang the doorbell and kissed Evie hello, dumped his bag in the front hall. I ran downstairs wondering how he knew where Evie had moved to, but nobody was at home. I went into all the rooms, feeling I had never seen any of them before, looking for Dad. Fernando found me curled into a ball on the bathroom floor.

I have been here three weeks and I hate it. I feel like a child and nobody knows how to treat me. I am too old for chicken soup and magazines and sympathy. But they don't seem to be able to talk to me like an adult. Evie has given up drinking on my behalf and removed all the alcohol from the house. I am dying for a drink but I am too scared to go to the shop. They have car bombs in Jerusalem all the time. There is no reason for that not to start here. We are always under threat. And my body is rebelling against me. I feel a tumour in my brain that is heavy when I stand up, but the doctor just says I need to rest. I will have plenty of time to rest when I'm dead. My heart pounds so much I think it might burst inside me. I spit the pills into a bin under the bed. I need to stay lucid.

They tell me that Eden calls every day. Wants to come and talk to me. But I don't want him here. After all, this is the first place they might look for him. I email Joshua morning and night and sometimes I call him to leave a message so that he can hear my voice. He doesn't contact me but I understand. He is very busy at the moment and, anyway, he doesn't want to put me in any danger. I know he will come for me when he can.

Evie says there was no bomb in my bag in Qatar, that I got scared and imagined it. Perhaps it's true. I can't tell any more. I have lost the ability to distinguish between truth and lies. I don't know what's real and what isn't. So much of what happened in Iraq seemed real and meaningful at the time, only to shift slightly and reveal that it was hollow and empty. I believed lies, I ignored the truth. Only it never came clear.

One day Nur phoned and talked to Evie. I wasn't taking calls. She'd heard I wasn't well, was in London, wanted to check in. Hugo is in hospital with heart trouble.

'She says her brother is talking to the Americans about elections by

July,' Evie said. 'Like I'm supposed to give a shit.' Clearly time had not healed everything between these two girlfriends of Dad's. I did not plan to be a part of Nur and Hugo's London life. Not that Hugo's sounded as though it was going to be all that lengthy.

I went to see a shrink. Evie took me in the car and she waited outside. I lay on a single bed and faced a bookshelf. There were volumes and volumes of Freud all in the wrong order. And a fat yellow paperback called *Do I Dare Disturb the Universe?* On the wall next to me was a painting of a mountain.

I told the shrink about Baghdad and about Joshua Klein and Eden and Bonnie Hernandez.

'That must have been very difficult for you. And frightening,' he said.

'Not really,' I told him. The man's an idiot.

After a long pause he said, 'I think you are frightened that I won't understand you.'

'You won't,' I said.

'I think you do feel that. That must be a very lonely and worrying feeling for you,' he said. And I burst into tears and cried until my fifty minutes was up.

'I'm afraid that's all we have time for today,' he said, and handed me a bill for forty quid.

Evie said she thought I should see him again. I wrote Joshua a long email about it in bed on my laptop. I think he will find it funny.

The next day the shrink asked me if I had been frightened for my father when he was away.

'Yes,' I said. 'I think I was always frightened. I could never sleep. I need to stay alert all the time.'

'And you felt this even when you were a little girl?' he asked.

'Yes. Always,' I said.

'And yet you went into the same profession as your father. Do you think that on some level you are looking for him?' he asked.

And I burst into tears again. But that evening I went out to the shop on the high street and bought a packet of cigarettes and two vodka miniatures. I sat and watched television with Evie and Fernando. I phoned Carly who was now bored out of her head and set to be hospitalised for at least another six months.

'Hear you went mad,' she said. 'Told you he'd send you insane. They can't resist youth and beauty but then they realise they're not good enough for it.'

'Sod off.' I laughed. I got Evie to send her some grapes as a punishment.

Fernando offered me a spliff. I hate the taste but smoked it anyway.

'What happened to Ziggy?' Fernando wanted to know, taking a deep drag and coming over all bleary. I was wearing a pair of Mo's stripy pyjamas. Does he almost count as a stepbrother? Not really. He's away at school and Evie sends him fruit cakes in tins. He's taking his A levels this year and she is crazed with worry. I planted my bare feet on the stripped boards and leant back in the sofa. Fernando was lying on the rug, a huge blood-red Bokkhara.

'I don't know. Joshua took him back to the States, I think. Why?' I asked.

'He was a fucking psychopath. Scary bloke.' Fernando shrugged, but didn't elaborate.

When the news came on I had to go back to bed. I emailed Josh and told him I hoped Daniel was doing OK. Then I took the Effexor. The doctor said I should take Valium as well for the first week so as to counter the disturbing side effects of the anti-depressant.

'I'm not depressed,' I told him and he smiled.

'We don't really know how these drugs work but they can be very useful for anxiety,' he said.

'I'm anxious because the American government is trying to kill me. Not because I don't take enough drugs,' I told him and he looked at

Evie who had come with me. She was wearing a tight white trouser suit and he'd been looking at her a lot anyway.

In the morning the shrink asked me about Mum. I told him about the drink, that she was an alcoholic, and that she tried to kill me one night, to suffocate me, if my memory is reliable – I don't know any more. I told him about being taken away from her to live with Dad and Evie. I remember turning up on the doorstep and Evie taking my suit-case, Dad behind me with the car keys.

'That must have made you very sad and afraid,' he said.

'You're a genius,' I told him. 'You'd have to get up pretty early in the morning to get one over on you.'

'Are you flirting with me?' he asked.

'You wish,' I said. I was getting better.

That night I called Eden and asked him if he wanted to go out for a drink. I took a taxi to Piccadilly and met him at the Palm Court at the Ritz. He was waiting for me and had ordered a bottle of champagne that sat glistening in its bucket. There was a very old woman in lipstick and a wheelchair at the next table, with a white dog in her lap. She was sipping an enormous multicoloured cocktail with an umbrella and fruit in it, through a long straw. Making the most of the last couple of months, by the look of it.

'Hey,' I said, a bit sheepishly, plonking myself down. Evie has staff, so my jeans were pressed down the front, my T-shirt had been bleached and ironed and my cowboy boots had been polished. I had tied my hair back and couldn't have been cleaner. Also I'd hardly had a drink for ages.

'Wow,' he said. 'You look great.'

'Yeah. Feeling a lot better. What a fucking nightmare,' I admitted. 'Don't know what's wrong with me.'

'Breakdown,' he said. 'It's been a shit year.'

'Yeah.' I laughed, and he poured us both some champagne a second before the waiter reached us with his white napkin. A string quartet was playing Boccherini. And there really are palms. Funny little ones in pots, scattered about in the pink and gold décor. Not much like the ones in Baghdad.

'Heard from Klein?' Eden wanted to know.

'No,' I said. 'Not really.'

Well, it was true. I hadn't actually heard from him but I did feel as though I had. I dreamt about him almost every night and I could hear all the lovely things he'd said to me in my ears most of the time. The good things felt true, the bad things I forgave him for, assuming him to be confused or weak or incapable. Or all three. I was consumed by Klein. Had I heard from him though? No. Or at least . . . well, he did reply to one of my emails. I had been writing to him for weeks, from the gloom of my curtained room at Evie's. And one day I wrote, 'I wish you would come and see me. Can't you come over and see me, darling?'

And for the first and last time, he replied. His email said, 'I will be in Sacramento, CA, on business for the next eight days.'

Uh-huh. OK. Hmmm. Conflicted? Weak? A wanker? Tough call.

And yet I couldn't believe that he didn't love me. He had seemed to love me. Why couldn't I let it go?

'I think this is a pattern,' the shrink said.

'What kind of pattern?' I asked.

'Well, I think this man represents a father figure to you,' he said.

'He's nothing like my father. My father was shabby and chaotic and wildly promiscuous and usually pissed. My father was gentle and funny. My father was a mess,' I said. 'Joshua Klein works in an office and wears suits. He got married and lived up to his responsibilities. He probably wipes his kitchen surfaces down. He probably collects Chinese screens or something.'

The shrink said, 'Hmm.'

I took a sip of my champagne and looked at Eden. An elderly couple had got up to dance.

'Sorry,' I said.

He rolled his shirt sleeves up and laughed. 'Listen, Faith. I understand that you've exhausted yourself mentally and physically and you need a rest. But don't get weird on me now.'

'No. I mean it. I'm really sorry. I fucked up,' I said, smiling and lighting a cigarette.

'Stop it. You're giving me the creeps,' he said, and took my hand.

'It could be the Effexor,' I said and snatched it back.

'The what?'

'It's like Prozac.'

'Yummy,' he said, licking his lips.

'It is actually,' I agreed, licking mine. 'It works anyway. If being aware that the world is basically shit and that Joshua Klein fucked me over is sanity then, baby, I've got it.'

He laughed. 'Faith Zanetti! You're back.'

I blew my smoke out and felt back. At least halfway.

'Hey. I lost my head before I heard what happened to Bonnie. Did you ever hear anything?'

'Well, she turned up again,' he said. 'Back at the hospital a few days later. No memory of where she'd been and no record of her disappearance. No sightings. Nothing. It stinks. I spoke to her parents and they said she was doing well. I got the feeling they didn't much want to talk to me. Shame. Bonnie's a nice girl.'

I hate it when he describes his lovers as a 'nice' or a 'lovely' girl. I hope he has never said that about me. Firstly, why are they girls? Already he has them in his mind sucking a lollipop and needing a pat on the head. And then nice? Lovely? Who wants to be either of those things? It's like saying someone's sweet. Charismatic, passionate, gorgeous, amazing, wonderful, captivating, hilarious, fascinating – fine. Nice? No thanks.

'Wow,' I said.

'Anyway, I did a whole first person thing about it and there's going to be an investigation but nobody cares any more. It's all about trying to get water and electricity back to the Iraqi people and then there are these grenade attacks on the American soldiers. We've pretty much been forgotten about. Do you think Klein knew?' He leant towards me on his elbows, smiling a bit.

'Yes. He knew. He thought it was necessary. I don't know. Maybe it was,' I said, sighing. It seemed such a long time ago already.

The shrink had said this to me: 'Things aren't as dangerous as you think they are, nor as safe as you want them to be.' And it helped. No idea why.

Eden was going to Liberia the next morning so it wasn't long before he'd kissed me goodbye and I was standing on Piccadilly in the rain waiting for a taxi. It was freezing cold and by the time I finally sat down in the back of a cab I was soaking wet. It seemed like time to get the fuck out of this country again. I called Tamsin.

'Hi, Tamsin. It's me, Faith. I'm better and I want to go to Liberia,' I told her. There was a long pause.

'It's great to hear from you, Zanetti. We've got Liberia covered,' she said, and I heard some muffled discussion as she put her hand over the mouthpiece. Then she was back. 'How about the UN?'

This is like saying to someone, 'How about you watch a late-night arts discussion programme over and over again until the end of time?' I mean, how about I just chop my toes off and fry them all up with some mushrooms? God Almighty. Does she think I don't know what it means to be covering the UN? It's like covering the EU. Standing there in some lobby asking some really boring people some really boring questions so that you can write a really boring piece that they either won't run or they'll run it on page 9 as two paragraphs in the bottom left-hand corner. The only job I can think of more boring than this is writing trend features. You know, like, there is a new trend for people to bring up their children bilingual. The rule is, three people make a trend. If you can find three examples, so three sets of parents who are bringing up their children bilingual, then the piece stands as indisputable fact – this is a new trend. Two people is not enough and you don't need four.

'Great,' I said.

CHAPTER TWENTY-FOUR

Evie and Fernando were glad to see the back of me. She was delighted to have a friend to hang out with now the kids were away at school and her husband Alexei (whom I have met a total of seven times) seems to spend more and more of his life in Hong Kong. Fernando had finally found himself a mother figure. A dope-smoking, American, stupendously wealthy ex-model mother figure at that. Somehow I'd imagined that I'd been the maternal one, finding somewhere for him to go until Carly was out and all that. I'd been usurped. I suspected he'd be staying put even after Carly reappeared. Or, more accurately, I knew he would.

Anyway, Tamsin had me upgraded and I sat back in my cradle seat watching films, drinking vodkas and wishing I could smoke. One thing about the Effexor was that alcohol seemed to have much less effect. The stewardess looked worried when I ordered my tenth vodka on ice, but I was no trouble. Just kept my headphones on and kept smiling.

261

New York was blue-skied and beautiful and I was staying in a scuzz-hole flat that belongs to a photographer friend of mine who was off doing a big piece about China for *National Geographic* (who reads it?). The walls were painted a yellowy beige or had gone that colour over the years. The view out of the small window at the front (which didn't open) was of the bridge over the river to Roosevelt Island. You could almost see the cable car station but not quite. Out the back was just the blind wall of the next building. There was no air conditioning, only a couple of big old whirring fans on stands that chugged through the sleepless night. On the empty old fridge the size of a Buick was a magnet that said, 'Just think – what would Elvis have done?' Part of me was tempted to do exactly what he would have done. He would have taken a whole bottle of Valium and washed them down with some Jack Daniels.

'You have reached the phone of Joshua Klein. Please leave a message.'

'Hi. It's Faith again. I'm in the States at the moment and wondered if you wanted to meet up and have dinner.'

Surely he couldn't resist me if he could actually see me. Surely he would explain and it would all be all right.

I spent most of the time in the delegates' lounge bar, drinking vodka with the Russian ambassador. He told racist jokes and said I was beautiful. Meeting a Russian is like coming home for me. They are comforting and predictable. You know where you are with a Russian. Maybe I would call my ex-husband.

When an Arab colleague walked past us, the Russian ambassador would say, 'Saddam alekum,' and be helpless with laughter at his own sparkling wit. In a week I heard him tell the following joke a total of six times:

An old Jewish man loses his wallet. He knows to ask the rabbi for advice on everything so he goes to him and says, 'Rabbi. I've lost my wallet. What shall I do?'

The rabbi says, 'Son, the answer to everything is in the Torah. Open it and you will be enlightened.'

The man happens to open his Torah on the page of the Ten Commandments. His eye rests immediately on 'Thou shalt not covet thy neighbour's wife'.

He runs back to the rabbi and says, 'Rabbi! Thank you. I remembered exactly where I put my wallet.'

Oh. Ha ha. Ha ha.

'You have reached the phone of Joshua Klein. Please leave a message.'

'Hi, it's me again. You must be sick of hearing from me. Listen, please could you just agree to meet up with me? I need to see you. OK? Call me in Manhattan on 1 212 681 5905.'

I climbed into the soft, sweltering single bed that night in the nasty little cell of a bedroom, and I had drunk just enough to get me to sleep.

I dreamt that Joshua Klein had committed a horrible murder. It was on the news that a woman's body had been found in the woods somewhere near the house I lived in with Mum when I was little – before everything. I asked him about it but he denied it and refused to meet my eye. I tried to touch him but my hands went through him. I couldn't tell whether he was real or imaginary. I watched another news report and they showed a picture of the woman's body lying naked under a tree. It was me.

And it was in the morning that I decided to go to Washington DC and confront him. Let's face it, there'd be fuck all going on at the UN again today. I tried to book the Shuttle but it was full so I had to get the train. I couldn't tell whether I was nervous or excited at the prospect of seeing him again, but I was certainly agitated. I wondered if taking two of my anti-depressants would make me doubly sane. I emailed my shrink to tell him what I was doing. I couldn't imagine him being wildly impressed. His answer to everything is to spend more time with him, not to stalk people who clearly don't give a shit about me. After all, part of me told myself, if it's someone who doesn't give a shit about me I'm after, I could surely achieve that closer to home. Wherever the fuck that may be.

I don't like Washington. Too well-structured and neat. Too many American flags and men in sharp suits. One of those cities like St Petersburg – dumped on an inhospitable swamp for political reasons. No organic life. Does that sound arsey? Yes, I suppose it does. True though.

I had a couple of vodkas in a depressing bar and set off to brace myself for another call, feeling madder and madder as I went. It took me a long time to rustle up the courage to keep going, but I thought it might be the only thing that would mean a full recovery. Closure. I remembered all the times when he had set things straight, told me that of course he loves me, of course I'm wonderful, of course he hadn't been lying to me about Iraq. He explains it all so well that it can put a spring in your step. Couldn't he do that for me again? God knows I needed it. My mobile didn't work (haven't got triband) so I kept having to shove quarters into machines to call him and tell him I was here. Now I know it's not the most rational opinion to hold, but I genuinely believed he would be pleased to see me when he finally did. Well, I can't help it.

I got a cab from the station but it dropped me off a block away and I wandered around a bit trying to collect myself before it occurred to me to go to a bar. I bumped into a woman who was carrying shopping and she called me a bitch. The pavements were slabbed and English. I walked past a shop selling second-hand comics. OK, one last call.

I knew what I was going to say. 'I'm here. Please come and meet me at the bar on the corner.' I had practised sounding sane.

But this time, instead of the familiar message . . .

'Hello?' he said. I wasn't sure if I'd be able to speak but I did.

'Josh? It's me. Faith.'

He didn't say anything for a very long time. Then he said, 'Faith.'

I took a deep breath. 'Why don't you want to see me?' I asked him.

'What has want got to do with it?' he said.

'Why won't you see me? How can you let me suffer like this?'

He laughed. Not much, but enough for me to smile into the receiver of the pay phone. 'You're not suffering, Faith Zanetti. You are . . . well, this is part of your charm.'

'Ha! What were you going to say? I am what?'

'Wonderful.'

I didn't know what to say to that. I was crying.

'I love you,' I said. 'Don't you want me to love you?'

'Do you think I don't like hearing it? How could you think that?'

'Well, the responses haven't been all that forthcoming.'

We were both laughing now.

'I'm coming up,' I said, and put the phone down.

It was strange to see Klein's front door. A shiny black door with a brass lion's head for a knocker, the names of the building's four residents on their buzzers on the right-hand side. I rang. It seemed so unlikely that I might actually see him after everything.

'Hello?' Joshua F. Klein said.

'Hi,' I said quietly. 'It's me.'

And I wish I had walked away and it would never have happened. I could have walked away then. And he would still be alive.

He coughed, or perhaps he was even crying.

'Faith, darling,' he whispered, and he pressed the buzzer to let me in.

CHAPTER TWENTY-FIVE

I reached up to push the door open and as I did so I heard someone shout and run up the steps behind me. Before I had time to react, Daniel Klein had pushed the barrel of a gun between my shoulder blades. He was wearing a long brown mac and he stank. His breath was rancid and I could smell booze and cigarettes and days and days of sweat and filth. He smelt like a tramp in an alley. I once wrote a piece about a medical drop-in centre for Moscow's homeless. I was standing there talking to a young doctor when an old man came in, his long beard yellow with nicotine and saliva and vomit, and took his sodden boots off. His legs were bandaged, army style, instead of socks and he unwound the right-hand bandage very, very slowly. His hands were red and swollen and raw from twenty freezing winters, this one included. Perhaps he hadn't taken this stuff off for years. Anyway, when he finally exposed his foot I actually threw up in a metal dish on a stand by the doctor's side. It was covered in suppurating sores and was a hideous lilac colour. But it was the smell. The smell was completely overpowering. This was how Daniel Klein smelt. Like that old man's foot.

'Hello, slut,' he drooled, sounding a lot madder than he had done in Baghdad. He was very much alone. Anita had obviously seen the light. He pushed me in through the door into a creamy carpeted hall with a marble table on the right for the mail. Above it a painting of horses, the kind of thing Americans think English people have. Like bowler hats and trilbies and bow ties and tweed suits and brogues. Actually only Americans and Pakistanis have these things. The upper half of the walls were painted a perfectly tasteful dark green. Almost British racing green. The carpets were deep and cream, at least until Daniel Klein and I trod on them.

Even then it didn't occur to me that someone was going to get killed. I had realised back in Iraq that Daniel had serious mental health problems and that his father tried to manage the situation. I assumed we were going in for a confrontation that could be settled by somebody being straitjacketed by nice healthcare workers, summoned with a phone call.

On the other hand he was pulling my head back by my hair now and it hurt.

'He goes out. He comes in. No visitors. Never. Need to get him in there with somebody else. Some whore. Never thought I'd get this lucky,' he said, choking the words out as though something was stuck in his throat.

'Where's your mother?' I asked, taking the carpeted stairs with difficulty since I couldn't look down to see them, hoping now that she might be in there too, three against one. Though Klein's tone and the fact that he had let me in did not offer much hope of that.

'You slut,' he said, unhelpfully.

I kept walking.

'She's been in hospital all my freakin' life,' he spat.

Oh, I see. I thought it but I didn't bother to say it. Shit, but that explained a lot. Why didn't Klein bloody well tell me? How could he not have told me? Now that I would have understood. He was always asking me to understand incomprehensible things but that I could have grasped.

When we reached Klein's landing he was leaning his head out of the door and smiling, expecting me. Oh, beautiful sparkly man. It was almost enough to make me feel optimistic just looking at his smile. In the present circumstances though, not quite. I think if I had been on my own he really might have taken me in his arms. But it was not to be. The smile was completely wiped off his face by the look on mine, and by the realisation that Daniel was behind me. Only half dressed and very obviously rattled, he went into deal-with-Daniel mode.

A police car wailed by outside. We were in Georgetown in a leafy turning just past all the shops and bars with their stripy awnings and their rich white clientele, uniformed in khaki shorts, white T-shirts and baseball caps, drinking lattes and reading the *Post*. I heard someone calling their dog. 'Joooooey! Joooooooey!'

'OK. Let's everyone be calm and come on inside,' Joshua said, opening the door wide and showing us in as though we'd come for dinner and were the special guests. The hallway was tiled in black and white marble and a big gilt mirror hung on the wall. I glanced into it and saw Daniel over my shoulder, unshaven, his face contorted with hatred. His eyes looked druggy, though maybe just very mad.

'Josh. Joshua. He has a gun to my back. Could you ask him to take it away?' I said, trying to sound a bit normal. Which wasn't easy. The stereo was turned up very loud indeed and Klein didn't move to turn it down. Perhaps he thought Maria Callas would calm his son. Perhaps he knew there was no time to lose.

Daniel pushed me through into the living room, which had a view over the quiet street, parked cars and tall hedges. There were a couple of abstract paintings on the walls, big Iranian rugs on the polished parquet floor and a big Shaker dining table.

'Danny,' Klein said quietly. 'Danny, come on.'

Danny spat on the floor but didn't loosen his grip on me.

'You know what my name is, Dad,' he said.

'You're right,' Klein conceded. 'Ziggy. Let Faith go. She hasn't done anything wrong. Ziggy?'

So far it was going well. He let go of me, releasing my hair and taking the gun out of my back. At least, I had assumed it was a gun. And I had been right.

'I was going to anyway,' he said.

I was beginning to feel a bit relieved and I pulled my T-shirt down and drew my breath in. But then he lurched towards Klein, grabbing his head and shoving the gun into his temple. Klein's eyes pleaded with me for help but I didn't know what I was supposed to do. I couldn't stop thinking that it was a nice day. My brain was trying to do its thing of concentrating on some mundane aspect of my surroundings and it kept saying to me, 'What a lovely day. Beautiful weather. What a lovely day.'

'You!' Daniel said, almost foaming at the mouth. 'Go and open that drawer over there.'

I turned my head to look at a dresser in the corner, an oriental type of thing with lots of little lacquered drawers in it.

'Listen, Ziggy . . .' I started to say, but that seemed to alarm Joshua.

'DO IT!' Daniel screamed. Loud enough to make me hope a neighbour might call the police. Mightn't they?

OK, getting very nervous now.

I went over to the dresser and opened the drawer he had seemed to be staring at. There were some letters in it, perhaps from a bank.

'NOT THAT ONE!' he screamed. 'Jesus fuck,' he said under his breath as though amazed at the idiocy of the people he had to deal with.

Now this time I knew I had the right drawer because there was a gun in it. A little handgun with a silver barrel.

'Get the gun out,' he told me as I had known he would.

I got it out and held it at the wrong end, like a dirty hanky. I thought the less menacing I looked, the better. Joshua was now breathing very heavily and looking terribly pale. I thought he might be going to have a heart attack. Why wasn't he saying anything? Why didn't he do his presidential thing of taking control and calming everything down? Why was he accepting this? Oh, Joshua, do something, I thought. Always the man. Always the benign patriarch. Why not now?

There have been lots of studies about how people behave in a disaster and apparently nobody behaves as they think they are going to. Nobody is the hero they plan to be. You know that one where they fill a plane full of people and, trying to simulate an emergency evacuation, they tell them that the first thirty people off will get a hundred quid. They trample all over each other, fight and kick and bite and elbow small children out of the way. Nobody knows what they will do. Survival instinct is strong. Heroism is rare.

And then Daniel said, 'Now shoot him in the head and drop the gun on the carpet.'

Joshua's expression didn't change. I could see the bright gleaming surfaces of a kitchen behind father and son. I thought how hideously Daniel resembled his father. A grotesque caricature of him. It was a perfect demonstration of beauty being in your personality, the expression on your face. Not much to do with features at all. To do with enthusiasm for life and with . . . magic? Daniel's dreadlocks seemed to have matted almost into one piece of stinking hair. What a lovely day.

'No, Ziggy. I can't,' I said. 'Of course I can't.'

'OK,' he said. 'I will. You know I will.'

I thought he started to squeeze his trigger.

271

I looked at Joshua and asked him, 'Do you love me?' It was what I had come to find out, after all.

'Yes,' he said quietly, eyes down. 'I do.'

And all I could do was take aim. It was hardly a plan but I thought I might be able to shoot one bullet past Joshua and then try to take out Daniel. There was no doubt that he was serious. He flicked the safety catch off and Joshua closed those beautiful eyes, ready, as though he somehow felt he deserved all of this.

I stretched out my arm and took aim.

'Hurry the fuck up!' Daniel said. He can't honestly have thought I was going to kill someone for him.

I fired past Klein and something in the kitchen shattered. I lurched backwards with the force and the noise of it, like nothing I have ever heard before. I have heard guns, of course, hundreds of them, but not fired by me in a quiet apartment in suburban Washington DC. I was not so shocked that I did not hear the second shot though. I flicked my eyes over to see Joshua Klein fall. Daniel had known I wouldn't do it, and had tried to fire his shot into his father simultaneously with mine, perhaps in some mad attempt to cover himself. Or what?

I took aim again, still reasonably possessed, and pointed my gun at Daniel's chest. His father was on the floor now, lying on the carpet in blood-drenched spasm. I thought I might be sick. Daniel was looking down at the results of his plan, in shock. It was as though he hadn't realised what would happen. I couldn't tell where the bullet had gone in. Not, as Daniel seemed to have intended, into his head.

I fired at Daniel. 'Darling, please don't die. Josh, please don't die. Please don't die,' I was saying over and over again. Almost screaming it. 'I love you.'

Of course, this only happens in fairy tales. The ogre earns the love of a beautiful maiden and when she kisses his hideous face as he lies dying he turns into a handsome prince. And he doesn't die, of course, being the main thing. But I have experience of willing people not to die. It doesn't work.

When I heard the empty click of my gun, the blood drained out of me. No more bullets. Had Daniel known? I stood motionless for a second, staring at Joshua Klein dying in front of me. I looked at myself and saw that I had been spattered all over with his blood. I thought he tried to smile at me, but I couldn't be sure. And then I looked at Daniel, who had started to cry like a baby, his hands to his face, the gun with which he had shot his father on the floor at his feet. I lurched forward and grabbed it, still warm, from the carpet and that was when he kicked me hard in the head. He was wearing big rubber-soled lace-up boots and he kicked me once and then twice until I lay on the floor not far from Klein, who was choking and slipping away. Looking up at Daniel through the blood that had started to pour into my face, I fired.

I wasn't sure if I'd actually hit him or not and I was trying to get to my feet as I watched him run towards the front door of the apartment where he fell heavily to the marble floor, shouting, 'Mom! Mom! Mom! Mom!' over and over again. Poor boy. Really.

I ran the other way to the kitchen, leaving both of them, saving myself. I shoved open the door to the back stairs and pushed through the fire doors to the black metal escape. I suppose I maybe planned to climb down, to get help, to keep going. But I froze there, shaking, a gun still in my hand, blood pouring from my head into my face. I hoped I might pass out from the pain or the shock but I didn't. I just rocked there until someone came to get me.

He had to climb up. I couldn't move.

'Put the gun down, lady,' he said, not aiming his at me. He seemed genuinely concerned, looking up at my perch and sighing deeply when he realised he was going to have to come to me. At his initial suggestion that I go back inside I had shouted, 'No!' Obviously firmly enough for him to take it for an answer.

'Goddammit,' he said to his colleague who, I now realise, was crouching behind the car ready to shoot me in the head.

'Oh. Sorry,' I shouted down, and I put the gun by my feet and my arms in the air. I wasn't sure I had the strength to hold this pose, but it seemed to relax them a lot and my rescuer climbed into view uneasily, the whole fire escape creaking. He actually slung me over his shoulders. The blood rushed to my head and dripped down out of my wounds on to the ladder behind me. When the cop slipped on an upper rung, I was aware of not wanting to fall. This was a good sign. Even after everything, the belief that Joshua had infected me with was still intact. I wanted to live.

It was only when we were safe in the dismal stinking courtyard that he had a good look at me. 'She's going to need stitching up,' he said to the woman who had been waiting to kill me. She had her handcuffs ready, unclipping them from her belt – torch, truncheon, handcuffs. Gun in a separate holster. Bulletproof jacket. Odd-shaped hat. Is it a hexagon? The whole business.

My man shook his head at her and walked me round to the front of the building to get into an ambulance.

'Happened in there?' he asked me, as though casually.

The area in front of Klein's house had been cordoned off with police tape and there were blue lights flashing everywhere, well-to-do residents peering at us from their windows. There goes the neighbourhood.

'It was my fault,' I said heavily. 'But I didn't kill anybody. I hope I didn't kill anybody.'

'Not yet,' he told me with a grim shrug of his shoulders. Two of the ambulances screamed off with their cargoes and I could still hear *La Traviata* floating out of Klein's open windows, the white curtains billowing towards us, one of them spotted with blood.

A police escort came with me to get sewn up – thirty stitches in my head. It's only my mad hair that makes me not look like Frankenstein's monster even now. The little shaved bits don't stand a chance against this stuff. You'd have to go through with a nit comb to even tell. In the middle of being cleaned up, Sergeant Shukmann took a call and visibly relaxed. 'Looks like you're off the hook, Miss Zanetti,' she said, smiling across her big doughnut face. 'Klein had cameras all over the place. Guess he was a security conscious guy.'

'Was?' I asked.

'I'm sorry,' she said.

CHAPTER TWENTY-SIX

Eden and I drove up to the Lake District in his Spider, the roof down, an English summer day in our faces. Tiny though England is, the Lake District is a really long way away. We stopped somewhere vile and ate something disgusting.

I had a mouthful of cold pizza and was looking at a boy who couldn't have been ten yet playing a horribly violent video game where he holds a gun and shoots people on the screen. It was noisy and the little people screamed when they died, a splash of red coming up on the screen. I do hate these things a lot. Hate children with toy guns. I have seen enough children with real guns not to be able to find it funny or endearing. They are for killing people. How is that a good game?

Joshua Figgiss Klein died on the way to hospital. Daniel 'Ziggy' Klein was only grazed by my very bad shot and will be in a secure hospital for some time. He is too mentally ill to be tried for his father's murder. Which is something, for America.

We got to our hotel on Ullswater late at night and had to wake the owner to let us in, a dumpling woman in a flowered nightdress and greying ginger hair.

'Cooked breakfast in the morning?' she asked.

I nearly told her I'd prefer it raw but bit my lip and said that would be lovely. She gave us our big heavy room keys (odd these days not to get a plastic credit card to poke into the slot) and asked if we needed anything.

The poor thing had to flick the lights on behind the bar and waddle around in her blue fluffy slippers getting us some shots of vodka. It was warm and smoky in here with a thick damp beery atmosphere. It had probably been quite a night before we'd got there.

'Lights off when you've finished,' she said, and went back to bed.

'Wish it was you and me tomorrow, Zanetti?' Eden asked, lighting his cigarette.

'Fuck off, Jones,' I said.

'Well, we know you can do it now, at any rate, don't we?'

'Do what?'

'Love someone,' Eden stated, looking me straight in the face.

I didn't want to be getting watery-eyed.

'Yes,' I said.

My room had a picture above the bed of the view out of the window. Why do they do. this? I once went skiing in Zermatt, a Swiss village completely overshadowed by the Matterhorn (the mountain on the Alpen packet). In every hotel room and every bar and every restaurant the garish artwork always features the Matterhorn. Like you haven't seen enough of it already.

In the morning, little white clothed tables with bowls of sugar on them and elderly couples in walking boots peering at their maps, I sat on my own waiting for Eden and drinking what was going to have to pass for coffee. Nescafé! She'd brought me a sachet of fucking Nescafé and a metal pot of water. Oh, and a plastic pot of milk with a picture of a cow on top, suggesting that it actually isn't milk but tastes just like it. I put sugar in it and drank it black. The couple next to me was bickering.

'But if we start from there we'll not be back at the car till dark,' the man complained. He wore a checked shirt and some beige shorts. Shorts do not look good on the over-thirties. It dawned on me that they were planning to drive somewhere, park the car and then spend all day walking back to the car, very probably in the rain. Okey dokey.

'Zanetti, you're not fucking wearing that,' Eden told me from the dining-room door.

Everybody stopped eating and arguing to look first at him in his grey morning suit, a top hat in one hand, some boxes in the other, and then at me, in jeans and a T-shirt, pushing a sausage (only half cooked, as it turned out) around my plate.

'I knew you would do this,' he said, striding towards me. 'Here.'

He handed me two boxes. A shoe box and a big white flat one. 'Go and change.'

Bloody hell. I mean, I had had a shower.

I trudged back up to my room with a fag in my mouth, acknow-ledging that perhaps mine wasn't the perfect outfit for the occasion. I am just not very good at outfit planning.

I opened the shoes first. Not too bad actually. Just slip-on pointy things. He's good at this, is Eden. The dress was fine too. Perhaps I ought to go shopping one day. It was white linen, like a man's shirt but longer, knee-length, with only a few buttons at the top. I didn't look like a porn star or a TV presenter. I just didn't look like a war correspondent on the job either and I suppose that was a good thing.

279

We walked to the church, all the way round the lake and up a tiny, steep, winding path to this ancient grey stone thing packed full of hungover hacks in bizarre outfits. We were late and McCaughrean was already standing at the front, his morning suit straining round his back.

'Hey, Don!' I shouted to him and he turned round nervously, sweat pouring down his face.

'Sit down, Zanetti, you slag,' he told me and everyone laughed. The Russian side of the church was incredible. All the women were over six foot and they were dressed like an episode of *Dynasty*. Nearly all of them had expensive sunglasses on despite the reverent gloom, hair scraped back off their elegant faces and legs taking up most of the church. The men were short and stocky with shaven heads, gold jewellery and somehow slightly inappropriate Italian designer suits.

We all sighed (even me) when the bride came in. Her veil had tiny gold stars sewn into it and her dad was crying. Someone read out that Donne poem about how everyone else he's ever had sex with was 'but a dream of thee'. But when a soprano stood up and started singing 'Sempre Libera' I had to go outside and smoke. I walked up the hill through the sheep shit a bit and saw a carcass, the flesh all rotted off the head, the horns still on. It's odd to see so clearly how one's teeth fit into one's skull.

I was back by the church doors when someone handed me a bowl of rose petals. Don and Irochka came out arm in arm, grinning all over their faces. I threw the petals at them and someone took photos. A skinny bloke in sandals. Don walked up to him.

'Not like that, you twat,' he said and made him change the lens.

Then Don went back to Ira and chucked loads of gold coins in the air and the children ran around picking them up while he and his bride got into a funny little convertible car. They didn't drive away, though, and some ushers (well, two Russian models in Chanel suits) led us down through the woods to the edge of the lake where we were all given a

FAITH WITHOUT DOUBT

glass of champagne on the pier. All the trees and bushes on the way had been decorated with white ribbons and there was a little girl in a frilly dress and daisies in her hair directing us towards the drinks when we got there. Now I know the world's shit and there's no God and all that anti-Kleinian stuff, but it really was a beautiful day.

Then suddenly we saw Don and Ira driving down the hill at us, careering wildly towards the edge of the lake. Everyone gasped as they hurtled down to the water and then into it, apparently making no attempt to brake. The car gave a choke and a gurgle and then an engine started at the back of it and, having turned, James Bond-style, into a motor boat, it set off round the lake, Don and Irochka waving at us and laughing. We all cheered and roared and I found a tear in my eye.

Eden put his arm round me and said, 'It must be love.'

The reception was in some old mill house through another field. Don slapped me on the back when he came in and said, 'Fuck me, Eff Zed. I'm hot as a fucking kangaroo's cunt in this thing.'

'I'm sure you are, Don,' I said. 'Hey. Congratulations, you fat bastard.' And I threw my arms round his neck and kissed him.

'Thanks, Faith,' he said, and I've never seen him look so bloody happy.

Eden made a speech that was mostly about Don getting stuck under a car in a marketplace in Grozny while it was being bombed. We'd had to wait until the fighting stopped and a bloke brought his donkey to haul the car off the miraculously unhurt McCaughrean who lay whimpering underneath. The first thing he'd said was, 'Give us a fag, Zanetti.' Then there were his heroics in Jerusalem when he'd hidden a roll of vital film in his mouth while some thugs beat him up looking for it.

We were all falling about laughing and clapping. Eden had paused between side-splitting anecdotes when his mobile phone audibly beeped him with a message. The first few bars of *Eine Kleine Nachtmusik*.

'Excuse me,' he said, smiling. I think we all assumed it was part of the show. But as he read, his face went grey and we could all see that something was wrong. Somebody coughed and a fork fell noisily to the slate floor.

'Ummm,' Eden said. He looked around him nervously and I was holding my breath, my stomach lurching about inside me. 'Bonnita Hernandez just died in a car accident. Alone on a mountain road.'

He walked slowly out of the room and I followed him. The band started playing 'It Had To Be You'.

I put my arm round Eden's back.

'Bastards,' I said.

Eden put his hands through his hair and sighed. We looked out at clouds gathering round the green mountains.

'Maybe,' he nodded. 'Maybe not.'